TOURIST

Temenuga Trifonova

BLACK SCAT BOOKS
2018

TOURIST

by Temenuga Trifonova

Black Scat Books

ISBN-13 978-0-9992622-4-5

Cover & book design by Norman Conquest

BLACK SCAT BOOKS

Sublime Art & Literature

BlackScatBooks.net

For my mother and daughter

1.

THIS—THE FLESH THAT RUBS against the inside of a white shirt, the bones that crack, the blood that murmurs, the muscle that thumps predictably in the left part of the chest cavity, the cells of which he is comprised and which he will never see—is Jack Sturrett. He is the sort of man that reminds people of someone else. His mouth is the least noticeable detail about him. On the other hand, it would be unfair and imprecise to say that his eyes, nose, ears or any other part of his physiognomy deserve to be called "the most remarkable thing about Jack."

Jack liked to imagine he was a character in a film following the Hollywood three-act structure. He would make index cards and write on them the main questions that, according to screenwriting manuals, a writer should ask. What is Jack's long-term objective? What is his short-term objective? Are they in conflict? What are the main obstacles that prevent Jack from attaining his objective (assuming he has one)? What is at stake (if anything)? What is the worst that could happen if Jack fails to attain his objective (would he care)? How can one keep raising the stakes for Jack to make his story arc more dramatic? Who is Jack's antagonist? What is his objective and how does it clash with Jack's objective (assuming Jack is capable of clashing with anyone or anything in the first place)? What is Jack's conflict (assuming he hasn't gotten too comfortable living without one)? |Is it an internal or an external conflict? How can one re-rewrite Jack's character to make it more psychologically consistent and credible (does credibility depend on psychological consistency)? How much of his backstory needs to be interpolated into the main story in order to understand the motivation behind Jack's actions (assuming his actions are indeed motivated?) What is the inciting incident that triggers Jack's story i.e., the event—however seemingly random and insignificant—that upsets the status quo and sets things in (equally random) motion? How will Jack respond to the inciting incident: will he accept it passively and suffer the consequences, will he take a stand, will he feel disempowered and realize the futility of his attempts, or will he persevere despite diminishing returns? What will be the turning point at the end of act one of his life? How would he know when it happens? Will there be a memo? Or will he receive a statement from his insurance company and a little thank you note for leading a dull life and thus sparing the insurance company the usual costs associated with an eventful life? Will they give him an end-of-the-year bonus for leading a safely episodic life consisting of random, disconnected episodes that never add up to anything and fade out without a bang? Will the second act of his life hang flaccid, equally devoid of inciting and suppressing incidents? Will the *denouement* he had been living toward remain just another alluring French word with no adequate translation? Will all the little misunderstandings, mishearings, misgivings, misinformations, miscommunications and missed connections of the preceding acts add up to one vaguely defined and ultimately unresolvable conflict in the third act?

Occasionally Jack would get so used to thinking about himself in the third person that he would forget to switch back to first person. His carelessness with personal pronouns would sometimes produce amusing misunderstandings in his daily exchanges with others. One time, during the annual population poll, the municipal government sent out an employee from the Institute of Statistics to count the number of people in Jack's household.

"Does Jack Sturrett live here?" the employee asked.

"Yes, he lives here," Jack replied dutifully, blocking the entrance to his apartment as he was wont to do when speaking with government employees.

"And where do *you* live?" the employee inquired.

"He lives here," Jack explained.

"How long are you staying with him?"

"He's lived here since 2004," Jack said.

The employee erased what he had written and repeated impatiently: "What I need to know is when you moved in."

"2004," Jack said.

"You mean you've been cohabiting since 2004?"

"He is not cohabiting with anyone. He lives alone," Jack explained.

The employee raised his pencil.

"Sir, either you are living here illegally or Mr. Sturrett is unaware that you are living with him. In either case I am going to have to report this. Where is Mr. Sturrett now? When do you expect him back?"

"He is here," Jack said pleasantly.

The employee waved his hand dismissively.

"It's not my job to inquire into the specifics of your relationship with Mr. Sturrett. That's between the two of you. Since Mr. Sturrett is unavailable at the moment I will have to ask you to answer my questions on his behalf. What does Mr. Sturrett do?"

The man of statistics raised his knee to prop up the sheet of paper he was supposed to fill out.

"He is…" Jack began.

"Yes?"

"He is," Jack said conclusively.

"That's not an occupation," the employee remarked with certainty.

"He is plenty occupied," Jack insisted. "Even preoccupied."

"You mean he is working extra hours? Is his income above or below the national average?"

"Unfortunately being doesn't pay," Jack smirked. "And to be honest with you, it doesn't pay off either."

"Do you mean he is working extra hours but he is not getting paid for it? Is he volunteering?"

Jack wasn't sure 'volunteering' was an adequate description of his ontological status. He was preoccupied with being, yes, but he did not 'volunteer' to be. Before leaving the man of statistics informed Jack that he was going to put him down as "an occasional guest" of Jack Sturrett's household.

Over the next few weeks Jack noticed an inexplicable surge in the interest his neighbors took in his affairs. Some said hello to him in the hallway, something they had never done before, while others glanced at him suspiciously. Eventually he was able to piece together the rumor that was going around: apparently, his neighbors were under the impression that Jack was living with another man, a mysterious stranger of whose civic identity there was no public record and whose relationship to Jack was anyone's guess. And guess they did. Some believed Jack was hosting an illegal immigrant, others were convinced he was having a secret affair with a man, and then there were those who questioned the existence of Jack's mysterious cohabitant and claimed Jack had simply played a practical joke on the Institute of Statistics. But it was the fourth hypothesis—that Jack might have suffered a psychotic episode resulting in a split personality—that would eventually prove most pernicious.

Word of this must have gotten around because a few weeks later Jack was summoned to the Main Editorial Office of the major London literary magazine for which he worked as a freelance book reviewer. Apparently, the magazine had implemented a new policy that required all employees to undergo an annual psychological check up, a preventive measure designed "to nip in the bud any psychological problems caused by the inordinate stress under which everyone was forced to work, strict deadlines and all that," as the Chief Editor put it. After the Chief Editor assured Jack that everyone else in the office had someone they could talk to about "strategies for better synchronizing their personal and professional life," he assigned him to a counselor. Although it was not the business of the Main Editorial Office whom Jack was cohabiting (or not) with, it was surely understandable that Human Resources would need to be informed if there was any change in Jack's civic status. Jack pretended to comply with the new policy. During his sessions with the counselor assigned to him he continued to talk about himself in the third person, which he found to be a helpful strategy for keeping things—himself included—into perspective. Unfortunately, his counselor had a different take on the matter. According to the report she produced at the end of the first three sessions, "Mr. Sturrett exhibits symptoms of depersonalization and flat affect. The root cause of his condition is still unknown."

Needless to say the little game Jack played with the Institute of Statistics employee had not miraculously added a new person to his household, although in the city records there were now two people listed as residing at Sulfer street, "Jack Sturrett + 1 occasional guest". Yet, as time went on Jack began to think of himself not simply as living but as *living with himself*—not as a roommate with whom one shares all expenses but as someone he had to put up with, an unannounced guest who was supposed to just pass through but who had extended his temporary stay indefinitely and independently of—in fact, in total disregard for—Jack's opinion on the matter. Now, when Jack came back home after work, set *his* groceries on the kitchen table, went through *his* mail, drank *his* regular glass of wine and ate *his* pasta, he felt he was setting his groceries on the kitchen table, going through his mail, drinking his coffee, eating his pasta; in short, he felt as if he was usurping his own place.

He tried to spend less time at home, distracting himself with trips to remote parts of the city where he had absolutely no reason to go. Thus, he found himself spending a great deal of time waiting at bus stops. Invariably people would walk by and offer him some spare change.

Jack was not a beggar. He was simply waiting for the bus like everyone else. He had to conclude, then, that there must be something beggarly about him. Back home he would walk back and forth in front of the mirror in the living room (a strange name for a room, as if what one did in the other rooms of one's apartment did not qualify as 'living'), ruthlessly examining his reflection, trying to detect that elusive beggarly side of him. He observed nothing unusual: his movements were neither phlegmatic nor rushed, he wore his hair very short, which was quite common among men of his age and social status, his clothes were unobtrusive (grey corduroy jeans, a Scandinavian sweater, a brownish jacket). The look in his eyes was neither pathetic nor imploring. His nose, broken twice, was a bit suspect but Jack believed a broken nose created the illusion of an active man. Every part of him, as far as he could see as he waltzed in front of the mirror, was average and inconspicuous. No, there was nothing beggarly about him. Yet there had to be. Maybe it was the chin. Yes. It was a pointed chin, narrow and bony. Perhaps it made him appear underfed, even though he ate three regular meals a day, organic only.

He avoided bus stops for a while. At the end of his self-imposed quarantine he ventured back into the streets hoping that his beggarly persona would have miraculously vanished. Nothing of the sort—he 'earned' over 50 dollars in less than an hour. What finally put an end to his unlikely predicament was an impulsive decision to fully embrace the image others had assigned to him and live the life corresponding to it. Then something unexpected happened. After no more than a week of living like a full-blown homeless man cliché he noticed he was becoming invisible to people again. Taking that as a sign that he had been 'cured' he resumed his regular freelancing life.

This nondescript October morning he was fully immersed in that life i.e., he was fully immersed in staring out his home office window at a gigantic billboard announcing *10 TASTY BURGER CHOICES*

STARTING AT ONLY 1.39! The unnaturally yellow cheese that was supposed to melt seductively over the thick piece of meat squashed between the two buns had grown pale after years of exposure to sun, rain and snow, eventually acquiring an almost believable color. The letters of the billboard ad—stylishly elongated and slightly squished—did not match the succulent image of a double cheeseburger authoritatively occupying the foreground, little bags of pristinely crispy French fries stacked neatly in the background. Jack figured that from the perspective of the French fries his own head, along with the upper part of his torso, were positioned in the lower left corner of the billboard, which advertised a fast food joint that had long ago closed down.

8:51am. The new day sprawled, languid and fat, ahead of him. What would he do with all that time? He considered coming up with a list of things and activities to fill the time. Making up the list would probably take 10, maybe even 15 minutes i.e., not long enough to justify spending any time on it. No, what he really had to focus on were not small-scale activities that barely qualified as 'errands' but meaty actions that filled large chunks of time. The problem was that he had never learned how to pass time properly. Up until now he had been doing it in a sloppy, amateur fashion, devising short-term solutions for stitching the glaring hole of time he woke up to every morning: surfing the web, taking showers, going through the list of contacts in his phone, watching TV, going to the movies, taking out the garbage etc. He had been mostly improvising, nervously grabbing the first solution that came to mind and using it indiscriminately to patch temporal holes of vastly different nature and size. Trying to conquer time with such 'local' techniques was absurd. What he really needed was a comprehensive, conceptual approach—a strategy for passing time.

The renovation of the YMCA across the street was under way. Two workers wearing construction helmets and orange overalls were removing the building's top layer. Occasionally they would stop, point at a section of the wall and shake their heads i.e., they were approaching the wall strategically. In fact, isn't it true that in the field of construction… Jack caught himself on time, just before he got off on a tangent about construction workers. Wasn't this precisely what he was trying to get away from, this slapdash inventory of everything that happened to cross his field of vision, a tried and true method of passing time quickly by slowing it down to describe it in minute detail? Doing an inventory of the world is, like all amateur endeavors, cheating: focus your attention on something—the more trivial the better—so that after a while you stop noticing the passage of time i.e., you cheat time by forgetting about it, a cowardly approach that inevitably backfires, because even if you manage to forget time it never forgets you. You have to do just the opposite: instead of forgetting time you have to beat it at its own game by being aware of it *all the time.* One way of doing that is by slowing down actions that normally take very little time.

Jack closed his laptop and moved to the kitchen. The first trial runs were awkward—to his surprise, he was unable to control the tempo and rhythm of his most routine movements. Place the pot on the stove. Turn on the heat. Stop. Set the timer on the watch. Repeat. Place the pot on the stove. Turn on the heat. Stop. Look at the watch. 5 seconds. He repeated the sequence one more time, with even less conviction, since it occurred to him that perhaps he was doing just another inventory though not of things but of his own actions. He checked his watch. The above thought, which had threatened to sabotage his plan, had actually slowed him down a bit: 11 seconds! He remembered a shot from *Battleship Potemkin.* A sailor is washing a plate when he notices something engraved on it. He raises his arm and smashes the plate. The camera shows his action from several different camera angles thus extending its screen time. What if he edited his own movements in the same way? He picked up the coffee pot, raised his hand as far up as he could and began pouring the coffee slowly, keeping the coffee stream consistently thin so it took longer to fill up the cup. He stopped, twisted his hand slightly to the right, and resumed pouring. He stopped again, lowered his hand a few inches and resumed pouring. He kept changing the height and angle from which he was pouring the coffee until the cup was full. 14 seconds! That was double the time it normally took him! Jack looked around the kitchen. Every object, from the tiny teaspoon to the soup pot on top of the shelf, was a hidden reserve of time waiting to be liberated. With enough practice he could probably extend coffee-pouring time to 20 seconds, without even counting all the stages preceding and succeeding the act of pouring, from grinding the coffee to washing the coffee pot.

Never again would he wait for time to pass; from now on he would be totally committed to *actively wasting time* and—why not—even keeping a record of it. A few years back someone had given him a small digital camera as a birthday gift. He set up the tripod in the corner of the living room and mounted the camera onto the tripod head. After spending a few days recording representatively banal scenes of his daily life he decided to spice things up by performing and recording a series of dramatic reenactments of a select few of them. He was curious to see if the dramatic reenactments of simply enacted actions, such as the routine action of filling an empty ice cube tray, were more or less believable than the actions themselves, and he was keen to calculate the surplus amount of time the dramatic reenactment would add to simple enacted actions.

For the next few weeks he lived from 6am to 12pm, watched the rushes of his life from 12am to 6am, and edited them from 6am to 12pm. Ideally, he would have liked to keep the three activities—living, watching, and editing—separate, but given the limited number of hours in a day that was impossible. He simply had to accept the fact that watching the rushes from the day before and editing them would take up a considerable amount of the following day, which should have been devoted entirely to 'living'.

Sometimes he would reminisce about the 'good old days,' when he was first starting out as a freelancer and didn't have to worry about what to do with time simply because he was always short on it. He gradually built himself a reputation of being infamously good with strict deadlines, unforgiving editors and rigid page length require- ments, and as the book review requests kept pouring in he was forced to spend less and less time on reading the books he was reviewing. Constantly pressed for time, he would plunder his old book reviews for sentences or entire paragraphs that were general enough to be reused in the review he was working on at the moment. In many cases if he simply changed the title of the book, added a new plot summary in the beginning and reordered the paragraphs he could make the review of one book pass for that of another. Over time his writing came to be known for its 'close attention to the philosophical significance of books'—i.e., for generalizations about 'the human condition'—earning him the reputation of a 'humanist critic,' an honorary appellation that had gone out of fashion for a while and was, therefore, prime for resur- rection. Spending less and less time on actually reading the books he was reviewing meant he could dedicate himself to experimenting with his own writing style. As he was no longer constrained by the specifics of the work he was reviewing he was free to develop his 'writer's voice,' while the necessity to disguise the fact that he was essentially saying the same thing about a range of vastly different books motivated him to expand his vocabulary. If some of his colleagues criticized, surely out of resentment and envy, the abstruseness of his reviews Jack would remind them that obscurity is necessary to excellence; as Flaubert him- self recognized, "Pour être vrai, il faudrait être obscur, parler charabia."

It was perhaps inevitable that Jack's big break in the world of book reviewing came with a review he wrote without having read the book he was reviewing. After submitting the review he was overwhelmed with embarrassment and guilt, from which he later sought to extricate himself by reading the book twice, cover to cover. He was relieved to find out that that his review, written in total ignorance of the book, had not missed anything significant about it; in fact, his review, it was said, managed to distill the book's underlying meaning in a more thoughtful way than the book's author himself. The Chief Editor commended Jack for his "unusual perceptiveness" and "eloquent language." Encouraged by this feedback, which, appropriately enough, the Chief Editor had offered without having read Jack's review, Jack gave himself permission not to feel bound by the specificity of the work he was reviewing, which was after all purely incidental. Over the next few months he published fourteen book reviews of books he had *not* read. On the rare occasions when he did feel a vague sense of guilt or embarrassment he would go to a meeting of one of the numerous book clubs in the city and take notes from the public discussion of the book he was reviewing. Using this 'meta-data' made his book reviews even richer: since book club members generally came from very diverse cultural, ethnic, class and gender backgrounds he was able to appropriate a diverse range of opinions.

When the literary magazine published a reader's response to Jack's review of *Dystopia*, Robert Gallahan's latest novel, which Jack had, of course, not read, Jack knew he had struck gold. The anonymous reader congratulated Jack on a beautifully written review that, in the reader's own words, "questioned the supposed primacy of the literary text over the critical text" and "challenged the long-established artificial distinction between writing and reviewing." Indeed, the reader went as far as to suggest that Jack's review had inaugurated a new genre, 'fictional criticism' or 'creative criticism', and expressed a hope that other critics would follow Jack's lead in developing further "the art of book reviewing." The Chief Editor invited Jack to respond to the reader's letter, which Jack had not read—he had read the Chief Editor's summary of the reader's letter and he used it—the summary, not the letter—as a starting point for a series of reflections on the importance of paratexts. "There has recently been a renewed interest," he wrote in his response to the reader's letter, "in what we usually assume to be of secondary importance: book reviews, prefaces, dedications, afterwords, endnotes, et cetera. Perhaps it's time we stopped reading the book review with the hope of 'reconstructing' the book we might not have read from what is being said about it; instead, we should approach the book as nothing more than a blueprint for its own future review." In the months following the publication of Jack's review, the reader's response, and Jack's response to the reader, Jack's popularity in literary circles reached its peak. Writers began requesting that he personally review their books and he was invited to participate in roundtable discussions at several universities about the potential irrelevance of fiction and the future of 'fictional criticism'.

Just when Jack was beginning to feel suffocated by his sudden rise to fame Alexander G. made an appearance, diverting the media's attention away from Jack. Alexander G., an up and coming literary critic, had decided to follow Mazlish's recommendation that every book review be published along with its own review. Mazlish's best-seller *The Art of Book Reviewing* opened with a bold proclamation: "A book reviews the reviewer as much as the reviewer reviews the book." Mazlish then went on to argue that, "A book based on detailed empirical work and exhibiting more than a passing familiarity with ongoing debates on the subject calls for a reviewer equally versed in those debates and thus capable of evaluating the strength of the scholarship presented in the book. Ideally, every review should be accompanied by a review of the review. A single review of the review ought to be sufficient: publishing a review of the review of the review of the review et cetera would plunge us into infinite regress, though in a certain sense isn't this what scholarship is ultimately all about?"

On March 11th the magazine's Sunday edition featured Alexander G.'s review of Jack's review of *The Art of Book Reviewing*. Very little was known, at the time, of Alexander G. The reason for this was simple: Jack had practically invented him overnight. He had figured that once Alexander's review was published he would have all the time in the world to 'fill him out' but for now it made more sense to leave Alexander a bit underdeveloped: after all, he was supposed to be a Nobody who suddenly breaks out on the literary scene and pushes Jack out of the limelight. Sure enough, in the first weeks following Alexander G.'s dramatic entry everyone was talking only about him, mentioning Jack only in passing and quoting him only in order to underscore, by way of comparison, Alexander's superior intellect and unparalleled fictional criticism skills. Several months later, when Alexander had already fully assumed Jack's former place in the literary firmament, Jack decided to take it up a notch. On April 29, the literary magazine featured a certain Samuel Vlonsky's review of Alexander's review of Jack's review of Mazlish's *The Art of Book Reviewing*. At that point the magazine had to reprint excerpts from Mazlish's book since no one could recall the text all subsequent reviews were referencing. Robert Dull, another book reviewer, took it upon himself to write a comparative study of the writing styles of Jack, Alexander G. and Samuel Vlonsky, in which he demonstrated the underlying similarity in tone, rhythm and tempo between the three reviewers. Dull suggested that it was now possible to speak of a new school of criticism—the Fictional Criticism School (FCS)—of which these three critics could be considered the founding fathers.

Jack considered Dull his crowning invention.

2.

EVEN AFTER THE DAZZLING LIGHT of his newly found literary persona had dimmed into a more mundane but reliable fluorescence Jack had trouble getting accustomed to his own star power. One time he was browsing a bookstore, amusing himself by removing the 'staff pick' tags from prize-winning works and attaching them to Harlequin novels, when he overheard his name. Two young women, whose vocabulary and general demeanor did not suggest a level of intelligence corresponding to their physical attractiveness—over the years Jack had learned to judge quickly the ratio between the two—were discussing a book titled *Another Life*. One of them spoke enthusiastically of the book's intriguing premise—a work of 'speculative fiction' she called it knowingly, though she dared not speculate what that might mean—but the other one informed her friend, in a sober voice, that Jack Sturrett, yes, that Jack Sturrett, had criticized the plot as "insipid," the style as "relentlessly conventional" and the book's author as "precocious." They put down the book, grateful to Jack for sparing them the mental pollution caused by conventional stories by precocious writers.

As he watched the two women walk away from the book he had condemned Jack cringed at the sense of finality and self-importance underlying his almighty critical judgment, of which, incidentally, he had no recollection whatsoever. He couldn't recall if he had read *Another Life* but forgotten it, or if he had never read it in the first place, like so many other books he had reviewed without reading. He picked up the book and read the first paragraph. Suddenly, the earnestness of the language, the story, and the writer's voice, which he would normally dismiss as 'first-degree'—straightforward, devoid of irony and thus, presumably, of any depth—struck him as authentic. The 'staff picks', among which *The Collected Reviews of Jack Sturrett* occupied a prominent place, were spread out on a separate table. Jack removed the 'staff pick' tag from his own book and placed it on top of *Another Life*, but even that didn't seem enough in terms of atonement. He grabbed all copies of *Another Life* he could find on the shelf and made his way to the cash register.

If on that occasion Jack encountered the specter of his literary fame at a safe distance, still a matter of opinion and hearsay, he could not so easily escape from it several weeks later when, leafing through a book on the philosophy of time in another bookstore, he came upon a long footnote in which the author quoted a passage from one of Jack's rare film reviews (the film was *Museum Hours*). Jack stared at his name in 9 points Time New Roman, feeling his whole existence shrunk and compressed into a bibliographic reference in someone else's work. The quote was rather long: "The museum guard spends his time or, rather, his shift, in the company of dead things—a commonly used euphemism is 'relics'—in various stages of ruin. He stands in the vortex of temporal decay, surrounded by abandoned things that have lost their purpose and use, whose value is now reduced to storing time, storing the decay of time, and representing the decay of time. He guards things from a particular time long gone, but he also guards the decay of time these things embody, and, on yet another level, he guards—and makes visible—the decay of time these already decayed things participate in right now, as items in a museum collection, a decay to which he, too, is subject. In short, he guards his own mortality, his own future death. And the longer he guards it the more he becomes it—his own death. Until one day he starts to believe he is already dead." In the footnote the author acknowledged having taken the passage out of its original context, Jack's film review, using it to advance his own argument. Jack thought of the author, one Thomas Reisenberger, reading Jack's film review and underlining promising passages that he could quote in his own book either to increase the word count or to beef up his sparse bibliography, the two main reasons for reading and quoting other writers. He imagined Reisenberger underlining this passage, attaching a sticky note and continuing the search for other relevant quotes to stitch together into his final quilt on the philosophy of time. Although he reread the quoted passage several times he neither recognized the words nor remembered writing them. According to Reisenberger, Jack had "used the figure of the museum guard in order to draw attention to the essentially conservative nature of time"—hence Jack's emphasis on the act of "guarding time," which, Reisenberger went on to argue, "is, for Sturrett, the museum guard's primary function."

Back in his apartment Jack searched his hard drive for the file containing his film review and compared the passage in the original review with the one quoted by Reisenberger. The two passages were identical yet Jack failed to recognize the thought as his own. One thing was clear: Reisenberger—and along with him the hypothetical reader of Jack's work—had filtered out Jack's morbid pessimism by purposefully ignoring the numerous references to death and decay in the original film review. Curiously resentful at this flagrant misinterpretation of a thought he could not even remember having had, Jack imagined the 'hypothetical reader' desperately grasping at what Jack's meaning must have been, but eventually he had to admit that he himself was unsure what he had meant to say in the first place. Jack wondered whether at the point where the hypothetical reader's uncertainty of what Jack might have wanted to say intersected (as it was bound to) with Jack's own uncertainty of what he had wanted to say, the reader's ignorance of Jack's intended meaning would be indistinguishable from Jack's ignorance of his own intended meaning. Would the reader's interpretation of Jack's text become part of Jack's unconscious/unintended meaning or, alternatively, would Jack's unconscious become part of the reader' interpretation? Perhaps Reisenberger was closer to the 'truth' of Jack's meaning after all, because 'truth' is something one arrives at through an act of interpretation whereas Jack was too 'close' to his own words to see them as something demanding interpretation. Perhaps other people are always at an advantage when it comes to understanding what one means, because they have the privilege of remaining on the surface of what one says and are thus able to interpret it.

3.

IT WAS AROUND THE TIME when he was beginning to feel that he was usurping his own life rather than living it, and beginning to fear that its rightful owner would attempt to reclaim it at any moment, that Jack began to flân in the streets of London. During one of his aimless wanderings he suffered a minor accident—a cyclist ran over him but thankfully didn't cause any major injuries. An ambulance picked him up and delivered him to the nearest hospital where a young doctor fixed his twisted ankle with a single abrupt and precise movement. While Jack was waiting for the status of his ankle to be recorded permanently in the public medical records he walked back and forth down the long hallway. The door of one of the rooms was slightly ajar—a pair of feet with long twisted nails protruded from under the white sheet thrown over the bed closest to the door. Jack entered the room and approached the bed tentatively. The feet belonged to an old man whose body was almost entirely buried under the sheet except for the pale forehead, the closed eyes, and some wisps of white hair sticking out at the other end of the sheet. Hooked up to the respirator by a number of tubes of different length and width the man resembled an aging octopus. Jack was about to leave when the aging octopus extended one of its soft arms and the moist suction cup at the end of it wrapped itself around Jack's wrist. The octopus opened its left eye and stared unintentionally at Jack, who simply happened to be in the octopus's line of vision. Jack tried to pull his hand out of the suction cup's tight grip. The eye grew wider and the grip tighter, suggesting that the octopus was coming into some kind of awareness of the world around it. A tear formed at the edge of the octopus's left eye but since the eye was physically incapable of blinking the tear could not move across its surface in order to drain at the edge and instead remained still on the eye's glossy surface like a surplus sclera, a surplus layer of protection the octopus no longer seemed to need.

Suddenly the octopus-man lifted his body slightly, grasped Jack's hand even tighter, and said in a shockingly clear voice: "Seventh row, south-west, number 673." The octopus arm retreated, sinking back in between the folds of the bed sheet. A nurse poked her head into the room.

"Is this a bad time?"

Jack pulled out his hand from the suction cup. This time there was no resistance.

"He is dead," Jack said.

The nurse raised her hand to her mouth.

"I am sorry. You must be the nephew. He talks…talked a lot about you. I will leave you two alone," she said, incorrectly, as there was only one of them now.

Jack arranged the two octopus arms on top of the chest, which provided a stable support now that it was not moving any more. The nurse poked her head into the room again.

"I am sorry, could I just grab your ID. I need to fill out some forms while you are saying your goodbyes," she said, incorrectly again, as only one of them was going to say goodbye to the other.

Without turning back Jack clasped the dead octopus's hands.

"I'll be down the hall. Just let me know when you are ready," the nurse said.

When he was alone with the octopus-man Jack glanced around the room. There were no personal belongings except for an old black and white photograph of a boy playing on a deserted beach but there was no way of telling if it was a photograph of the old man-octopus himself or of the nephew he had been talking about.

"A long time ago," a feeble voice said inconclusively but unexpect-edly enough to startle Jack.

The octopus-man unclasped his hands as if it was the most normal thing in the world for a deceased man to do and pointed at the photo-graph.

"He must have been 9 or 10," he said without clarifying whom he was talking about. "Do you remember what you were like at that age?"

Jack tried. Nothing came to mind.

"I remember," the old man said. "You liked to cut things."

Octopus man, whose brain was apparently still sending signals though the signals were completely scrambled, went on to tell Jack about his, Jack's, childhood. When Jack was little, octopus man said, he used to receive gifts quite often but didn't know what to do with them. If someone gave him a book Jack would ask for a pair of scissors and cut the pages into various geometric patterns. He didn't understand that the book was meant for reading, not for making paper decora-tions. His grandfather, i.e. octopus man, would piece together the pa-per fragments and read to Jack from the recomposed book, a difficult endeavor as he had to constantly twist and turn the pages to make certain sentence fragments match others and to match the beginning of sentences with their endings. Jack's first encounter with reading was thus an encounter with a complex, recursive process of interpretation that required the reader to construct the meaning of words, sometimes literally matching individual letters that had ended up on different pages as a result of Jack's cutting technique, which ignored semantics and instead followed only the logic and beauty of abstract geometric forms. Sometimes a sentence would begin on one page and end on the reverse side of another page, which Jack had transformed into the hypotenuse of a right-side triangle. His grandfather would patiently unfold the pages one by one and recreate for Jack the correct sequence of letters, words, sentences and paragraphs. Jack would nod, apparently following the logic of language, but when his grandfather would then fold the pages again, severing all connections between words and sentences, and ask Jack to recreate the passage he had just rebuilt from Jack's fragments, Jack wouldn't be able to do it. From the incoherent jumble of words he could just produce another, equally incoherent jumble, a word soup that had so many spices mixed in indiscriminately that it was, ultimately, tasteless.

Jack's grandfather/octopus man took Jack's difficulties with language as evidence that he was incapable of abstract thinking, although his predilection for abstract geometric forms, to which he reduced every book that ended in his hands, suggested otherwise. Jack did eventually learn to read, but only after undergoing a long training period at the end of which his reading patterns remained somewhat peculiar. He never grasped the idea of language as a convention: he could not make the connection between a series of black dots on the page and the meanings people ascribed to them. Since first-degree reading—assigning particular meanings to particular black dots on the page—eluded him he developed his own reading technique, which consisted of cutting the page into individual words and then combining them into sentences. Given that the 'right' order of the words was not self-evident, he would always end up with multiple versions of the same page. When his teachers asked him to summarize a page in a book he had read he would ask them to specify which version they wanted him to reproduce, for he had many. He always glued the words of each version to the page: he had to touch the rough edges of the words to understand their meaning. Tracing a sentence with his finger across a regular page did nothing for him: the page was too smooth and thus illegible. How could one speak of 'text' and 'subtext' when the page was so uniform and singular? He needed the words to literally come off the page, half-unglued, in order to feel the sub-text.

Jack's difficulties were not restricted to reading, the dying octopus man continued; he also had trouble understanding what it meant to use language figuratively. He could not, as they say, 'wrap his head around it'. The first time he heard that expression Jack thought they wanted him to wrap a piece of cloth around his head when speaking. He was convinced speaking required a special kind of outfit. His grandfather then explained to him that this was just a metaphor, a figure of speech, but that confused Jack even more—why was he allowed, even encouraged, to use words to draw figures while cutting the pages of a book into abstract geometric figures was frowned upon?

At this point in the story of Jack's childhood, in which Jack himself was beginning to believe, though he was not sure whether it was because he recognized himself in it or because the dying man playing the role of his grandfather was a very good storyteller, the hospital room door opened and an old woman walked in. Failing to take notice of Jack she sat at the edge of the bed, pulled out a small plastic bag from her pocket, took something out of the bag and dropped it in the glass of water on the bedside table. The dying octopus man's artificial teeth sank to the bottom of the glass and then floated up again, opening up slightly in a grin aimed at no one in particular. Jack wondered how the old man had managed to speak to him without his prosthesis and whether he had actually said a single word. When the old woman finally noticed Jack he apologized, without specifying for what he was apologizing, and sneaked out of the room before she had time to call security.

He walked one floor up and found himself in the Department of Neurological Disorders. The doors to most rooms were open for visiting hours. Men and women he had never met were lying in bed, asleep, staring at the ceiling or mindlessly watching the TV screens positioned above their beds. The bed sheets under them were suffused with personal bodily fluids, smells and memories. In one of the rooms four men were sleeping on their backs, tucked under the covers, as if their bodies had been arranged that way for the sake of visual symmetry. Jack took turns sitting at the edge of every bed—a solitary dark spot moving through the white cube of the room like a black ball in a pinball machine—straightening out the wrinkles in the bed sheets, repositioning the sleeping men's hands, crossing and uncrossing them over their chests, as if to see whether they might look better dead (hands crossed over their chest) or alive (hands on the side of the body). As he was arranging the hands of one of the sleepers Jack glanced up at his face: the man was watching him silently with no expression on his face other than a vague curiosity as to what Jack would do next, as though Jack had the final say on whether the man would live or die depending on the way he arranged his hands for him.

Visiting hours were just beginning and the hallway, completely dead until moments ago, suddenly came alive, anxious relatives opening and closing doors, looking for their loved ones, getting the room numbers wrong, finding other people's loved ones, who, therefore, meant nothing to them. As Jack hurried down the stairs someone called after him. It was the nurse, the one who was an expert at peeking into rooms. She motioned to him to come back and told him, in a confidential tone of voice, as if she was sharing a secret with him that he himself did not know, that she knew he was not related to the old man in room 312, and perhaps to none of the other patients he had visited (she had been watching him) but that he ought not to worry about it because she would not tell her superiors about it on the condition that Jack agrees to do this regularly, or at least once in a while. Do what, he asked. Keep the patients company and, if they need it, pretend that he is a relative of theirs, provided they don't recognize him of course (most of them wouldn't anyway). The nurse was convinced this charade would cheer them up. Although the idea of pretending to be a part of someone else's life was tempting, Jack was afraid that the very fact the patients were still alive would prevent him from seamlessly inscribing himself in their lives. While hospitals, located somewhere between the reality of life and the surreality of death, were not conducive to the kind of fictionally realistic existence Jack was after, cemeteries, on the other hand, seemed the perfect choice. If life resisted the encroachment of fiction, the vacuum left behind by death welcomed it.

In the course of his first forays into cemetery flânerie Jack imagined himself the leader of a reconnaissance team sent to explore a foreign territory before the actual planned invasion, although he was not so much interested in exploring the topography of the cemetery as much as he wanted to simply soak in the atmosphere, get used to the surreality of death before attempting to fictionalize it. He wandered through cemeteries as though they were museums, stopping in front of the most elaborate tombstones, reading the names of the deceased as if they were captions placed next to art works to explain their provenance and significance, noting differences in tomb styles, cross styles, and funerary portrait photography styles.

One day, as he was leaving yet another cemetery, he watched a dozen black limousines file in slowly and park in front of the cemetery gates. Four sturdy young men carried the coffin to an empty grave in the northwestern corner of the cemetery; they were followed by a long procession of mourners, walking together, in pairs, or small groups, separate in their pain, which had twisted their faces into dramatic masks worthy of a Greek tragedy. Jack followed the mourners at a distance, trying to replicate the slowness and gravity of their gait, the lowered head, the hollow gaze, the stoic face on the verge of cracking up. The mourners formed an irregular circle around the coffin by the side of the grave. Jack stood a little to the side, trying to guess their relationship to the deceased and to imagine the fragmented memories of the body inside the coffin running through their heads. The circle opened into a line as people began taking turns to say their goodbyes. One of the mourners standing close to Jack stepped aside and motioned to

Jack to go ahead of him. Jack hesitated. Failing to come up with a credible explanation for crashing a stranger's funeral he stepped forward. His head felt hollow, like a tent stretched too tight, the sound of wind reverberating between its walls. In front of him a pair of elegant stiletto shoes sank deep into the mud, came out, and sank back into it again. Somewhere behind him a woman was crying softly. In the distance the polished chassis of the black limousines were heating up. Leaning against the cars, the drivers were smoking, checking their watches, readjusting their hats and ties.

The stiletto mourner in front of Jack stepped aside. The coffin now loomed big in front of him, a funereal Space Odyssey monolith. The mourners, grim and statuesque like the women in Visconti's *La Terra Trema*, waited to hear his final words to a body he had never known. He bent forward and touched the coffin but immediately withdrew his hand—the lid was burning hot. The pain brought tears to his eyes. He didn't fight them back. Someone tapped him on the shoulder and a friendly male voice reassured him that "Karl is in a better place now." Jack stepped aside and assumed a respectable pose. Several female mourners looked at him approvingly, touched by what they interpreted as his silent and understated goodbye to Karl.

The interment was quick and people headed back to their cars. Once there, the mourners were divided into two camps: the first camp—presumably Karl's closest relatives—lined up to receive the other camp's condolences. People shook Jack's hands. They were so sorry for his loss. How difficult this must be for him. Every time someone shook Jack's hand they would share with him one or two things they knew about Karl. By the end of the hand-shaking ritual Jack had accumulated a respectable collection of adjectives describing Karl and, he would venture a guess, a better knowledge of Karl than he had of other men he actually knew personally. He tried to disappear discreetly during the ensuing general confusion over the correct ratio of mourners to black limousines but a young man, who speedily appointed himself the overseer of the most efficient distribution of people to cars, pushed Jack toward one of the cars and even opened the door for him. Jack had no choice but to take a seat inside and be driven to a house where the farewell-to-Karl dinner was scheduled to take place.

Now that the majority of mourners had seen him at the funeral he was accepted as one of them, which granted him a certain freedom of movement throughout the house and unlimited access to all alcoholic beverages and catered snacks. Soon they all gathered in the living room and someone clanked a glass with a spoon. Everyone was invited to say a few things about Karl and share their memories of him. It occurred to Jack that Karl was not that different from one of those books he had reviewed without reading: after all, wasn't writing a personal eulogy for a man he had never known similar to reviewing a book he had never read? All he had to do is stay in the safe realm of trivialities and generalities and leave enough gaps between his invented memories of Karl, into which people could project their own, real memories. For a brief moment he wondered if the other mourners were as fake as him, if they had all been hired to attend Karl's funeral and pretend to suffer for his loss. If only there was a photograph or some other incontrovertible evidence to make explicit the reality of the person they had just put in the ground. But there was none.

When it was his turn to speak Jack raised his wine glass and smiled bitterly: "Karl was not an easy man to know." Several people nodded in agreement. His confidence boosted by the wine Jack went on to tell a story about Karl, carefully avoiding any specific details and connecting the dots of Karl's fictional and prematurely finished life into an abstract pattern that could be superimposed upon anyone and so described no one in particular. His eloquent speech rendered Karl's life, undoubtedly as banal as everyone else's, full and round, like a deflated balloon that had been inflated again. The benefits to be reaped from

Karl's death and from his posthumous inflation, were numerous: all of a sudden everyone else's life was slightly inflated simply by dint of its association with Karl's. Years of trivial conversations and difficult communication with what probably had been a taciturn old man were now rewritten in everyone's mind as 'seemingly unimportant conversations in which Karl and the particular mourner in question shared a moment, an understanding, or just a cigarette.' Jack was surprised by the ease with which he was composing, on the fly, the story of Karl's life, and too shocked by his own extensive vocabulary of sentiments to be as disgusted with himself as he would have normally been under the circumstances. The more fake the sentiments he described, the more earnest his voice sounded, the less self-conscious he felt, and the more moved his audience seemed to be. Near the end of his speech, looking around the room, he caught his own reflection in the mirror above the mantelpiece and could barely recognize himself: his face was red, his shirt unbuttoned, and two large sweat stains marked the sleeves of his jacket. He raised his hand to wipe off his forehead and was surprised to find that not only his forehead but his eyes, too, were wet. Tears. Real tears!

Someone clapped. The applause spread across the room, carried over from mourner to mourner as they wiped off their tears—tears of aesthetic appreciation of Jack's funereal rhetoric?—and reached for another glass of wine. Jack felt sadness, melancholy, regret, self-pity, pity for Karl, and pity for everyone who knew Karl, but he couldn't tell which of these sentiments, if any, was real. Was he really devastated by the death of a man he had never known? Had mortality, including his own—something he had always accepted as a fait accompli and thus not warranting any sentimental response—suddenly moved him to tears, and was he really moved by the death of a stranger or by the beauty of his own funerary rhetoric? What did it matter that the reasons for these sentiments were made up if the sentiments themselves were real, as evidenced by the real tears in his eyes?

The organizing mourning squad had hired a DJ 'to celebrate Karl's life' because 'Karl would have never wanted anyone to be sad when he is gone.' A middle-aged woman, who likely got more complimented on her inner beauty than on anything else, stumbled toward Jack, stopping at every table on the way to refill her wine glass and swinging her hips to the music. Slurring her words and switching indiscriminately from formal to informal speech she wanted to know whether Jack was available on July 12 for a similar function. It was actually a birth, not a funeral, but in a way weren't they both an occasion to celebrate life? Jack had no idea what she had in mind. She confessed that she was 'impressed'—no, 'moved'—by his speech and wanted to know what his hourly rate was. She hoped he was not only excellent— 'terrific really!'—but also affordable. "Life is full of defining moments," she informed him. Granted, birth and death were the two universally accepted 'biggies', but in-between them there were numerous mini-events that also deserved some sort of signposting, no? She told him she was surprised she had never run into him at 'the company' given that she knew all the other employees and they usually arranged to car-pool to the event. Jack assured her he did not work for a company. "Oh, you are a freelancer?" she exclaimed, apparently even more impressed with him. Before he could correct her she went on to tell him about all the incompetent crooks she had had the misfortune of working with, how many cliché funeral speeches she had had to sit through, and how many cheap glasses of wine she had consumed, damaging further her poor liver. Jack said he was sorry to hear that she had had so many people close to her die. No, she reassured him, there hadn't been any deaths in her family. She was talking about the funerals she had worked at over the last few years.

'Worked at'?

After refilling her glass she went on to explain to him the ins and outs of the new offshoot of 'Events Planning', known as 'MLEP' (Major Life Events Planning), a growing new field in which she had made a career. The company she worked for was an innovator in the field of MLEP and had even won the Audience Award at last year's international MLEP contest for introducing the concept of 'MLE Extras' (Major Life Events Extras) modeled after film extras. The company had established a subsidiary called 'RLE' (Real Life Extras), which functioned like an acting agency, maintaining a database of RLE i.e. people one could hire to fill in the background of MLE such as births, deaths, marriages, circumcisions etc. Clients could go on the agency website and select from a wide range of extras—classified by age, race and ethnicity—the ones most closely fitting the nature of their event.

The woman, who introduced herself as Rachel, pulled out her iPhone and showed Jack her profile on the RLE website. She had come upon the announcement for Karl's event (under the rubric 'Death in the Family') while she was browsing for event opportunities: *"67 year old man, white, upper-middle class, survived by his wife and two daughters, two separate rates for RLE extras on site (the cemetery) and RLE extras post-event (the house of the deceased)' Contact by phone only."* Now that the field of MLEP had expanded beyond the original two or three companies, one had to browse the website regularly in search of event opportunities in order to stay competitive in an overcrowded market where new MLE were constantly being added, forcing RLExtras to become increasingly specialized as they tried to find their own niche.

Rachel pointed discreetly at some of the men and women around them, counting them under her breath. The company had hired 35 RLExtras, an average number for an event of this size, but she counted only 27. The remaining 8 were probably back-ups, on stand-by somewhere in the neighborhood, a phone call away. In the company's records the 35 RLExtras would be noted down as "mourning personnel" and further subdivided into several categories depending on their specific duties, e.g. weepers, condolence providers, wake help, emotional supporters, etc. RLExtras pursued these different career paths according to their previous vocation and educational background but their personal psychological profile was also taken into consideration: e.g., those of a melancholic temperament were more likely to pursue training as weepers or condolence providers, while those with previous experience as maids, waiters or housewives proved better suited as wake help (post-funeral catering).

Jack wondered how a RLExtra could distinguish herself from the rest given that, unlike the real film business, acting skills could not serve as a criterion of judgment. That was a misconception, Rachel hastened to correct him. RLExtras underwent a training period as grueling as that of any professional actor; in fact, the training was far more challenging since what RLExtras had to learn was how to be present, no questions asked, which was probably the most difficult thing in the world. "Try it!" she challenged him. "Am I not doing it already?" he asked. She laughed, lost her balance, and fell against the wall behind her. As much as she had been impressed by his rhetoric she could see that, like any amateur, he still felt uncomfortable simply being. She knew the feeling because she had experienced it herself, *before* her training as a RLExtra. Back then, she told him, no matter where she was, she always felt like a little cardboard figure imperfectly glued to a drawing, the edges constantly coming unglued, making her stick out of the background instead of seamlessly disappearing in it.

RLExtra training, usually lasting several months (or more, if the RLExtra was too self-conscious) consisted of several stages. The final goal was to make the RLExtra as inconspicuous as possible, integrating her maximally with her environment. To that end the RLExtra was first released into a heavily populated environment—e.g. a train station, an airport, or an amusement park—where the RLExtra could easily get lost among all the other people and not draw attention to herself. From then on one gradually decreased the density of the host environment, eliminating distractions (such as other people and objects) and thus raising the visibility of the RLExtra, forcing her to actively struggle to erase herself and recede into the background without however—and this is important!—disappearing altogether. The aim was to achieve a level of 'presence' that was inconspicuous but nonetheless thoroughly warranted, to be justifiably present, or simply 'to be, no questions asked,' something only the most highly regarded—and highly paid— RLExtras were capable of. The ultimate test of a RLExtra's skill was the ability to achieve this kind of warranted presence in the most rarified environment imaginable: an empty room. Imagine a prison guard looking through the peephole into a cell and not seeing the prisoner inside—*that* is the ultimate testimony to the talent and skill of the best RLExtra.

4.

TAKING ADVANTAGE OF RACHEL'S next wine-glass-refill trip to the table with refreshments Jack managed to sneak out of the crowded and palpably less mournful house and to jump into a cab. The conversation with Rachel had brought up thoughts he had purposefully tried not to indulge in for a long time. The truth was that he had always felt that while others seemed naturally immersed in life he had to make a special effort to *insinuate* himself in life, like an uninvited guest or a distant, long-forgotten uncle no one is particularly happy to see after a long absence. He was incapable of simply-being-present-no-questions-asked. When he looked at a photograph his eyes were always drawn to the people in the background, random people passing by, unaware of being the background of someone else's life even as they lent that life an existential density it would not otherwise have. When others complained about being photographed without permission Jack could barely suppress his resentment: he would give anything to be able to see himself like that, an extra in someone else's life. He had never had the good fortune of coming upon a random photograph and suddenly recognizing himself as one of the blurry details in the background. Not that he hadn't tried: he would often choose a particular tourist attraction, wander around it, on the lookout for tourists, and as soon as he saw one preparing to take a picture he would casually walk into the frame. However, the tourist would either patiently wait for him to walk away before snapping the picture or politely ask him to step out of the frame. Simply being in the frame, entering or exiting it: god, wouldn't that be something!

Passing through the requisite phase of self-doubt and self-hatred, though slightly faster this time, he made a few phone calls, checked a few websites, and finally created a profile on a Film Extras website. He thought it prudent to start with the basics—working as a regular film extra—before trying his luck as a RLExtra. He was just about to settle into a long wait during which he would no doubt torture himself with a fresh new batch of fears and regrets when he received an email inviting him to work as an extra on a low-budget film shoot. The scene to which he was assigned was supposed to take place in a bus station. He was a passenger, along with dozens of other extras, whose only reason for be-ing—in the scene, that is—was to convey the impression of rush hour.

On the day of the shoot Jack woke up at 5am and took the Tube to the film set in a state of acute coffee-deprivation. A few gaffers, key grips, dolly grips, lighting technicians, best boys, costume assistants and camera assistants were milling about. There was another group of people whose function on the set was not immediately clear—as far as Jack could tell their sole occupation was to stand at a respectful distance from the man sitting in the Director's chair. The Director was a man of small stature, whose awkward incongruity with the excesses of his spirit left some people, especially talented female Production As-sistants, nothing short of breathless. He wore a pair of pants a little too short for him, as if to underscore the sublimely ridiculous nature of his physique, and a tastefully crumpled shirt that was a size bigger and that, when filled with air by the strong ocean breeze, made him look like a beautiful little sailboat floating gracefully from one end of the set to the other. The rolled up shirt sleeves, with their suggestion of revolutionary toil, provided one last touch to his general image of unstoppable, creative élan vital. At present, he was rubbing his fore-head with one hand, drawing mysterious figures in the air with his other, and gently rocking in his chair. His body was moving to a grand symphony only he could hear. The rocking got more and more vigor-ous. Just when it seemed that the symphony was going to explode in a glorious display of mental fireworks the Director froze in his seat. First, he puckered up his small face, then his messy eyebrows touched each other, remolding his face into a frown that was meant to express the creative turmoil and self-sacrifice he was known for and, finally, a little beatific smile alighted on his thin, colorless lips. It was a performance worthy of a Kabuki actor.

Jack stood by one of the bus station's side entrances, feeling like a young horse before a rodeo as he waited for the man in the rocking chair to say *Action!* - the most beautiful word Jack had ever heard. That single word had the power to endow every involuntary movement of his body, every random glance, with meaning and motivation. It would make the adrenaline course through his body. His heart would beat stronger. His jaw muscles would contract. On the other side of that little word — 'Action!' — was a world of certainty, in which every gesture or movement was padded with enough significance to reassure even the most neurotic man, a world in which Jack's existence was not under question even for a second but was, on the contrary, absolutely necessary to sustain the film's illusion of reality. The word appointed him, no, anointed him, as the irrefutable—precisely because contingent—ground of existence of 'Sarah' and 'John', the two romantic leads in the movie. The contingent nature of the movie extra—Jack's unnamed character just *happened to be* at the bus station where the two lovers part—actually guaranteed his existence. It was precisely because he happened to be there that he was incontrovertibly there. Contingency is unreliable, unpredictable and, thus, beyond suspicion.

"Action!"

Jack stretched out his hand and opened the door to the bus station with an air of casualness, even laziness, free of any self-doubt. He let the door slam behind him with a bang and walked toward the ticket counter, oblivious to the other movie extras crossing his path. Every step he took had a purpose. When added together his steps constituted an 'action' simply by virtue of that magic word, which justified everything he did as meaningful and worth doing. Although he had not come to the bus station with the express purpose of buying a ticket to Canterbury or Brighton, although he was wandering around the station because he had nothing else to do, because he was bored and the only way he knew to pass the time was to hang around public spaces, watch other people and wonder, resentfully, about their reasons for being there—despite all that, everything he did still counted as 'action.'

So this was what it was like to be present, no questions asked!

"Cut! Cut! Cut!"

One of the PAs, a college student enamored with the headset he was wearing to communicate with the production manager, a symbol of his hard-won film industry membership, pointed to the side door.

"Back to your spot."

The PA gestured to him to wait while he listened to the instructions delivered into his headset. "Roger that," he said and turned to Jack.

"Don't walk so fast next time," he instructed him in a confident voice.

Jack explained that it was more believable to walk fast and without direction so as to convey the impression of a busy, crowded place. The PA informed him that no one expected him to worry about issues of realism—that was the Director's job. Although that was not the time to discuss the nature of cinematic representation the PA wished to remind Jack that, "walking in a realistic manner in a crowded bus terminal was not the same as walking in a real life crowded bus terminal."

"When you hear 'Action!'" the PA said, "it means 'Start acting as if you are walking in a bus station.' It does not mean 'Start moving!' There's 'action' and then there is 'action,'" he concluded enigmatically.

"Action!" someone yelled, without specifying which kind they meant.

The two romantic leads were kissing several feet away. Jack made a few uncertain steps forward.

"Cut!" the director yelled, signaling to the PA. The PA waved at Jack and pointed to the exit.

"He wants you off the set."

"I can try again," Jack pleaded.

"It's no use. You are too self-conscious," the PA said in a tone of voice usually reserved for the delivery of tragic news.

"First you tell me I am not acting enough, then you tell me I am over-acting. Which is it?"

"Sir, all you have to do is enter and exit," the PA shrugged. "You can't draw attention to yourself. You are background, for God's sake!"

And that's exactly what Jack wanted to be.

"Let me try again!"

The PA shook his head and walked away. Jack watched the next several takes from the sidelines. How did the other extras manage to move so casually without appearing to 'act casual'? How did they manage to disappear in the background?

Leaving the film set Jack walked to the nearest bus station to practice walking in a real crowded bus terminal. Taking position outside the entrance he whispered to himself "Action!" and proceeded to walk into the station. As he made his way to the ticket counter everyone around him was off, moving either too fast or too slow. After rehearsing several dozen entrances and exits he noticed the security guards observing him with suspicion.

A double-decker bus was about to leave from platform 2. The driver was counting the passengers on his list. Jack walked toward the platform, not entirely sure if he was still in rehearsal mode or not.

"Do you need help with your luggage?" the driver said without looking up.

"No, thank you."

Jack paid the fare, walked to the back of the bus and sat down. He felt calm, as if he had done this before, as if there was nothing extraordinary about getting on a random bus and leaving town for no reason.

The bus pulled out of the station, made a left turn and stopped at the major intersection leading out to the highway. Jack saw his apartment building, not more than 200 feet away. His apartment faced the main street—if he strained his eyes a bit he could actually see his kitchen. He had left in a hurry this morning and hadn't had time to wash the coffee pot and the plates from last night's dinner—they were all piled up in the sink, soaked in bright orange dish detergent. The spare set of keys was hanging from a nail on the wall. The electricity bill he had been meaning to pay was on the kitchen table. The cat—whose name was Cat—was stretched out obscenely on the floor in the middle of the room, her feet twitching, something she always did in her sleep. The chair, the sofa, the dresser, the plastic hangers in the closet, the forks, spoons, Ikea tumblers, cat dry food, garbage bags, dull pencils, lightbulbs reaching their expiration date, avocados reaching their expiration date, socks that had been lying at the bottom of the laundry basket for over two weeks, a few pubic hairs on the toilet seat—all of this was still there, infused with his body odor.

The bus made a sharp right turn and the driver stepped on the gas. They were on the highway now.

5.

JACK HAD NEVER BEEN GOOD at dramatic entrances and exits. Whenever he was invited to a party or a book launch the hosts would be the last ones to notice he was there. Toward the end of the evening, when the party was already winding down and the hosts assumed the obligatory position by the door for their goodbyes, they would be genuinely surprised when he walked up to them to ask for his coat. "We didn't even know you were here!" they would exclaim, insisting that he come back and see them another time so they could catch up. He would smile and lie that 'this would be lovely', there would be some mix up with the coats, he would stand aside awkwardly while his hosts diligently rummaged through the pile of jackets, sweaters and scarves, he would try to reassure them that he was really fine without his jacket, it was not that cold out anyway, but they would insist that he wait, because giving him back his jacket was 'the least they could do' given that they had missed the chance to chat with him the entire evening. The following day he would wake up and remember absolutely nothing from the evening before. He would wonder if he did indeed go to that party. If his jacket had gone missing he would have been able to deduce that he must have forgotten it at the party. But his jacket would be hanging inside his closet, neither denying nor confirming that he had ever left his apartment the night before.

The mild surprise his entrances provoked was matched only by the timidity of his exits. It was all the more peculiar then, he thought as the bus sped down the highway, that he had failed so miserably at being a movie extra. Why was it that his real life entrances and exists were so natural and believable—that is, invisible—while he struggled in vain to disappear in the background of a film set? Perhaps the problem was that on a film set he was expected to pretend to be what he actually was in real life, invisible. It would be equally pointless to ask a depressed person to play the role of a depressed person: on one hand, 'acting depressed' might actually pull him out of his depression by forcing him to objectify his depressed state and thus transcend it but, on the other hand, it might make him see his own depressed state as a mere 'act', plunging him into a deeper depression about the inauthenticity of his own experience.

As the bus carried Jack through the night the word 'despair'—despeiren, from Middle French *desperer*, from Latin *desperare*, from *de-* + *sperare* to hope; akin to Latin spes hope—hung like a small but efficient guillotine over the top of his dirty bus seat. It was the kind of word that made for an excellent title of a treatise: there was something monumental, 'treatisely' or 'discoursely' about 'despair' (whoever heard of a treatise on joy or happiness?). 'Despair': a word that did not need any qualifications or explanations. It stood on its own. It weighed in its place. It evoked noble sentiments and extreme measures. In fact, it demanded a different font altogether: **DESPAIR.**

In "Sickness unto Death" Kierkegaard points to the deeply ambivalent nature of despair. The capacity for despair is a testimony to man's spiritual destiny and to his relation to God, yet despair is the most miserable state to be in: "To despair is a qualification of spirit and relates to the eternal in man. But he cannot rid himself of the eternal: no, never in eternity. [...] The eternal in man can be demonstrated by the fact that despair cannot consume his self [and]...precisely this is the torment of contradiction in despair" (353, 356). If Kierkegaard regards despair as a revelation of our relationship to the Absolute, while still recognizing the misery this revelation brings us, for the philosopher André Comte-Sponville despair delivers us from what he considers, under the influence of Buddhism, an ever greater misery: hope. The enlightened man has freed himself of all hope and embraced despair as the greatest happiness there is: "Que ce désespoir puisse être lumineux, oui paisable et lumineux, comme un ciel de printemps, c'est ce que j'ai essayé de montrer. […] Seul est heureux celui qui a perdu tout espoir; l'espoir est la plus grande torture qui soit, et le désespoir le plus grand bonheur" (291-292). Despair is the greatest happiness because it does not promise anything. As we no longer expect or hope to be happy, we find ourselves, paradoxically, already happy: "Telle est la bonne nouvelle du désespoir...précisément parce qu'elle n'annonce rien" (285-86). To live in despair is simply to live life as it is: "La béatitude n'est pas autre chose que le désespoir, et je l'avais dit en commençant; ni pourtant, avouons-nous, tout à fait la même chose : elle est le désespoir *sub specie aeternitatis*, si l'on veut, c'est-à-dire la vie elle-même, cette vie, la vraie vie, la seule vie, avec ses tristesses et sa finitude, mais délivrée enfin de l'attente, du manque et du sens: la vraie vie, donc, mais vécue enfin en vérité" (279). In despair all distinctions disappear: sadness becomes indistinguishable from happiness, justice from injustice, hope from despair. All feelings have a limit at which they lose their value—the 'positive' or 'negative' value ascribed to them—and revert back to their intrinsic neutrality or anonymity. Despair then becomes beatitude, the greatest happiness, the absence of all hope. In his later book, appropriately titled *Le bonheur, désespérément*, Comte-Sponville goes beyond comparing despair to certain states of Eastern religious enlightenment to consider despair on analogy with Nietzsche's 'gay science', calling it instead 'gay despair': "Le désespoir 'ce n'est pas la tristesse, encore moins le nihilisme, le renoncement ou la résignation: c'est plutôt ce que j'appellerais volontiers un gai désespoir, un peu au sens où Nietzsche parlait d'un gai savoir" (54-55). There are no traces of regret, *ressentiment* or self-pity in despair. To be in despair is to have attained 'le bonheur de celui qui n'a plus rien à espérer. Parce qu'il est perdu ? Non: parce qu'il n'a plus rien à perdre' (57). For another philosopher, Pierre

Michel, despair also functioned as a sort of self-defense mechanism: to be in despair is to guard oneself against deception or self-deception. Jack, however, did not subscribe to such a therapeutic, recuperative understanding of despair that neatly brushed aside all pain, reducing it to a placid contemplation of ultimate reality, to one eternally smug "Ommm."

Jack put on his headphones and leaned back in the uncomfortable bus seat. Listening to world music was a routine he had gotten into recently to allow his mind to wander, free of his constant internal commentator, the imp that even now sat—legs dangling, arms akimbo, a sly, cynical smirk spread evenly across his baby-fat, malicious face—at the end of this sentence, ostentatiously yawning his know-it-all smile, because he already knows how this sentence is going to end and he takes pleasure in reminding Jack that he knows it too, that he can't surprise himself.

He remembered reading a story about an amnesiac once. The man had tried to deal with his condition by inventing new memories. Following the loss of his memory he had begun dreaming of his memories. Of course, he was never able to remember any of those dreams. The reason he was able to realize—*realize*, not *remember*—that he had begun dreaming of his memories was simple. In the course of a single day the amnesiac would catch himself wishing for various things, that is, thinking about the future. Those wishes were so strong, and the realization that he could not fulfill them so painful, that through some inexplicable but enviable self-gratifying mechanism he was able to convince himself that everything he wished would happen to him had actually, at some unidentified point in the past, already happened. The pain he felt when thinking of those unfulfilled wishes had to be, the amnesiac reasoned, the sense of nostalgia normally produced by memories. Time passed. Eventually, all his thoughts about the future— all his wishes—transformed into self-manufactured memories. There was one unwelcome side effect, however: the future began fading away. The amnesiac's life was no longer framed by the past and the future: 'behind' him there was nothing, since he didn't remember anything, and 'before' him was his 'past,' his wishes-turned-memories, which could never take him by surprise.

The bus had slowed down. Jack peered out the window: there were signs—malls, parking garages, fast food joints—that they were entering a town. He checked his ticket: the town's name was abbreviated as 'Abberc.' It didn't ring a bell. He was born and raised in London and with the exception of a few unavoidable brief funeral trips he had never left the city. The other passengers started pulling their bags down from the overhead compartments, stretching, putting away their entertainment magazines, blowing their noses, thinking about dinner. Jack checked his watch. They had been on the road for five hours and judging from the landscape—which did not merit any description thanks to its monotony—they had been going north, possibly northeast if one took into account the sea breeze. Of course he could simply ask the driver or any of the other passengers to identify the town, and there was likely a map of the county and the town in the travel magazine in the pocket of the seat in front of him. Jack decided, however, that clarifying his whereabouts at this point would impose artificial limits on what had started out as a spontaneous journey into the unknown.

It was only after the other passengers had left the bus that the driver remembered to remind them to remember to take all their personal belongings with them and to have a pleasant journey forward or a pleasant stay if this was their final destination. Jack's personal belongings, of which he now thought it reasonable to make an inventory, included his ID, two credits cards, one debit card, some cash, a key to the apartment he was no longer living in, a bag of stale chips, a bright orange messenger bag bearing the name of another literary publication for which he used to freelance, an umbrella, and a pair of clean socks.

He never left home without a pair of clean socks: it was an old childhood habit, courtesy of his mother, that over the years had failed to
benefit him in any way.

He asked the driver if he knew of any hotels nearby and was given
the names and addresses of two, not far away. A couple of cab drivers whose lives were spent at bus terminals waiting for passengers approached him but he waved them away. He preferred to walk. Most of
the streetlights were broken but he didn't mind walking in the dark.
Arriving in a new town at night is always a surreal experience. Everything is unfamiliar and as much as you try you cannot imagine
what the town might look like in broad daylight. You have nothing to
compare it to yet, no memories of particular experiences or events, no
memories of what certain buildings look like in the daylight that you
can match to their respective silhouettes against the night sky. There is
also something uncanny about the experience—in the dark you can't
be absolutely sure that this is really a different town, not the one you
have supposedly left behind. And yet you feel with absolute clarity that
you really are a stranger here. The day is coming to a close, a day in the
course of which the town's inhabitants have done what they do every
day—getting born, running errands, dying—but you were not a part of
that, and yet here you are now, walking the same streets that the locals
have walked just a few hours earlier, feeling the same gentle breeze on
your cheeks, tripping over the same holes in the road, seeing the same
tree branches sway in the wind.

The hotel room, overlooking the parking lot, was small and stuffy.
The vending machine in the hallway was empty except for a few pack-
ets of chewing gum and a stale soft cookie in a plastic wrap. It was not
even midnight but the hotel bar was closed. They closed it down early
in the off-season if there were no customers, the hotel receptionist told
him. Jack wondered what was considered 'peak season' in Abberc.

The following morning he woke up very late. He rolled over the wrinkled tourist brochures strewn on the bed and checked his phone. No new messages. This wasn't all that surprising: only a day had passed, not enough time for anyone to notice his disappearance. Is that what they would call it? Had he really 'disappeared' or had he simply left? He dared not reflect further on his own motives.

Breakfast was still served in the modest hotel café, which was surprisingly crowded. Most of the hotel guests were of retirement or dying age; a few were disturbingly close to not being at all. Except for a couple of two over-energetic sixty year olds, who were busy making a schedule of activities for the day, the rest of the guests sat alone at separate tables. Jack chose a table in the back—he was not yet ready to face Abberc., glimpses of which he could catch from the big café window. At the table next to his an old but well-preserved woman with an impressive hairdo that seemed several decades old, put a single sugar cube in her coffee, took a sip, stirred the coffee, took another sip, put another sugar cube, stirred the coffee again, took a sip. She repeated the procedure several times before determining that seven was the number of sugar cubes that best agreed with her. Jim Morrison's *Break on through to the Other Side* played incongruously in the background, though it was perhaps not entirely out of sync with the senior breakfast crowd the majority of whom were, indeed, on the cusp of breaking through to the other side.

After breakfast Jack checked out. The receptionist asked him where he was off to next and offered to give him some suggestions for tourist attractions he could check off his 'must-see list' in just under two hours! Jack informed her that he, in fact, lived here. He was only staying in a hotel for one night because he was going to surprise his wife, who was not expecting him to return home so early. The receptionist smiled conspiratorially and congratulated him on such a thoughtfully executed surprise plan. Outside in the parking lot Jack opened the local newspaper he had picked up in the hotel foyer and thumbed through the apartment rental listings on the last page. The very first landlord he called accepted his offer. Things were moving along smoothly, as if he had planned the trip to Abberc. a long time ago and knew exactly what he was doing there. He asked the cab driver to make a quick stop at the Tourist Office (TO), where he bought a 72 hour pass for the sightseeing double decker bus and collected a few more brochures about Abberc.'s attractions where "lasting memories are made." As he was leaving TO he noticed a sheet of paper stuck to the bulletin board. "SEEKING TOURIST ASSISTANT: excellent communication and social skills, a pleasant demeanor, extensive knowledge of Abberc.'s history, and an intimate knowledge of the local entertainment scene strongly preferred."

The apartment he had rented over the phone was on the top floor of an old brick apartment building. It was modestly furnished but had all the basic amenities and, most importantly, three big windows overlooking the courtyard and the rooftops of the adjacent buildings. Jack did a mental fast-forward—he tried to imagine himself waking up every Sunday morning to the sound of church bells (the church was right next door) and to the sprightly steps of the lithe members of the church's Sunday yoga class. He imagined the yoga devotees leaving the church, an hour later, rolled up yoga mats under their toned arms, hair pulled back in buns, Lulu lemon yoga pants rolled up to the middle of their ankles in a casual display of the challenging physical activity they had been engaged in over the last hour.

He spent the first few days in his apartment staring at the ceiling, not thinking about anything, neither daydreaming nor reminiscing about the past. Since he had hardly ever travelled he wasn't sure what one was supposed to do on vacation, assuming that vacationing was what he was doing in Abberc. (the alternative explanation of what he was doing there was too existentially disconcerting to acknowledge). On the fourth day since his arrival he called a cab and asked to be taken to the Public Library. The library assistant at the circulation desk informed him that travel guides and brochures could not be checked out but he was welcome to read them in the Reading Room. He spent the next couple of weeks in the library, reading through every local travel guide until he had learned by heart all the 'culture and entertainment options' offered by Abberc.'s "incredibly diverse neighborhoods." Before too long he knew everything there was to know about Abberc., from general facts about the town's history to first-hand accounts and anecdotes of the scandals, marriages, deaths and weddings the locals took to heart (he gleaned this information from perusing the local yellow press).

To prepare for the job interview at the Tourist Office he rented several instructional videos, which featured mock job interviews illustrating the difference between acceptable and unacceptable behavior in the work place. Having never worked with other people (as a book reviewer sending and responding to emails had been pretty much the extent of his communication with others) Jack found the level of deferment to other people's needs that was generally expected of employees indistinguishable from obsequiousness, but in the end his curiosity about his newly chosen 'career' outweighed his knee-jerk intolerance for politeness and hypocrisy, the two personal qualities most highly valued in the service industry. He was determined not to allow such trivialities sabotage his plan (even if he wasn't sure what his 'plan' was).

The day after submitting his resume he was invited for an interview. The HR person interviewing him was impressed by Jack's exhaustive knowledge of Abberc. and of "everything the town had to offer to the curious traveler." How long had he been living here? Was he born here? Jack told her he had lived in Abberc. all his life and that his friends considered him the "go-to" person whenever they were looking for advice on where to eat and drink or where to take their guests from out of town. He complemented his answers with innocuous jokes, exactly as he had practiced in front of the mirror at home. The HR person asked him if he could kindly account for the unexplainable gap in his work experience (in revising his resume Jack had taken out the years during which he had worked as a book reviewer and critic). Jack made a long pause before telling her, in a stoically sad voice, that during the period in question he had been dealing with a 'family situation', a pro-longed illness that unfortunately resulted in the death of... He paused to consider which family member to kill off first for maximum effect. In the end he went with his mother, to whom he had been "very close" (he considered adding another 'very' but decided that the effect of a single 'very' was stronger as it seemed to intentionally minimize his 'pain'). He was offered the job on the spot. The HR person began talk-ing about salary requirements, benefits and retirement planning but Jack was too exhausted by the social aspect of the interview and nod-ded mechanically. They expected him to be in the office the following Monday at 9am. As Jack was leaving the HR Office it occurred to him that he didn't know how to get to the Tourist Office from his apart-ment. Since his arrival in Abberc. he had been taking cabs, postponing the day when he would have to immerse himself fully in the town's life and admit to himself that he was now living in Abberc. for reasons not entirely clear to him.

The idea of using tourist buses, instead of public transportation, to go to work occurred to him when he came out of the Tourist Office, after the interview, and saw three large double decker buses parked in the front. He couldn't have asked for a better solution. Every morning he boarded the TO bus one block west of his apartment and got off the bus two blocks before TO—the risk of being seen commuting to work on a TO bus was too big. When the weather was nice he liked riding on top, from where he could survey the town but never feel a part of it. To blend in with the other tourists he bought himself a small Kodak camera, which he hanged from his neck in traditional tourist fashion.

The only other thing he needed to complete the picture was a city map. Since was not that concerned with the absolute veracity of his tourist persona any map would do. He purchased three maps of Abberc., chosen at random, from one of the second-hand shops lining up the cobblestone streets behind his apartment building. They were all from the 1970s but when he folded them in a particular way it was impossible to tell how old they were. The final touch to his carefully constructed tourist persona—someone he was pretending to be even though he actually *was* one—was a pair of sunglasses he got in a second-hand shop, a model that was retro but not in a hip(sterish) way (it was now hip to wear retro non-ironically).

During his brief funeral trips outside London Jack would sometimes keep a travel diary in which he would record his passing impressions of the city to distract himself from the ennui of funeral rituals. The one he remembered the most was a two day trip to Rome to attend the funeral of a second cousin who had moved to Italy twenty years ago and whom Jack had not seen since they were both kids. His memory of the funeral itself was blurry but his impressions of Piazza Navona were as crisp as on that day years ago. A Japanese tourist eating gelato runs after a well-fed Roman pigeon, trying in vain to get the pigeon to taste the gelato. An octogenarian Italian dances to an old Italian song he is playing on a modern looking record player he has piled up, along with his clothes and an umbrella, in a half-broken supermarket cart parked next to him. There are technical difficulties: all of a sudden the song stops but the music continues. The octogenarian, who has been lip-syncing, is forced to sing for real while he tries to identify the reason for the technical glitch. His falsetto voice and strange dance moves endear him even more to the tourists who have gathered around him to snap pictures of his absurdly sincere performance. A ray of light moves across the walls of the Pantheon. A couple of tourists equipped with professional tripods and cameras methodically take pictures of the ray of light as it hits the next section of the Pantheon. When the ray comes full circle they turn the cameras on themselves, like conscientious cinema verité directors. They take turns taking pictures of each other, each proudly holding up their photographic weapon in front of the other's camera. Gelateria on the Spanish Steps: An American family is taking a group selfie licking differently colored gelatos. First they take a picture of the four scones only, each scone representing one member of the family; only then each family member enters the frame and assumes position behind their respective gelato scone. A middle-aged Italian businessman with silvery hair sits on the bench next to the American family unit, licking his gelato and clutching a leather business bag in his other hand. Elegant lawyers in expensive suits swoosh past on colorful Vespas. A dramaturgy workshop in one of the oldest theatres in Rome: attractive Roman youth, at different degrees of dishevelment but uniformly tanned and artsy-looking, lounge on the stage, discussing character motivation and dramatic arcs. About 500 meters away east of them, in the Pantheon area, Antonioni shot *L'Eclisse*. Pigneto. Necci. Pasolini's café. Black and white photographs of the *Accattone* film shoot. Almost every street bears a sign of a Pasolini film shot there. The air is heavy with the smell of jasmine and linden trees. Late night thin crust pizza and Aperol spritz. In front of the Coliseum muscular men laid off from their regular jobs sweat profusely inside their Roman soldier costumes. Creepily credible wax figures of various popes revolve around themselves, non-stop, in the window of the Curate Museum, looking up to Heaven i.e., to the ceiling of the Papal Museum and Gift Shop. Rome is espresso and real leather. Rome is Midwestern Americans with dirty, swollen feet trying on Italian leather Greek-style sandals. Rome is baristas checking customer satisfaction in operatic sentences: "How was your espresso?" "Era marvelloso!" Rome is blasé illegal street vendors selling Prada knock offs, staring indifferently past the Roman ruins that are the object, at this very moment, of hundreds

of cell phone cameras. Rome is 12 year olds with puberty voices butch-
ering a religious hymn in the Pancreas catacombs, while their friends
giggle in the back pews over someone's Facebook status update. Rome
is a middle aged, unattractive man gazing respectfully at the Caravag-
gio murals in the French church, squeezing a tourist brochure between
his hands. At the first sounds from the church organ his unmemorable
face is filled with beatitude, humility and awe at the sublimity of the
music and of the golden-covered icons looking down on him. His previously inexpressive face now turns expressive—what it expresses is
the simple awareness that he is too simple to appreciate all this beauty.
All he can do is weep helplessly overwhelmed by it. Rome is a desolate
Christian summer camp, plastic Bible figures lying abandoned in the
courtyard, outsider art drawings telling the story of Jesus along the
crumbling walls. Rome is a fat man looking like a blind pigeon, his
thick neck sagging into several layers of flesh, stuffing his mouth with
cannoli and throwing crumbs to the pigeons.

Although Jack could take the bus that passed by his place at 9:30am
and dropped him off at TO at 9:55am, he preferred to take the 8:30am
bus so he could listen to the tour guide's trivia-ridden lecture. He
would sit in one of the plastic chairs on the upper deck, put up his
feet and listen to the tour guide drone on about the movies that were
shot in this or that building, in this or that street, about the series of
noir novels that had recently become all the rage, "all based on a series
of murders that took place on the corner of this street right here," the
tour guide would say in a voice devoid of any excitement, pointing at a
non-descript street corner now occupied by a mom and pop's grocery
store and a branch of Western Union. Skipping all the gory details, and
keeping only the skeletons of the murder story, the tour guide would
offer his international audience just enough trivia to whet their appetite, throwing a fictional gauze over the otherwise forgettable street.
Sometimes Jack would listen to the tour guide with his eyes closed,

marveling at the guide's ability to fictionalize the real city they were traveling through, strip and skin it of any urban meat and grit, blow out and pulverize its graffiti-covered walls and pot-filled roads into a hypnotic stream of words that erected another, second city on top of the first one, a city in which sociopathic serial killers rubbed shoulders with sophisticated, worldly housewives and second generation hipsters, where the most unassuming corner store was the site of an erotic encounter, and the most expensive hotel the setting for a brutal murder. As they traveled through this constantly shifting fictional landscape (the tour guide's stories were updated every couple of months to reflect the most popular stories in the media)—a landscape made up of trivia that miraculously transformed the city into anything else but trivial—Jack would take out one of the old maps he had bought at the second-hand bookstore and try to locate the tour guide's stories on the map, whose growing anachronism nudged it closer and closer to that unnameable point where history turns into fiction.

After a while Jack stopped looking out at the real streets the bus was moving through and barely noticed the real people hurrying down there, two bus decks below, toward their offices, extramarital affairs, business meetings, parent-teacher meetings, grocery stores, cemeteries, kindergartens, and dental offices. His senses no longer registered the physical particulars of each individual trip, the sunlight falling across the row of French windows they were passing by, the dog drinking from the rain-filled pothole in the middle of the road, the garbage bins turned upside down, the crumpled pages of yesterday's newspaper floating, Antonioni style, down a little side street, the old woman with curls in her hair drinking her morning coffee on the balcony, under the laundry line—all of these 'real life' details would eventually drown under the hoppy, *interesting* surface of trivia. Where did George Winshaw use to get his morning bagel while shooting his latest psychological thriller in this very street two years ago? What was TV anchor Mel

Deamon's favorite pizzeria? How many people did the notorious serial killer known only by the area code within which he 'worked', kill? In front of which pastry shop did the lovers from that famous romantic trilogy kiss for the first time, and what kind of pie did they share to seal their love?

Every morning at 8:30am the bus took Jack and the other, real tourists on a 20- pound journey through the repository of cultural consciousness. The real people down there, in the street, would glance up at the tourist bus, indifferent or slightly condescending, convinced of their own privilege of knowing the city inside and out, having lived here all their lives, while the tourists were getting a barely palatable trivia version of 'the real Abberc'. And yet, it seemed to Jack that trivia offered the quickest and most authentic access to the 'real city'. The trivia the tour guide dished out over the mike consisted of facts seamlessly mixed in with fiction: it was an unadulterated expression of the fantasies of the city's inhabitants, the way they perceived themselves, and the way they wanted others (tourists) to perceive them. The stories that made it into the two-hour bus tour had been carefully selected on the basis of their popularity, that is, they were indicative of what the city's Tourist Office considered most unique about the city. Over the last several decades there had been a real push in the field of tourist literature toward offering tourists increasingly marginal experiences, getting them to explore places and experiences 'off the beaten path', getting them to see how 'real people'—i.e., the locals—live. Numerous off-the-beaten track tourist guides targeting the 'true travelers,' the 'true nomads' who pledged allegiance to no country or nation, those who didn't mind sleeping in a haystack and eating with their hands, lined up the bookshelves of the most popular bookstore chains. The word 'tourist' had gradually fallen out of favor: it was now offensive to be called 'a tourist'. Those who still expressed an interest in visiting the 'tourist attractions' were looked down upon as boorish amateurs with no real flare for adventure. As the new breed of 'world travelers' flocked toward the margins of the cities, eager to experience the real city as they had never experienced it before, the city centers, where most of the tourist attractions had been traditionally concentrated, had turned into wastelands, abandoned even by the locals who considered them already 'contaminated' by tourists and thus made no attempts to reclaim them for themselves.

Occasionally Jack would stumble upon one of the few remaining newspaper kiosks that still sold stamps, *par avion* envelopes and earnestly generic, picture-perfect postcards. These kiosks seemed like prehistoric creatures that had survived the Great Globalization Era, which had swept across the globe leveling down old-fashioned notions of the exotic and the picturesque and replacing them with the post-National Geographic concepts of the Travel Nomad and the Urban Explorer. He had wondered if he was the only one who looked back on that bygone postcard era with nostalgia or there were others, like him, who dreamt of resurrecting the lost art of tourism and the long lost art of postcard writing. People no longer sent postcards back home when they traveled; instead, they went out of their way to take photographs of deliberately un-photogenic 'non-places', the kinds of places that would never be included in a travel guide and whose value derived precisely from their unrecognizability. With the decline of interest in the generic tourist postcard an entire form of social life was also in danger of being lost. The continued use of clichéd pictorial representations like the aesthetically vacuous tourist postcard used to be evidence of the existence of a shared imaginary—a common picturesque space, a common 'elsewhere'. However, now the tourist postcard was increasingly mocked as inauthentic, ideologically suspect and clichéd. In the past, when friends and family went on a trip to a distant destination, everyone back home would receive one and the same postcard from the distant place: the only difference would be the date, the season, and the name of the sender and addresses. Now, when people travelled to the same location they would send back home highly personalized, photo-shopped photographs of the place, which would itself disappear under the burden of the sender's originality.

But the tide was turning. The 'real city' that had lured tourists off the 'beaten track' was now gradually losing its allure, its 'real' streets trampled by converse shoes and Greek style sandals, its 'authentic' little restaurants becoming more and more exclusive venues for which one had to make a reservation weeks in advance, its 'real' locals becoming more and more vaguely cosmopolitan. Abandoned by locals and tourists alike the 'beaten track' had now entered a strange phase in its lifetime: it was no longer associated with a sense of urgency as it had been before, when its enjoyment was considered mandatory, but neither had it yet become overgrown with weeds or claimed by drug addicts and the homeless. Its existence had shrunk down to a few pages in the tourist guide, a few stock photographs reproduced from older guidebooks. In short, 'the beaten track' had reached that stage when its overfamiliarity promised to slip into its opposite, rendering it strange, uncanny. The town, of course, continued to invest in preserving the appearance of everything that belonged to 'the beaten track': even as the monuments, the buildings, the art museums and other tourist attractions were losing their audiences, they retained their polished, magazine-worthy look. Tourists were still signing up for the two-hour tour, and they still snapped pictures of the historical buildings and art museums, but the real reason they were there in the first place was because they enjoyed sitting in the sun, on the open upper deck of a luxury bus, drinking chilled wine and listening to someone else tell them a story. The bus tour was their break from their exhausting sightseeing 'off the beaten track'. The beaten track had become their lunch break from a long tourist shift, two precious hours when they could sit back and relax from the intense pursuit of local flavor.

Jack got off the TO bus and walked two blocks south to the Tourist Office. He sat behind the tourist brochures display, exactly as he would do every day from now on, Sundays excluded. Mornings were generally busy, while the afternoons dragged on, interrupted only by a short coffee break at 4pm. Over time Jack learned to distinguish between different tourist types. There was the dedicated type, determined to 'do' as many tourist attractions in as little time as possible, crossing them off his mental list of errands so he could sleep better at night, having fulfilled, to his satisfaction, the tourist quota for the day. The challenge with this type was not to let them indulge their neurosis, the constant anxiety that they are missing out on something despite their best efforts and their excellent planning skills, that some little known trivia fact about the town would slip away from them, and that they would discover it only when it was too late, sitting on the bus to their next destination just as they are closing the wrinkled pages of the guidebook they thought they had put to such good use. They would arrive at their next destination, another picturesque little town, check into their hotel, locate the tourist office, start the whole work of exploring all over again, but the nagging sense of not having completed their mission in the previous town, of being inexcusably negligent in letting an old fresco, a romantic bridge, or a famous person's grave slip away, would pursue them, keeping their stomach in knots, never allowing them to relax and enjoy the new place. They would walk the streets, cameras around their neck, pockets refilled with new tourist brochures, feeling like complete and total failures. They would pretend to get excited about 'discovering' the items listed, in alphabetical order, in their new travel guide, its pages still fresh and crisp, but no matter how hard they tried to stay in the present moment, a mental image of the attraction they had missed in the previous town would superimpose itself over everything they were looking at, filling them with resentment and regret and leaving them blind to the new tourist sights surrounding them. A few days later, sitting on the bus to their next destination, they would discover, to their disappointment, that while they were busy reminiscing resentfully about what they had missed in the first town, some other tourist attraction in the second town had slipped away from them.

Then there was the 'seasoned tourist' type, the one that went to great lengths not to be taken for a tourist by dressing down, not making a public display of their photographic skills, never asking for directions and never, under no circumstances, carrying a map. They would 'drop by' the tourist office, *not* looking for help, self-consciously ignoring the numerous tourist brochures, maps and guidebooks, deliberately looking bored, not in a hurry to 'discover' anything. Occasionally they would pick up a brochure or a guidebook, glance at it absentmindedly, skeptical that they could get anything out of it, lazily put it back in the wrong slot, pick another one, this time not even look at it, with a well rehearsed automatic movement of the hand. In those rare cases when Jack somehow managed to overcome his disdain for them and ask them if they needed any help, they would say, curtly, no, and ask where the bathroom was.

Third, there was the 'know-it-all' type: they would roll out a map of the city in front of Jack and ask him to recommend places to eat or things to see, but would then question his every suggestion, informing him that, according to their research, this or that restaurant was not what it used to be, that the fastest way to this or that place was not the one listed in the guidebook but rather the one a friend of theirs had recommended, or that the average temperature in July was not 23 degrees but more like 34 degrees. If he tried to convince know-it-all types that the guidebook's authors had spent years researching the book and were among the best in their field, the know-it-alls would respond that this only proved their point: if the research had been done years ago surely the information in the guide was no longer reliable.

Why had they come to him for help then, Jack would ask. They would inform him that he was rude and thus not well suited for this kind of job, which—in case he wasn't aware—demanded excellent people's skills. One of Jack's colleagues would then step in and try to diffuse the tension, smile politely and inquire what the problem was. The know-it-alls would explain the problem indignantly and the colleague would reassure them that their helpful suggestions would be forwarded to the TO manager and taken into serious consideration in the next, updated edition of the travel guide.

Finally, there was the 'innocent-abroad' type, curious to explore but easily confused. They would 'stagger' their trip to the Tourist Office into several stages: first they would verify the location of the office without yet going in; they would return a few hours later, still not entering the office but reading all the advertisements posted on the walls and taped to the glass doors, writing down a few things in a little notebook; stage three was when they actually entered the office but instead of approaching one of Jack's colleagues they would head directly to the stacks of tourist brochures. Their approach to tourist literature was exhaustive and methodical: they would collect copies of every brochure available, and if any of the brochure slots happened to be empty they would request that they be replenished. Finally, when they had spent at least an hour in the office, collecting and reading every brochure, folding and unfolding every map, they would dare approach Jack "with just a few quick questions." Jack would spend the next couple of hours going over every single brochure, correlating brochures, representing various tourist attractions with red dots on the map, drawing all possible routes connecting the red dots, repeating walking and driving directions, drawing new maps on napkins if the official map proved 'too confusing', and correcting their pronunciation of the names of streets and menu items to avoid any possible misunderstanding. They would be impressed by Jack's intimate knowledge of the town and its surroundings and ask him if he was born here. Yes, he would lie, he was born and raised here, never left town. They would nod as if to confirm that it would be very difficult to leave a town like this, a town that had so much to offer that there were not one but two (!) tourist guides written about it, not to mention the numerous maps of different size and color one could purchase at very reasonable prices at the Tourist Office.

Sometimes, when Jack was in the mood, he would draw their attention to a specific street on the tourist map and tell them one of the stories he had heard that morning on the tourist bus; usually it was not the story corresponding to that street. He would keep remapping the city through switching and mismatching stories: the intersection of King and Queen street, where a brutal murder had taken place in the late 1970s was now the corner where the two lovers in a famous romantic comedy first met, while the cute French pastry shop where the president's current wife used to go for croissants when she was a graduate student became the secret location where money laundering gang leaders met secretly to do business before the police raid of 1992 that put an end to the whole thing. Every time Jack heard those stories, on the upper deck of the tourist bus, the streets and buildings with which the stories were associated receded further and further from view until there was nothing left to uphold their existence except for the tourist guide's monotone voice.

Every time Jack retold the stories to a tourist he would revise or embellish them a bit if he found them unsatisfactory from a dramatic point of view. Eventually he knew the stories so well, having retold them so many times, that they no longer seemed to him just stories— they began to seem like stories that had happened to him, not to someone else, like personal memories he would recall every time the tourist bus passed by this or that building or street. Once the stories began feeling like memories, their earlier versions seemed to him like distant, hazy versions of those memories that had gradually come into focus, like Polaroid photographs. This is not to say that he was beginning to feel at home, that he was making the town his own, that he was beginning to associate certain places with certain memories, even if they were fake ones. On the contrary: by appropriating public—and often fictional—memories, and transforming them into his own, he was able to remain as removed from Abberc. as he had been from the day he arrived. It was not that his private life was beginning to extend and dissolve into the town's everyday public life; rather, with every new memory he attributed to this or that part of town the physical space of the city became more and more abstracted into a mental space.

Things were a bit more complicated when it came to human beings, that is to say Jack's colleagues at work, the only human beings with whom he was forced to enter into, and maintain, some semblance of a relationship. Unlike buildings and streets, human beings resisted his attempts to ascribe to them, even to just loosely associate with them, particular moods or memories. He began to see his colleagues' incontrovertible materiality i.e., their self-sufficiency as an obstacle: the more he tried to keep his images of them schematic and vague, to think of them simply as avatars of the real people he would never have the displeasure of dealing with directly, the more aggressively they assaulted him—involuntarily of course, which made matters even worse—with their insurmountable, unsublatable particularity, both physical and psychological. Things finally came to a point where he found each colleague's individuality so grating and overblown that he perceived it as mere eccentricity rather than personality.

There were four employees working with him at TO but whenever he thought of them—whenever he was forced to think of them because his job required it—he couldn't think of them as individual human beings but only as one vaguely defined entity with several different facets instead of faces. They made even that difficult by showing up at work wearing very different noses, ears, mouths, clothes, necks, arms, fingernails, shoes, teeth, and cunningly playing with all of their attributes—he was sure they did it on purpose, to spite him—to create various, unrepeatable combinations, which they referred to as different 'temperaments', 'moods', 'dressing styles' and 'states of mind'. As much as he tried to ignore the green shirt of one, the deep dark circles under the eyes of another, the greasy hair tied into a bun of a third, and the cashmere sweater of a fourth, as much as he tried not to perceive the difference in their gender identities, he registered all of these and much less obvious material details of their being. He was aware that in spite of himself various correspondences and associations had already begun to form in his mind between the green shirt and a raspy voice, between the greasy hair and the sickeningly sweet smell of an expensive perfume, between the cashmere sweater and the squeaking of Italian leather shoes, between the dark circles under the eyes and long legs in black stockings. Sometimes, when he arrived in the office before having had his morning coffee, he perceived these various attributes as one indistinguishable entity but eventually the perceptual fog would lift and each attribute would come into focus, associating itself with its corresponding person.

He was grateful for busy days when everyone was preoccupied with their own customers; alas, the majority of the time there were significant intervals between peaks of activity, which the other four took advantage of to 'get to know' Jack, to make sure he was adjusting well to his new job, and to insist incessantly that should he have any questions about the job, or even about the town, he should absolutely, they mean absolutely, let them know because, as Jack could surely tell, they were a bunch of really laid back, really cool, really hip people and he should never, ever, feel like he would be imposing on them or bothering them, because, as they had mentioned earlier, they were a really laid back, really cool bunch. They were keen on qualifying everything they did, felt or were with 'really'—the job was 'really challenging but also really satisfying,' the weather today was 'really amazing', the town was 'really something'—as though they themselves were not entirely sure of the reality of their feelings and statements and needed to confirm them over and over again. He really *did* mind that but he also knew that openly expressing his irritation would be tantamount to indicating a willingness to engage them in a conversation, something he knew from experience was not as harmless as it seemed. Not that he had to make any attempts at striking a conversation: they took the initiative from day one, first asking him general questions (how long does it take him to get to work in the morning, how does he rate the amount of traffic during rush hour) in a friendly, predisposing tone, then moving on to more personal questions (what is his favorite place on earth, where would he like to travel if he won the lottery, does he prefer the window or the isle seat, how many times does he have to use the bathroom over the course of a six hour flight, does he think the colors in the Thailand brochure are a little off) and, eventually, going the distance with intimate questions such as "does he think it's morally objectionable to fly to Paris with your mistress while your wife is stuck at home with the kids, like that client earlier today, the one wearing the expensive Italian suit," and "is there someone 'special' in his life at the moment." Although he *strategically* answered their questions with a single 'yes' or 'no' they took his monosyllabic answers as an invitation to expand on their personal opinions on the matter at hand. When these conversations by the cooler became insufferable he toyed with the idea of hiring people to act as tourists and having them come to the tourist office where they would keep Jack's colleagues occupied.

That plan was difficult to execute, however, since Jack did not know anyone in Abberc. He didn't make any—not even half-hearted—attempts to socialize, preferring to spend his evenings at home alone, in front of his laptop. He would often close his eyes, click randomly at websites and let chance dictate his online path. It was during one such evening of virtual flânerie that he accidentally clicked on a website called Maher Studios. At the top of the webpage, in bold red, he read: "If you are considering the purchase of a new pal, please check out what I might have available." The site contained an impressive collection of 'pals', male and female, all freshly painted. Despite the variation in size and clothing, they all shared the same facial expression, one of good-natured amazement and over-friendly disposition conveyed by the asymmetry of eyebrows, one of which was invariably raised higher than the other. Jack appreciated the fact that no attempt had been made to make the 'pals' look more human; he especially liked the deep wrinkles around the mouth concealing the thin invisible wires through which one could make their pal speak. The pal's characteristics were described in great detail: "Head tilts, nods, and turns full circle, open & close mouth, side-to-side moving eyes (self-centering), and raising eyebrows. Handcrafted mechanics operate smoothly from hardwood finger controls mounted on hardwood head post. Ball and socket neck (chamois lined socket for silky smooth quiet head movements). Lifetime return springs. Sturdy, lightweight, fully lined body, with naturally shaped and expanded chest area. Deluxe hands, arms, and legs. Designed to sit alone safely. Dressed as pictured. Head and hands exquisitely hand-painted and detailed. Finest glassine eyes. Lifelike wigs, eyelashes, and eyebrows. Two year warranty: satisfaction guaranteed! A complimentary 48 page instruction book is included!"

Jack filled out the online order form but as soon as he was forwarded to the confirmation page he was overcome with doubt. He imagined getting the UPS notice and walking over to the post office to get his lightweight pal with naturally shaped and expanded chest area. The whole thing suddenly struck him as ludicrous. If he had gotten his pal by accident it would have been a different matter altogether. For example, it could have been delivered to his address by mistake.

One day he would have opened the door and found the UPS box at his doorstep. He would have taken the box into his apartment, placed it on the table and walked around it, puzzled yet pleasantly tickled by its un-announced arrival in his life, by its hidden potential to derail it. After savoring the pleasure of being taken by surprise, one that he had not orchestrated himself, he would have taken a kitchen knife and care-fully sliced the box open. He would have taken out the differently sized plastic bags, in which his pal's body parts would have been carefully packaged, and arranged them on the bed as he struggled to contain his excitement at the thought of making, by mistake, a 'pal' that was designed to channel someone else's voice but that, from now on, would channel his voice instead.

6.

SIX MONTHS HAD PASSED since his arrival in Abberc. Jack knew that thanks to the big calendar hanging in the Tourist Office. He had arrived in April; according to the calendar it was now October. Jack had no recollection of anything happening during these six months but he did not find that a cause for concern. He had not come to this town to lead a productive life, to 'find' or 'rediscover' himself or to 'start over.' He was not trying to live as if today was his last day; he was not determined to seize the day or take the bull by the balls. He was simply in exile from himself, with no intention to return.

But the world would not let him.

After six months of working at the Tourist Office and living like a tourist—tentative, detached from everything and everyone around him, ready to leave at any moment—and after working out numerous algorithms of inefficiency to help him pass the time, his freely chosen precarious existence suddenly came to an end one October morning as he was getting off the TO bus at his usual bus stop two blocks south of the office. The cashmere sweater, also known as Lizzie, came out of the building across the street from the bus stop and saw Jack climb down from the upper deck of the tourist bus. Later, the cashmere sweater would congratulate herself for not missing the irony of the situation: a tourist guide using a tourist bus as public transit to get to work every morning. The Head of the Tourist Office, however, did not care about the irony of the situation; he was more interested in the abuse of job privileges of which he found Jack guilty. For six months Jack had been passing himself off as a tourist in his own town, an affront on the dignity and honor of the entire tourist industry, and on this office's dignity and honor in particular. Jack argued that he had faked being a tourist as a way of identifying with his customers so he could better understand their needs. The Director did not buy that—he had been following Jack's 'performance' over the last six months and it was his impression that Jack was not particularly concerned with his customers' needs. Nevertheless, the Head of Office believed there was something valuable in Jack's idea and he would look into implementing a similar program, with the approval of the Tourist Board of course. As a sign of acknowledgment of Jack's contribution to the development of a new marketing strategy based on the psychological identification of travel guides with tourists, the Director announced his decision to demote rather than fire Jack—as he ought to, given Jack's egregious violation of TO rules and procedures—from a front desk job to the position of Publishing Assistant in charge of promotional materials.

That evening Jack walked home from work for the first time. Demoted to street level, disoriented, he shuffled down the street hesitantly, glancing with resentment at the double decker buses passing by. Everything down here looked and felt distastefully real. After wandering in the streets for an hour, failing to recognize any of the streets or buildings that he had become used to seeing from above, he had to admit to himself that he was lost in this town where he had lived and worked for six months.

He walked into a bookstore. The Travel section carried not only the latest editions of local maps but also some older maps piled on the top shelf, in the back, out of reach. He pulled out a map at random, faded and rough around the edges. The year was penciled in in the lower right corner: 1972. The cashier smiled at him with the edges of her mouth but not with her eyes, and looked in vain for the price tag. Instead she found the year of publication and informed him that he had picked up an old map by mistake but he told her he was collecting old maps for an art project he was working on. On his way out Jack stopped by the Photography section, which also featured a mixture of new and second-hand books. A book lying on top of a pile of glossy catalogues caught his attention: *Abberc. Then and Now: 1972-2015.* The book consisted of photographs of Abberc., each one followed by a caption identifying the exact address of the place photographed. If the cashier was surprised when he walked back to the counter and requested to return the 1972 map and get the photography book instead, she didn't show it. She scanned the map, then the book, and calculated the difference in price, which was negligible. She wished him a great day and walked to the Travel section to return the old map to its briefly interrupted bibliographic oblivion.

Over the next several weeks, when he walked past the Tourist Office Jack would no longer see the freshly painted red brick house with two plastic palm trees on either side but, instead, the primitive looking concrete building of the old school that used to stand there 40 years earlier. When he sat at his new desk, in the back of the office, he would no longer see the modern six-level parking lot but, instead, the old fish market, its bloody floor littered with fish heads. And when he walked home at night—following the imaginary route he had reconstructed in his head by mentally mapping out the connections between the no-longer existing places in the photographs—he would no longer pass by a small café crowded with hipsters but, instead, by a grocery store with an attractive display of fresh produce in crotchety wooden crates.

He enjoyed living in this imaginary city, which he now viewed not from the height of the upper deck of the tourist bus but from the distance of time, keeping the real city safely displaced, just the way he liked it. He wondered how others could stand walking in the street, where 'walking in the street' was exactly 'walking in the street' and nothing more. How could one be content with passing by the same department stores, cafes, newspaper kiosks, fast food restaurants, bus stops, tram stops, liquor stores, dog parks, churches, art + design offices, used bookstores and tennis courts, when an album of old city photographs could transform one into a time traveller so easily?

Using old photographs as a quasi-map had the additional advantage of extending the amount of time it took to travel from point A to point B since the spatial relationship between different buildings, streets and boulevards had changed considerably over the last 40 years. Street names had also changed: Jack would start walking down one street but end up in a different street after crossing the intersection, or he would plan to go to the small watch repair shop on page 42 only to end up in front of a posh hair salon for poodles, which would set him off on another false trail to a bakery where a five star hotel now stood. With the exception of a few stable referent points—the city hall, the courthouse, the department store—the majority of places floated around, unmoored signifiers that kept deferring his arrival at the Tourist Office every morning, false leads that initiated a series of false movements as he bounced off from one to the next, like a ball in a pinball machine. Instead of worrying about positioning and repositioning himself in this constantly changing city landscape his mind was actually at rest. His thoughts crawled through this unstable cityscape, slow and light, leaving no impression and failing to connect with the thoughts preceding and succeeding them.

Standing in front of a poodle hair salon, watching through the window one of the hair assistants in a crisp white apron brush the hair of a demure grey poodle in a modest (by poodle standards) blue outfit with matching shoes, Jack wondered how the brush must feel against the poodle's skin, how it would feel against his own skin, and how he would never have the guts to kill himself, which meant he would have to find another suicidal person, kill him, and then quickly confess to the murder so as to be sentenced himself to death. That way both of them would get what they want. Of course he would have to meet up with his victim in advance to discuss the rules of the murder/suicide agreement. But where would he find him (her)? It might be necessary to hold auditions in order to make sure he gets someone reliable, not one of those posers who are all talk and no action. The hair assistant turned the poodle's head slightly to the left and tilted it up so she could reach the area under his chin. The poodle looked at her dispassionately, not the least bit interested in the whole procedure but willing to go along with it if it mattered so much to his owner, an old woman petting the poodle on the head and talking to him to distract him from the absurdity of the procedure he was being subjected to. Jack wondered what her constant stream of words must sound like to the poodle, whether the dog registered, let alone understood, any of it. He recalled all the times in his life when he had decided to learn a foreign language, all the Beginner I classes he had signed up for, all the dictionaries he had downloaded on his hard drive. His fascination with learning foreign languages was not pragmatic; neither was it motivated by an interest in other cultures. Even if he were forced to remain in the country where he was born all his life, he would still want to learn other languages just so he didn't have to speak in his own. At one point, right after he had finished Intermediate French and was already taking Portuguese for Beginners, he had devised an ambitious plan of never going back to his native English and, instead, studying every new language from the foundation, however shaky, of the previous foreign language he had studied: he would study French as a native speaker of English, Portuguese as a native speaker of French, Russian as a native speaker of Portuguese, Greek as a native speaker of Russian, Chinese as a native speaker of Dutch, and so on. When he made a mistake in Russian, when he confused one case with another for example, it would be because Russian cases reminded him of some obscure law in Portuguese, not because in English there were no cases. Eventually, he would learn to speak Russian with a Portuguese accent, he would curse in Chinese with a Dutch accent, he would recite poetry in Greek with a Russian

accent. His dreams and nightmares would not only be a jumble of images but a cocktail of languages and dialects. He would, for example,
dream of jumping into an empty swimming pool in Dutch—*springen
in een leeg zwembad*—riding through the prairie on a mustang in Portuguese—*andando através da pradaria em um mustang*—and walking,
alone, through the snow in Russian—*ходить, один, по снегу*. When
he arrived at a new airport he would line up in the "Visitors/Foreign-
ers" line and answer questions about where he was coming from and
what the purpose of his trip was in the language of the country he happened to be coming from. If a more attentive immigration officer were
to remark that Jack spoke French with a German accent, or Greek with
a Dutch accent, he would explain that he had travelled a lot when he
was growing up because his parents, both diplomats, were periodically
reassigned to diplomatic missions in other countries. If the immigration officer happened to be female—which was very likely since wom-
en are generally more perceptive than men—she would comment that
she wished she had been as lucky as him to have had such an exciting
life, and she would look for an empty spot in his colorful passport filled
with stamps and signatures. Perhaps he would ask her for her number.

The poodle's session had ended. The assistant removed the protec-
tive sheet that she had hung from the poodle's neck and carried it over
to the trash basket, carefully balancing it between her hands as if it
were a precious artifact she didn't want to damage. The poodle's owner
ran her hand through the poodle's hair with a critical expression on her
face, which gradually relaxed into an approving smile. The poodle's expression remained as disaffected as before. Jack stared at the dog's tail.
He was alert, waiting for the next involuntary thought to pass through
his head, determined to catch it at its source, identify what exactly trig-
gered it. Surely a thought cannot just spring into existence. There must
be something in the present situation—him standing in front of a dogs'
hair salon—or in his present perception—a disaffected poodle leaving

the salon—that will either link up to his next perception or recall an older perception or memory. He wondered if he could write a book review by rearranging all the words in the book he was reviewing. The hair assistant was sweeping away the remaining dog hair off the floor. The poodle was gone. Perhaps there were only non-sequiturs after all.

He arrived at work late. The Director had stepped out, the other four informed him, but he was not happy with Jack's tardiness and with his lack of enthusiasm for the graphic design of the new Shanghai brochure. Jack spent 8 hours sitting in his ergonomic office chair. At 5pm he stood up from the chair because the workday was over.

This evening he decided to explore a different false route but somewhere along the route he stumbled across an entire intersection, with the café, grocery store, restaurant and library branch on each of its four corners, untouched, exactly as it appeared in the photograph on page 14 of his book-map. This little piece of untouched reality tripped him. He stood in the middle of the intersection, unsure what to do about this perfect alignment between the past and the present, then turned around and tried to retrace his steps back to the periphery of this tiny island of Reality. But the island proved bigger than expected: it took him at least twenty minutes to get comfortably lost again. After wandering the streets for what seemed like hours he stopped to rest in a little green patch of grass designated as "Thorncliffe Park." Across the street was an old gas station that looked like it should have been closed down a long time ago. In his improvised city map it corresponded to "Plate # 19." The photograph was taken straight on, showing the gas station in its entirety and some patches of grass, burned by the sun, on either side of it. If Jack strained his eyes he could see the little store inside the gas station, faded calendars from previous years still hanging on the wall, the cashier flanked by a plastic stand with snacks, whose brand names he did not recognize, and another plastic stand with newspapers and magazines announcing the news of a world long dead.

The four pumps were empty. The sun came down hard on the station's steel roof. The only sign of life in this photogenic urban wasteland was the human figure standing still in front of the station, one arm raised to his mouth and the other buried in his pocket. The man, balding and timid, wearing the typical faded blue overalls one would expect any gas station mechanic to wear, was smoking. The smoke from his cigarette twirled in front of his face and floated up, disappearing in the air above his head. The collar of his shirt was covered with gas stains.

Jack rubbed his eyes. The gas stains on the man's collar had spread out: they had almost reached his shoulders. The man continued to smoke, the cigarette smoke twirling in front of his face and floating up. There was nothing unusual about this fact except that it was a *fact*, not a feature of the photograph's composition. Jack was looking at a real man, not a photograph.

The empty lot in front of the gas station was drenched in sunlight, and so were the four empty spots by the pumps. The age of the man in the photograph was difficult to determine: no shadows cutting his face into sections, throwing into relief some parts while sinking others into the shadows. His face was overexposed, indistinguishable from any of the other surfaces that had left their impression on the photographic plate 40 years ago. He could be 19 or 59: the big denim overalls covered up any indications of resiliency, softness of skin, or musculature. Apart from the change in size of the gas stain, the man standing now in front of the gas station—Jack could now swear on it—was the same man photographed there 40 years ago.

The man finished his cigarette, turned around and walked back into the station, opening up an irreparable rift in Jack's carefully de-signed buffer zone. Reality came rushing back in, unceremoniously sweeping away his crutches, his fictional routes through the city, his futile attempts to be more present in his own life by living it as if he were a movie extra rather than the central protagonist, his experiments with incorporating movie dialogue in his conversations with others and phasing out 'real talk.' All of this was now irrevocably compromised. He had to do something fast to reclaim the gap between the real and the imaginary.

Jack walked toward the station, stepping over the man's cigarette butt. The man came out through the gas station's side door and walked toward the restrooms, which were housed in a separate building. Jack took advantage of his momentary absence to take a look inside the station. In place of the old calendars on the wall there were equally faded calendars from this year, as if the moment calendars were brought within the confines of this station they aged, in fast motion, by the decades, as if there was something in the drywall that derailed time's natural course, causing it to turn into the past before it had even become present.

"Can I help you?"

Jack had not expected to find anyone else there. A middle aged man, who could actually be younger but whose double chin and thick beard made him look a lot older—or was it simply the fact that he was sitting inside the vortex of time that this gas station appeared to be—raised his head above the counter.

"I was curious about the price of your unleaded gas," Jack mumbled.

The man glanced at the four empty pumps outside.

"Where are you parked?"

"I didn't park....I didn't drive here."

"I see. You have no vehicle," the man said. Jack couldn't tell if he was mocking him.

The man in the denim overalls came out of the restroom and turned on the water in the small sink outside to wash his hands.

"Do you work here?" Jack asked, aware that he was only making it worse.

"You are a curious fellow, aren't you?" the man observed.

The man from the photograph was now walking back toward the gas station. There was no time.

"Listen, I thought I could be discreet about this but apparently I can't. I am working on a documentary, sort of like *A Day in the Life of.* I'm doing gas station attendants now."

Jack pretended to drop the book of photographs and bent down to pick it up, hiding briefly behind the counter. The man from the photograph was at the door now. Jack could now see that he was in his sixties or even older.

"William, pick up a rag and clean up those restrooms already, will you?!" the thick-bearded man yelled at the old man in overalls. William turned around and walked away without saying anything.

"You are a filmmaker?" the thick-bearded man said, with a little less hostility in his voice. "I am Norbert. I own this place. William here is my only employee."

Jack took out a piece of paper and pretended to take notes.

"How long have you had this place?"

"Not that long, a little over three years. But William has worked here for over 40 years I think."

"Did you buy it from him?"

"William has never owned anything in his life, other than those denim overalls. I swear he must have sprung into this world wearing them."

"When did he start working here then?"

Norbert scratched his head.

"I don't really know. He was already here when I bought the place. I think he started working here when he was very young and never left. He must have come to work every morning, eaten lunch at noon, taken a nap in the afternoon, and went home in the evening."

Norbert glanced out the window.

"If you'll excuse me, I have customers."

"Sure. Could I just ask you not to tell William that I was asking questions about him? It will be easier to build rapport with him if he trusts me completely."

Around dusk William left the station. He hadn't changed out of his overalls. Jack followed him at a distance. Several cigarettes later—William's, not Jack's—William entered Jack's apartment building and, much to Jack's surprise, climbed to the third floor. Apparently, William was not only real. He was also a neighbor.

This new piece of information had not fully been processed by Jack's febrile brain when, a few days later, a late-night local TV news report informed him that a 60 year old man, a gas attendant, was found murdered in his own home. The cause of death was a head trauma, likely caused by a hit to the head with a heavy object. The motive for the murder had not yet been established and no one had been charged with the crime. The police had started a preliminary investigation.

Jack switched to another channel, but as much as he tried to distract himself with a documentary about an endangered species of sea turtles on some far-flung island he couldn't shake off the image of William standing in front of the gas station where he had spent the better part of his life. To distract himself he had to fully immerse himself in something else, so he switched off the TV, turned on the camera, and hit Rewind to review the footage of his life from the preceding weeks. The 'recording phase' that had started in London had turned out to be not just a phase after all. If anything, his obsession with monitoring the amount of time he spent on habitual activities and developing algorithms of inefficiency to slow them down had only grown stronger. He stopped rewinding at random and pressed Play. The time slot was 8am to 9am: making coffee, watering the plants, smoking a cigarette on the balcony, washing the dishes, checking the weather online, erasing his Internet history. He had already seen that footage several times.

But something was different this time. As he watched himself pour the coffee into a cup something caught his attention. It was not the timing of the action. Over the last several months he had managed to extend the amount of time invested in pouring coffee by 10-12 seconds, a fact he was very much aware (and proud) of, and which he took into account when reviewing the footage. Apart from the slight changes in the timing of actions, the actions themselves and the order in which they were performed had remained consistent: he could perform any of them with his eyes closed. He hit Rewind, waited, released the button and hit Play. He watched himself pour the coffee, rewound again, and hit Play again. This time he watched the whole thing in slow motion. Something was definitely off—a slight variation in the movement of his arm, in his posture as he leaned against the kitchen counter. He pressed Forward. Here he is on the balcony, smoking: he raises his hand to his mouth, puts the cigarette in his mouth, breathes in, takes the cigarette out of his mouth, places his hand on the railing, shifts his weight from one foot to the other, turns his head to the left, back to center, raises the cigarette to his mouth…Wait. He hit Rewind and rewatched the sequence. An almost imperceptible movement of the head to the right had somehow sneaked into the sequence.

He spent the rest of the night examining and re-examining the footage. He rewound to the day before, and to the day before that. He then went back a week, a month, a couple of months, trying in vain to identify the moment in which the reliable, consistent sequence of movements had become corrupted by the slight variation. Things were even worse: this variation was not the only one. As he fast-forwarded and rewound, rewound and fast-forwarded, over and over again, he began to notice other minor variations in the sequence of his automatic movements, which, in turn, produced other variations that became perceptible only if he compared the very first recording of an action with its latest iteration. The variations grew by barely recognizable increments, spreading through his automatic behavior like a virus, corrupting the expressionless surface of his bodily automatisms with ambiguous looks, half-completed gestures, slight modulations in his facial expression, little facial ticks, a slight shaking of the hand, a pursing of the lips and a flaring of the nostrils that seemed to express a sudden determination. What were previously automatic movements devoid of any meaning suddenly seemed imbued with another, hidden meaning. A slight turn of the head to the right now struck him as expressing fear and uneasiness.

He remembered reading in a history of Photography about the profound effect instantaneous photography had had on people's belief in themselves as rational beings. By arresting what people had assumed to be motivated, purposeful, meaningful movements, instantaneous photography had unexpectedly revealed something immobile, automatic, unconscious—dead—at the very heart of life, undermining the idea of a singular, absolutely self-present self. Not only did photography afford views previously forbidden to the naked eye—it showed the human body as nothing more than a soulless mannequin, a puppet involuntarily going through a series of maladroit, contorted postures over which it had no control.

What Jack had just witnessed, however, was the exact opposite of this. His daily records of his life did not reveal something automatic or unconscious at the core of his actions; on the contrary, his movements and gestures, which he had assumed to have become automated and unconscious through repetition had unexpectedly revealed an active consciousness, a reasoning—perhaps calculating!—mind. And yet, somehow, this self-conscious self had, so far, remained inaccessible to him.

No matter how hard he tried he could not reconstruct the exact progression of these variations in order to establish their possible causes. The variations did not occur in a chronological order but rather popped up unexpectedly here and there only to disappear again. It was impossible to establish any correlation between them or construct some sort of narrative around them. They happened in an isolated manner, never repeated themselves, and never underwent further elaboration. Although there was no visible reason for their existence, their appearance reorganized everything around them, their ambiguity spilling over into preceding and succeeding movements and gestures, pointing to a shift in Jack's mental and emotional life that had remained—and, even more disturbingly, continued to remain—off-camera.

Memory was of no use to him either. He tried, in vain, to mentally reconstruct his state of mind at the particular moment whose record he was now reviewing but he was barely able as it is to hold together in his mind all perceptions, impressions and memories that made up the present moment. Every moment was already so dense that the idea of adding previous moments to it and holding them all simultaneously in one's mind seemed to verge on the miraculous. Trying to remember how he felt or what he was thinking about when he performed this or that movement would not help him decipher its meaning or motivation. All he could rely on was a formal analysis of his movements, as recorded on camera, in terms of composition, pacing, lighting etc. A detailed analysis of his past life's mise-en-scène was the only clue to understanding the psychological import of the slight variations in his behavior over the last six months and, perhaps, their relevance to William's murder.

Nonsense. What did William have to do with any of this?

Jack pressed Stop. His image on the screen froze: standing on the balcony, he was looking right, his right hand, suspended in the air, holding a cigarette. The date at the bottom of the screen was June 14. He rummaged through the waste paper basket under the desk until he found the wrinkled receipt from the bookstore. According to the receipt he had purchased the photography book two weeks before he stumbled upon the real William at the real gas station. He supposed it was possible he had seen the photograph of the gas station, while leafing through the book, though he had no recollection of that. And if he had seen the gas station photograph, it was also possible that he had passed by the real gas station, on one of his numerous wanderings through the city, without recognizing it. And if that was possible, it was also possible that he had passed by William on his way back home after work. And if that was possible, it was also possible that he knew William was his neighbor. Now he was no longer sure if he was truly surprised that evening when he followed William back home only to find out that they were neighbors.

Jack rolled his chair away from the desk, inadvertently pressing Play. He watched himself again finish his cigarette, throw it over the balcony, take a sip from his coffee, raise the cup to his eyes and inspect the strange shapes the coffee grinds had formed at the bottom of the cup. He must have pressed the Zoom button by accident when he was recording himself that morning, because the rest of the balcony sequence was shot in extreme close up. He pressed Full-Screen mode. His eyes filled the screen. Abstracted into a series of dots they still seemed to retain—or convey in a concentrated form—a certain expression. Was that regret? Determination? Fear? Guilt? Was he thinking about what to do about William, with William, to William? Or had he already done it?

He was not the only one asking questions. A few days after the murder there was a knock on Jack's door. A man, who introduced himself as Inspector Block, in charge of the preliminary investigation into William's murder, requested to have a few words with Jack. They were talking to all of William's neighbors to find out if he had had any enemies, anyone who 'might have held a grudge against him', anyone who 'might have taken things a little too far' (which was apparently Block's definition of murder). Block declined the invitation to sit down: he liked to walk around when talking to people, he said. It relaxed people, made them feel more comfortable. Jack noted that he had no reason to feel uncomfortable. Block said nothing. Cigarette in hand, he stopped in front of Jack's laptop, intrigued by the image frozen on the screen: it was an image of Jack, cigarette in hand, standing in front of the laptop, looking down at the screen, on which was frozen the image of Jack smoking, standing in front of the laptop, looking down at the screen. Block pointed at the screen wordlessly.

"Mise-en-abyme," Jack said.

"I see," Block replied humorlessly. "Why you are recording yourself?"

"It's something I've been working on. An art project."

"I am something of an artist myself," Block said in the same dispassionate voice. "An amateur. Nothing so involved or, rather, self-involved," he added pointing at the screen.

"I am not really an artist either," Jack said. "I dabble."

"Is that so?" Block said, apparently convinced the opposite to be the case. "What is it that you do then?"

"I used to be a tourist guide."

"You must know the city like the back of your hand," Block remarked.

"Down to the smallest nooks and crannies," Jack said with conviction that took him by surprise.

"How long have you lived here? Do you know your neighbors well?"

"I suppose I know them to the same extent they know me," Jack said.

Block killed his cigarette.

"As much as I want to have a deep philosophical conversation about how well we can know another human being this is not why I am here."

Jack told him he knew all of his neighbors, although he was not particularly close to any of them.

"If you knew Mr. Frampton why did you question the owner of the gas station on the corner of Adelaide and Church street about Mr. Frampton four days before the murder?"

Jack felt his eye twitching.

"What do you mean?"

Block took out a tiny notebook, opened it and tapped on the page with a broken pencil.

"Isn't it true that you went to the gas station where Mr. Frampton worked to ask the owner, Mr. Norbert Richardson, a series of questions about the victim?"

"I wouldn't say I was 'questioning' Mr. Richardson. We were having a conversation about a new project I am beginning to work on, a documentary tracing the history of gas stations."

"So you are a filmmaker as well? Or is filmmaking also one of those things you just dabble in?" Block asked sarcastically.

Jack loosened up his collar. He felt Block's material presence with every fiber of his body. He smelled Block's deodorant, he saw, in close up, all the little hairs sticking out of Block's nostrils, and he felt, without touching, the rough surface of his hands and the dried up snot on Block's handkerchief inside his pocket. Block's presence in the room was as irrefutable as William's presence that day in front of the gas station. Jack stared at Block intently, without blinking, hoping that if he stared long enough he would stop seeing him, that Block would disintegrated into dots like his own eyes in that frozen computer image of himself. Nothing like that was happening: Block was still there, definitely a man in his early forties rather than a pointillist portrait or a random combination of geometric shapes in space.

"We would appreciate it if you do not leave town while the investigation is ongoing," Block said before leaving.

"I am a suspect," Jack said in a tone of voice that did not at all sound interrogatory.

"Everyone is," Block reassured him.

Block wrote down his phone number on a piece of paper and left it on the desk, asking Jack to give him a call if he remembers something, anything. Jack locked the door behind him and resumed his own investigative work, looking for visual clues, comparing dates, and trying to reconstruct the chronology of events since his arrival in Abberc. Every movement, every gesture, and every facial expression he had recorded now seemed suspect, including his decision to keep a daily visual record of himself. Had he decided to record himself so as to have an alibi in case of a police investigation? The idea didn't seem that far-fetched under the circumstances.

There was nothing he could do except wait for the investigation to run its course. There was no point going back to work now, but there was no point in not going either: either way it was a matter of weeks, perhaps days, before his life in Abberc. came to an end. And so he continued getting up at 6:30am, turning on the camera, going through his morning rituals, descending the stairs, passing by William's apartment one floor below—it was now cordoned off with a yellow Do Not Cross sign—and emerging from the murky interior of the apartment building into the broad daylight. Sometimes the door to William's apartment was open and he could see the crime investigation team swiping the key locks, the bed and the furniture for fingerprints, collecting hairs off the floor and carefully putting them into small plastic bags, or kneeling down to smell some unidentifiable stain on the floor. Block would be there too, walking slowly through the rooms, hands in pockets, stopping in front of a wall, looking at it intently, his eyes travelling along its crevices as if following some invisible route on an invisible map, walking over to the window, turning around, his eyes tracking a past, hypothetical movement that might have happened on the day of the murder in that space, taking a few steps back to get another angle on the same hypothetical movement, and shaking his head as though disagreeing with himself. Jack would wait for Block to notice him and wave him in for further investigation but if Block acknowledged him at all it was only with a little nod of the head, after which he would resume his methodical attempts to resurrect the past.

At night, Jack would review the daily digital rushes of his life, looking for new variations in his behavior, fleeting body tremors, a slightly faster flapping of his eyelashes, an uncommon twitching of the nose, any involuntary signs betraying his guilt. The more methodically he reviewed himself the more tentative his recorded movements and actions seemed to him, a tentativeness that would then infiltrate the same movements and actions when he performed them the following day. The tentativeness of his movements slowed them down until the number of movements that could 'fit' into a given time slot began to decrease. While earlier he was able to take a shower, get dressed, make coffee, wash the dishes and put on his shoes in half an hour, now the same amount of time was barely sufficient for making coffee. His apartment was like a turbine that was running down, making slower and slower revolutions, until one day it would stop, all in accordance with the second law of thermodynamics. As his movements got slower and slower the apartment seemed to expand. He could not imagine traveling the distance from the bathroom to the kitchen, or from the balcony to the bedroom, in less than two minutes. As he stood in the middle of the living room, it seemed to him that the walls were bending backwards, that the space between him and the apartment door was filled to the brim with extra air, pumping up the density of the space around him. Physically exhausted by the effort it took him to cross all that extra space he scaled down his morning routine to the bare necessities, excising this or that morning ritual so he could at least complete the basic ones. Every morning there was time for one fewer action, one fewer movement, one fewer gesture. He stopped showering. He stopped brushing his teeth. He stopped washing his face. He slept in his clothes to save time in the morning. He stopped making coffee at home, even through he felt drowsy the rest of the day. He stopped brushing his hair. He still walked to the Tourist Office every morning, but he had to leave his apartment at least two hours earlier to arrive on time. He knew his colleagues at work had sensed something. They politely stepped back when he walked a little too close to them, held their noses, exchanged meaningful glances, and wiped the seat of a chair he had happened to sit on. He knew he smelled. He was not ashamed of it. His smell was truthful: he smelled like he was supposed to smell, like a condemned man.

Eventually the Director of the Tourist Office called him into her office and told him he should take some time off (to her credit, she managed to do it without holding her breath or stopping her nose). He knew why but he asked her nevertheless just so he could watch her squirm as she tried to come up with some plausible explanation that would not offend his sensibility. He was obviously dealing with some personal issues, she said, but she respected his privacy far too much to ask him what they were. He assured her he didn't have any issues, personal or otherwise. She remarked that it was normal for people to deny that they have an issue. He countered by saying that it was she who was denying the obvious, namely his statement that he didn't have any personal issues. When she couldn't help herself any longer and opened the window Jack lost interest in his little game and agreed with her: he did need some time off.

Although he no longer performed many of his habitual movements they did not vanish immediately. He would wake up in the morning and remain in bed for hours, mentally going through all the habitual actions he no longer had the will or time to perform: they were like the imaginary limbs of an amputee who still feels he is moving his arms and legs in a coordinated, purposeful manner when in fact he is lying, perfectly still, in bed. He would lie there for a long time listening to his own breathing, amazed and grateful that his breathing alone could fill so much time, that he had to do absolutely nothing to maintain it: it happened of its own accord and it continued on its own. No one could credit him with the reasonably paced rising and falling of his rib cage. Of course he could stop it, which he did once in a while if he was bored or if he was trying to fill some time. But it would eventually start again, despite him, and to spite him.

After a while he could no longer get up from bed so he remained there. All he could do now was reach out, from under the bed covers, to the camera on the night table and press the Record button. In the evening he would repeat the movement but press Stop, then Rewind. He would watch the record of the day, which consisted of him lying in bed, and eventually fall asleep to the sound of the record of his breathing. He slept soundly, without dreams, without nightmares, and he woke up free of anxieties, doubts, and desires. He imagined this is how he would feel in prison, once the trial and all other formalities were over and done with.

He was ready.

A few days later, feeling a slight spurt of energy, he turned on the TV. The news report was on. He watched the natural and human disasters of the day condensed in one eventful minute, the weather forecast, the stock exchange report, the celebrity siting of the day, the crime report. The investigation into the murder of William Frampton, a gas attendant, had concluded successfully with the capture of the perpetrator, one Lionel Pensky. Pensky, Frampton's neighbor, had confessed to the murder and was currently undergoing medical examination. There was reason to believe he was mentally challenged.

Jack sat up in bed. His head was spinning. Pensky. Pensky. Lionel Pensky. The name sounded familiar. He massaged his temples with the tip of his fingers. Suddenly the name appeared clearly before him.

He walked to the door of his apartment and opened it. The name was written out neatly on a small piece of paper glued to the door opposite his apartment. Apparently Lionel Pensky lived across from him yet no matter how hard Jack tried he could not recall the man's face.

Jack ordered a large pizza and while he was waiting for the delivery he began going through all the online updates on the murder case in reverse chronological order. Apparently, no relationship had been established between Frampton and Pensky. They had never been anything more than neighbors and it was not even certain that they had ever exchanged a word. Pensky had never had a driver's license and, as far as the police could tell, had never been to William's gas station. The perpetrator had no relatives, distant or close, and had been living on social welfare for the last 20 years. He had made no attempts to hide his deed: as soon as the police began questioning him, along with the other neighbors living in the building, Pensky confessed to murdering Frampton. He had explained to Inspector Block that he needed Frampton's body to test an idea he had for a human ventriloquist figure, because he didn't find the wooden one he had purchased online—mind you, handmade—realistic enough. He had then enumerated all the flaws of a wooden ventriloquist figure and listed all the advantages of a real human version. When asked why he had chosen Frampton as a prototype of his human dummy Pensky had confessed that he had chosen Frampton at random. Any human body would have done just as well—Frampton's simply had the added bonus of being more readily available as he lived in the same building, one floor below.

Inspector Block, the online article went on to say, known for his indefatigable devotion to the job and for his intimate knowledge of human nature had not stopped there. He had continued burrowing into Pensky's personal history until his investigation finally paid off. Intrigued by the absence of anything in Pensky's past that could explain his peculiar obsession with ventriloquist figures, Block had interrogated the accused further, knowing that criminals of his type often viewed their obsessions as proof of their intellectual and moral superiority over the law-bound crowd of 'normal' people and thus often took pleasure in sharing their abnormal obsessions with representatives of the Law. However, much to Block's chagrin Pensky's interest in ventriloquism did not have a long history. When they searched his apartment the police did not find any other ventriloquist dummies or any books on the practice of ventriloquism. Pensky's conversations, all his neighbors testified, had never been peppered with half-hidden references to the lost art of ventriloquism or to the exquisite pleasures of scooping out a human body to make it function as a dummy. The story turned out to be a lot simpler. Pensky confessed that one day, some months ago, he had received a Fed Ex package that was not addressed to him but to someone else (in fact, to his neighbor living across the hall, one Jack Sturrett) but that was delivered by mistake to Pensky's apartment. Although he was well aware of the mistake Pensky, his curiosity aroused by the contents of the package, did not return it to its rightful owner. He had never heard of ventriloquism—luckily the package contained an informative brochure (in color!) with specific instructions on using the dummy and even a few exercises meant to improve the ventriloquist artist's craft. Pensky began practicing right away and even purchased all the DVDs in the "Masters of the Art of Ventriloquism" series.

Pensky confessed to Block that he found talking through someone else a pleasant way to pass the time as well as an opportunity to finally have an actual conversation with someone, even if that someone was himself. Over the course of time, however, Pensky apparently grew increasingly disappointed with the obvious limitations of a wooden dummy. He found it infuriating that the makers of ventriloquist figures seemed uninterested in creating more human-looking dummies. It then occurred to him that he could try to make one himself. After all, all one needed to make a dummy was a body and there was no dearth of those—they were everywhere, including in his own apartment building, literally a few feet away from him. One evening Pensky waited for Frampton to come home from work, struck a conversation with him and followed him inside his apartment. Only after he had killed him did he realize that turning Frampton into a dummy would require all kinds of tools that he, Pensky, didn't have. It also occurred to him that, even if he managed to scoop out Frampton's insides and fill him up with pharmaldehyde, it would be very difficult to shove his arm through Frampton's throat: Pensky was a small man with short arms while Frampton was tall and skinny, with a long torso. Pensky's arm would likely remain stuck inside Frampton's torso and Pensky would have a hard time manipulating Frampton's dummy's facial muscles.

The long article summarizing the main stages in the murder investigation ended with a quote from Block, who commented on the irony of the situation: apparently, he said, the man who had ordered the ventriloquist dummy, Jack Sturrett, but who didn't get it by mistake, had been a prime suspect in the early stages of the investigation. Although Pensky's confession had completely exonerated Sturrett, Block reminded readers that the court had ruled that Pensky be sent to a psychiatric institution. However, whatever doubts the confession of a mentally ill man might raise, they would be dismissed as 'circumstantial' now that the case was closed.

Jack grabbed the photography book and went out for a walk to clear his head. The sun blinded him but he found that pleasurable. The light breeze caressed his cheeks and pleasantly tickled the inside of his arms under his shirt. Strange how easy relapsing into life was after all the hard work he had put into withdrawing from it. He was walking at a leisurely pace, allowing others to catch up with him and pass him by. He enjoyed those brief moments when a stranger, having walked behind him for minutes or sometimes longer, eventually caught up with him. The stranger would walk next to him, as though they were walking together, neither of them saying anything to the other, their movements and the direction in which they were moving miraculously synced for a while, until the stranger picked up the pace and passed him by. Jack would continue walking alone, following with his eyes the stranger who was now walking beside someone else, soon to overtake that someone else. Eventually another stranger would catch up with Jack and the whole thing would repeat itself. In that small window of time when a stranger walked beside him Jack felt as though something unspoken remained between the two of them, that they were both in on some secret they were guarding from the rest of the world, that this is why they didn't speak to each other. They were like spies working for a top-secret organization that had arranged a meet-up between them so they could exchange a secret piece of information. As they walked side by side each one of them knew the other one was thinking about the same thing, waiting for the right moment for the exchange, but somehow they always missed the moment and one of them had to continue walking forward so as not to draw attention to himself. And so it went, stranger after stranger trying to, and failing, to pass on the secret to Jack, as if they were all participants in an embarrassingly inefficient Olympic relay race.

Sometimes, when he didn't think of them as secret agents or failed Olympic relay runners, Jack liked to imagine that he had known these strangers for a long time and that this short walk, side by side, was the last moment he would share with each one of them. In a matter of a few strides he would reconstruct the entire history of his relationship with each stranger, from the moment they must have first met, months, years or decades ago, through the various stages in their evolving friendship or love affair if the stranger happened to be an attractive woman, their tedious arguments, passionate fights, late night phone calls, increasingly irregular emails, long periods of silence interspersed with blips of re-connecting, re-discovering, followed by even longer periods of oblivion, from which they would be finally awakened only thanks to a random encounter in the street, the two of them now walking side by side, having finally discovered, after all these years, the one thing they shared, silence. When he grew tired of imagining backwards, that is experiencing the brief moment of walking side by side with a stranger as the coming to an end of a long history that cast its shadow somewhere behind him, Jack would switch gears and imagine forward, that is, think of the present moment that had brought him and a stranger together as the inauspicious beginning of a relationship whose end was still far ahead in the future, on another sidewalk perhaps, where he would walk at some point in the future reconstructing the history of the now still non-existing relationship.

The area around the department store was crowded. He followed the crowd into the store but before going in he pulled out the photography book, which he had been carrying all this time in the inside pocket of his jacket, folded in two, and dumped it in a garbage bin. Its black and white photographs of streets, people, churches, drugstores and shops had lost their power to displace the real streets, people, churches, drugstores and shops that were now weighing back in, claiming their places all around him, re-situating him.

The spacious isles separating the rows of clothes' racks—arranged by color, function and price—on the floor with the top designer merchandise, got a lot of traffic in the afternoon, mostly upscale housewives of a certain age strolling past the racks of designer clothes with a slightly bored expression on their puffy, botox-injected faces. Most of these women knew one another—they had all spent the better part of their sixties taking long walks down these isles, a small but tasteful Prada bag under their arms. Occasionally they stopped to inspect a piece of clothing, feeling the fabric between their manicured fingers, holding the dress up in front of their eyes to see whether it would cover up their bony, wrinkled knees, and never checking the price tag (that would be vulgar). They could easily afford any of these dresses, in fact they could probably buy all of them—all sizes, colors, and variations—but there was always something about the dress, some small detail—the color of the button that one could not even see because it was discreetly positioned in the back, or the shape of the décolletage—that disappointed them. As they walked from one rack to the next they felt let down, cheated out of a pleasure they felt entitled to, afraid to hope that the next rack would hold the surprise 'find of the day'. But the dresses hanging off the next rack were the same ones they had seen the week before; in fact, now they looked worse than the week before simply by virtue of the fact that they had already been seen once and so were as good as used.

Jack took the escalator to the last floor, part of which was cordoned off with a red band. On the other side of the red band a group of women sat in a circle, engrossed by a presentation delivered by a short woman in a business suit.

"Raise your hand if you consider yourself a winner!" the woman said with an inspirational smile.

The women hesitated.

"Come on, ladies, who here is a winner?" the short woman repeated, raising her voice to an authoritative pitch.

A couple of women raised their hands tentatively.

"That's more like it!" the short woman said, smiling coldly. "Now, which one of you loves shopping? I mean, really loooves it!"

All women raised their hands.

"You go ladies!" the short woman congratulated them.

The women in the audience smiled at each other as if they had just gone through a most difficult ordeal and had come out on the other side unscathed. The short woman looked around, clearly satisfied with the effect of her inspirational presence.

"And now raise your hand if you love doing your finances as much as you love shopping!" she teased them.

The women chuckled. They knew they were expected to acknowledge publicly, through a commonly produced, agreed-upon sound, that this was a joke. Jack walked away before he could find out the specific banking services for 'winners' the short woman was there to promote. He wandered between the isles of designer clothes, occasionally coming upon a small island with a cash register. The store was purposefully designed so as to hide the cash registers: any thought of having to pay for anything here had been banished so as not to reduce the clothes to mere merchandise. At one of the cash registers two customer assistants were having a tête-è-tête. The older one, a middle aged woman with a small, concerned face was trying to convince the other one, a plump teenage girl, that she ought to cut down on refined sugar and eat more apples. Jack knew this to be a fairly common recommendation people liked to exchange at times of personal crisis or, alternatively, boredom.

Alas, removing refined sugar from one's daily life was not always the best solution to a personal crisis. Jack had read an article in the local newspaper about a worker at a sugar refinery, who had put an end to his life by jumping into the enormous cauldron of sugar whose refining he had recently been promoted to oversee. The story was brief and did not give any details about the man's personal life or make conjectures about the possible reasons for his suicide or about his peculiar choice of 'suicide medium' (sugar). At the time of his death the employee, whose name the newspaper did not reveal for reasons of privacy—although the act of drowning oneself in a cauldron of refined sugar was hardly a private one—had been employed at the sugar refinery for less than six months, making it highly unlikely that his decision to end his life in this particular manner was prompted by prolonged exposure to enormous quantities of sweetness that contrasted sharply with the sourness of his own existence, or at least with his existence as

Jack tried to reconstruct it from the few minor details provided in the newspaper article titled "Man Finds Sweet Death."

In the weeks preceding his suicide the now dead employee had shown no signs of depression or of any other psychological disturbance that might have attracted the attention of his fellow employees, who would have then brought up the problem to their foreman, who, in turn, would have referred the troubled employee to the Refinery's Health Center. The dead employee had punched in at work every morning, like everyone else, had taken his lunch in the cafeteria and joked around with the boys, like everyone else, had attended meetings with the foreman and undergone training to familiarize himself with the new machinery, like everyone else, and at the end of his shift had boarded the bus home, like everyone else. He had been generally liked among the other, alive, employees, and had even shared a beer or two with a few of them. His coworkers described him as a reliable worker with an average work ethic, neither a slacker nor a go-getter. As for his attitude toward his job, his co-workers unanimously agreed that he had had no strong feelings about sugar one way or the other: he took his coffee with one spoon of sugar and his tea with no sugar, but that could have been because he drank herbal tea, which was not as bitter as English breakfast tea and did not require extra sweetening. All in all, the dead employee had enjoyed his job, within the limits of what is expected in terms of enjoyment from this type of work, had been on good terms with his co-workers and his foreman, had not been diagnosed with any mood disorders, and had demonstrated a positive attitude toward sugar, which must count for something when you are faced with such enormous quantities of it on a daily basis.

Some time around 1pm, on the day of the incident that would render him no longer alive, the dead employee had been seen buying a pack of chewing gum from the corner store across from the refinery, something that arguably he would not have done if he had planned to end his life an hour later. He had even commented on the cashier's new hairdo—as she would later tell the police—and had seemed in a generally upbeat mood. He had entered the enormous refinery hall, turned on the sugar centrifugal, and assumed his usual position from where he could oversee the process and stop the machine if something went wrong. Around 2:20pm the foreman had called the other two men working with the dead employee up to his office, leaving the soon-to-be-dead employee alone. About ten minutes later the foreman had looked up from the plans he had been showing the other two men up in his office with a big window overlooking the refinery hall underneath and had noticed the top of the dead employee's head popping up, like a buoy, in the middle of the gigantic pile of sugar before sinking again. By the time the three men had reached the sugar centrifugal it was too late. All that remained of the dead employee were his shoes, which he had taken off before diving into the refined but deadly sea of sweetness.

'The sugar man's case', as it came to be known, quickly became a hot topic for debate in the media as well as in academia, where it was taken up by one Prof. Dooley, who came up with a bonus question for the final exam for IPHL (Intermediate Public Health Law) based on the case. Dooley had become somewhat famous for the peculiar first-person singular format of his multiple-choice exam questions. The exam question inspired by the sugar man's case, for instance, was formulated as follows: "I am a worker at a sugar refinery. I have a stable job record and I do not suffer from any mental disorders. One day I commit suicide during work hours, at my place of work, using the very substance whose production I am in charge of (sugar). My family, who believe my suicide to be a work-related accident, sues the sugar refinery. To make the case in my favor my family's lawyer points to statistically correlated measurements of the acceptable amount of sugar in the cauldron on any given day and to the deviation from this standard amount on the day of my death. Given the facts of the case, who do you think should receive a monetary compensation in this case: 1) the dead employee's family; 2) the sugar refinery, which claims the employee's suicide has cost the company an enormous amount of money (the sugar in which the employee committed suicide was obviously no longer edible and had to be thrown away); 3) the family's lawyer; or 4) no one?" Apparently, students got this question wrong so often—in fact, all the time—that Dooley resolved to organize a class trip to the sugar refinery so they could reenact the case on site instead of thinking about it in the abstract. Unfortunately, the university administration did not support the proposed 'field trip' for fear of any possible litigation should the reenactment turn bad and claim the life of another victim.

Jack stopped and looked around. He had been so preoccupied with the Sugar Man's tragic story that he hadn't realized he was no longer in the department store: he was now standing in front of the heavy glass doors of the Tourist Office. Handing in his letter of resignation took five minutes—the Director had gone out for lunch so he simply left the letter on her desk. In the letter he thanked the Director for giving him this wonderful opportunity to learn about the Tourist Industry from the inside out but did not specify his reasons for leaving.

Outside the Tourist Office a dozen tourists were milling about as usual but he was no longer one of them. Despite his best efforts to remain uncommitted to this place, without a map or at least with a fictional one, he had arrived at his destination simply by placing one foot in front of the other, his whole body already knowing instinctively the direction in which he was going. He had hoped the feeling of transience, of homelessness, would remain his only home. But the city had finally won: it had taken over his body and turned it into a map itself. He was like the rest of them now, a local, in sync with the city, seemingly unable to escape. Unless… He waved a cab and asked the driver to take him to the airport.

An hour later he was drinking an espresso in the Italian café in Terminal 1. He had hoped that the transient nature of the airport would be enough to jumpstart his nomadic existence, to bring back the feeling of being a tourist. However, within the general sense of the liminal produced by all airports there was still an unmistakable difference between the pleasant state of limbo in which a local finds himself while waiting to leave his hometown, and the state of disorientation a tourist feels when he first arrives at the airport of an unfamiliar city. Thus, instead of recapturing his nomadic sense of self the longer he waited at the airport the more firmly grounded he felt, as though he had lived in Abberc. all his life.

The café was empty except for a bespectacled man and what looked to be his son, a boy of about eleven with a small round face and an upturned nose. The man was reading aloud a math problem from his son's textbook; his pleasant voice came in and out amidst the clanking of cups and glasses behind the counter and the wheezing of the espresso machine. "You are filling a swimming pool with 200 gallons of water, using a rubber hose. You began filling the pool at 9am and you know you have to finish by 11am at the latest. How long would it take you to fill it up to the brim, taking into account the coffee break at 10am?" The boy leaned forward, cupped his hands and stopped his ears so he could give the problem the full attention it required. He flipped to the last page of the book and jotted down a few things with a pencil, occasionally stopping to reread the problem so as not to get any of the parameters wrong. He then lifted up his head, propped up his chin with his small hand, and stared ahead at some invisible point in the distance. Jack followed the boy's gaze. The polished white floor swirled before his eyes, becoming brighter and brighter, and the wheezing of the espresso machine grew louder. The floor fell through and a stream of water burst out filling up Jack's field of vision. The wheezing, having reached a crescendo, suddenly stopped, leaving behind a piercing silence punctuated by memory echoes of wheezing sounds that grew quieter before fading out completely. The airport, and the whole world in which the airport had existed, was now an empty, liver-shaped swimming pool at the bottom of which lied a thick rubber hose. Jack stared at the hose. Suddenly water burst out of it, spreading out from the center of the pool to its four corners until the entire bottom of the pool was under water. All of a sudden Jack was gripped by a sense of urgency he had not experienced in a long time. Nothing else seemed to matter now except figuring out, as fast as possible, how long it would take to fill up the pool. The rubber hose twitched and turned, as though it had come alive, spurting water in all directions. Everything that had, up to now, kept Jack's existence soft and unfocused—all doubts, ambiguities, uncertainties and regrets—came together as if attracted by some magnetic force, finally crystalizing into one single problem whose simplicity and urgency was enough to break his heart. All those long days, months and years of wondering, wandering, questioning, self-sabotaging, giving up, breaking down, coming together, falling apart again, drained of energy, even the energy to break down, floated by like pieces of debris after a shipwreck on the seductively blue surface of the pool, a superfluous weight that lacked the gravitas to even sink with a proper plunk. He saw himself standing by the pool, clip chart in hand, writing down formulas, adding and subtracting numbers, calculating square roots, crossing them out, writing them down again, drawing the line, putting down the final figure, a number that he had produced through a series of math equations and logical deductions, following mathematical laws he had learned in elementary school but forgotten right away, a simple number that bordered on magic, a number that made all his doubts appear preposterous, self-indulgent. He now saw clearly that he had been given the tools he needed to live very early on and that he had casually, contemptuously, thrown them all away, setting out instead on an imaginary, self-sabotaging quest for something 'more', something 'meaningful'...whatever the hell that was. The simple fact was, life was simple, as simple as a game of poker.

Peter, Sarah, Michelle, Josh and John are playing poker. Peter is sitting across from his wife, who is sitting next to her ex-husband. Josh is sitting to the right of his closest friend, the only right-handed person at the table. One of the five is cheating on their current partner with one of the other three, and one of the other three knows about it but keeps quiet because they, too, are cheating on their ex-partner with one of the other four. Given that John is the only single person at the table can you deduce the seating arrangement and the specific romantic or sexual relationship of each of the five players?

The firm of Harper & Robinson has recently hired seven new accountants, four women and three men. Their cubicles are located on the same floor but only one of them has a window. Two of the men come with the highest recommendation from their previous employers, while three of the women have slept with their previous employers to advance their careers. Two of the men—not necessarily the two with the best recommendations—have, at some point in the past, had an affair with a colleague, and one of the women—not necessarily the least attractive one—is divorced. One of the women always returns to work ten minutes late, after the lunch break, and two of the men arrive five minutes early. One of the men and two of the women spend, on average, twice more time at the office cooler than any of the other employees. One of the women wears Prada but her salary is the lowest of the seven. Three of all seven employees have brown eyes, two have blue eyes, one has green eyes, and one is handicapped. Only two of the seven employees use stick-it notes but all seven have at least one photograph of a close family member decorating the wall of their respective cubicle. Given these facts can you deduce who got the cubicle with the window, what measures they took to secure it, and who is most likely to get fired by the end of the month? Bonus question: Was the Prada suit a gift from a superior, a significant other, or a colleague?

Jen and Marc are going grocery shopping. Jen has $60.85 at her disposal but she would prefer to spend only half of that on groceries. Marc has $110.34 but he is willing to spend only half of that. She smokes, he doesn't. A pack of cigarettes costs $8.50. Marc likes vanilla ice cream. The average price for half a gallon of ice cream at the store is $6.50. Jen prefers Greek-style yoghourt to the 5% fat yoghourt the majority of other customers buy; however, she has recently decided to cut down on yoghourt. A pound of reduced fat cheese is $16.50. A loaf of rustic bread is $3.75. Organic lettuce: $4.30. Fish filets: $7.80. Light bulbs: $3.65. Plastic gloves, yellow: $2.78. Dishwashing liquid: $4.65. Swedish meatballs, frozen: $8.95. Sports Illustrated: $6.80. Condoms, flavored: $7.50. Aromatic candles: $5.00. Plastic bag: $0.05. Given these facts, can you deduce which product will provoke the Wednesday morning argument between Jen and Marc that will lead to their eventual divorce?

A construction company has signed a contract for a large sum of money to build a new condominium building near the waterfront. The number of employees exceeds 200 people. There are two foremen. The completion date for floors one through twenty is April 15, and that for floors twenty through fifty is July 30. In the construction business there are 2 work-related accidents on average every day. Three of the married couples to move into the new condominium will file for divorce within two years of buying their condo. 10% of the extra-marital affairs among condo owners begin in the condo gym or swimming pool. The average temperature of the water in the condo pool is 21 degrees but during the summer it is kept a few degrees cooler. 80% of condo dwellers report being happy with their lifestyle, 12% report increasing dissatisfaction after moving in, and 8% are unsure how they feel. Given these facts, what is the likelihood that Mary and Paul, recently engaged, both gainfully employed and possessing a healthy sexual appetite, living on the 27th floor, two floors down from Ann and Tom, another very attractive young couple, will stay married for more than 3 years and have sex more than twice a week? Hint: Ann and Tom have sexual intercourse less than half a time per week.

Life is nothing more, and nothing less, than a series of clearly defined problems like these with just enough information to help one arrive at the only plausible solution. All the data necessary to make the correct deduction is always readily provided; all one needs is the dedication and stamina to push through the series of logical detours purposefully planted in the way as a way of strengthening one's logical skills.

"Very good! Now do the next one."

Jack looked up. The problem-solving father flipped the page in the math textbook. The bus boy walked up to Jack's table and began clearing the dishes. Jack watched him silently for a while.

"I wasn't done," he finally said.

"I am sorry sir." The bus boy began unloading everything he had collected on his tray back on the table. There was no reason for Jack to make a scene. It was unlikely that the bus boy had any hidden agenda in clearing the table prematurely. The truth is Jack wanted to punish the boy not for failing to perform his duties but for his indifference toward the very peculiar personal crisis Jack was going through. That the bus boy had failed to recognize—through no fault of his own but other than his sheer absent-mindedness—Jack's superior talent for suffering in exceptionally nuanced ways only made matters worse.

Jack was suddenly struck by the monstrosity of his own 'fine sensibility' and repulsed by his passive-aggressive expectation to be congratulated, even admired for it. Why should his own constant sense of anxiousness, clearly a product of his unhealthy obsession with oneself, matter in the least to a boy forced to spend his days stroking other people's egos in exchange for pitiful tips? Jack looked around. People were walking through the terminal, either leaving or arriving but, unlike Jack, none of them exaggerated their departures and arrivals into a hyperbolic existential quandary, a whiny search for a more 'authentic' self. Wasn't it time to stop indulging in self-hatred, to accept, without a sense of resignation, his identity as a local, to stop perpetuating a romanticized image of himself as the eternal tourist?

And yet when the automatic glass doors of the airport closed behind Jack and a taxi driver stood in his way and said "Holiday Inn?" Jack replied automatically "Holiday Inn," and followed the driver to the hotel shuttle. Half an hour later the shuttle stopped in front of a Holiday Inn on the outskirts of town. A single hotel guest was waiting for the shuttle, smoking and talking on his cell phone. He walked away from his small black suitcase in the middle of the parking lot, gesticulating excitedly, oblivious to anything around him. The hotel was flanked on either side by fast food joints and gas stations. The opposite side of the road was still wild but further down the road Jack could see the massive, identical looking buildings of the Outlet Mall. The driver got back into the van and honked. Running toward the van the hotel guest waved at the driver to wait. Jack walked toward the entrance, past the small black suitcase in the middle of the parking lot. He retraced his steps and picked up the suitcase.

"Welcome to Holiday Inn," the hotel receptionist said without conviction. She hesitated before adding "Your home away from home."

Jack figured she must be new. Remembering a series of bland niceties and being automatically courteous to strangers takes time. She asked him for an ID. He watched her enter the number and expiry date into the system. Her facial muscles had not yet relaxed from the fake smile. He wondered if this was what she looked like in the middle of an orgasm, painted fingernails tapping impatiently on her lover's back, followed by a post-coital affirmative tap, a sign of gratitude that the whole thing was finally over.

"How many nights?" she asked, smiling at him or rather at the ideal hotel guest she had been trained to greet during the six month long Customer Service course she had been obliged to take.

"One."

"Pleasure or business?"

"Do you mean which one I prefer?"

She blushed.

"Pleasure," he said and immediately regretted it.

"It's too bad you are staying just one night. This town has so much to offer."

She spread out several tourist brochures on the counter, fanning her long red nails fetishistically over their glossy surface. He picked up a couple of brochures at random and stuffed them in his back pocket without looking at them.

Up in his room he sat on the bed and turned on the TV. Only now he remembered the suitcase. He lay down next to it and stroked its smooth leather surface. *This life* could be his, he thought.

He woke up late. The suitcase was under his head. At some point during the night he must have decided to use it as a pillow, an unwise decision as he discovered when he tried to move his stiff neck. He opened the window: life outside went on unimpeded, sure of itself. Downstairs in the lobby the receptionist's painted fingernails were wrapped around the telephone.

"Black? I see. Real leather. We'll give you a call as soon as we find it."

He checked out, went outside, put the suitcase down and lit a cigarette. When the airport van came by he got on, leaving the suitcase by the entrance. He got off at the downtown Holiday Inn and from there walked back to his apartment. He sat down on the bench next to the elevator. On most days one of his neighbors, an overweight man of uncertain mental prowess, would park his wheelchair by the bench and spend the entire day observing people going in and out of the building. He lived alone and the highlight of his day was the arrival of the mailman, between 10 and 10:30 every morning. The building's residents felt obliged to exchange a few passing pleasantries with the man and walked away feeling better about themselves on account of their voluntary display of magnanimity. The wheelchair was not there today, for which Jack was grateful.

He spent the day cleaning the entire apartment. In the early evening, when the light was most flattering, he took a few pictures to post along with the online ad. The latest trend in rental apartment photography was to isolate small, beautiful objects and photograph them tastefully while leaving the background out of focus, a trick that kept the potential renter unaware of the real layout of the apartment or its real size, and instead seduced| him with attractive but useless bric-a-brac. He figured he could charge at least a grand per month, which would probably be enough to live on for a month while looking for another job and a cheaper apartment.

7.

AFTER A BRIEF PHONE INTERVIEW with the first person to contact him, Jack was ready to hand over the keys. His subletter had collected all kinds of evidence certifying his maturity, reliability and financial solvency. After pretending to inspect the paperwork with the utmost seriousness Jack signed the contract he had written up himself and wheeled his suitcase out onto the street. At first he thought of checking into a hotel, perhaps the airport Holiday Inn, but the thought of having to explain his return and being forced to share his 'impressions of the city' as a first-time tourist with the red-fingernails-fake-smile receptionist put him off.

He sat down in a café and opened the daily paper to the Classifieds section. The rental sub-section was long and the font too small. He placed his index finger on the page and moved it down, occasionally stopping to circle an ad. The Rentals section was on the same page as the Obituary section, which seemed logical since both followed the principle of vacancy/no vacancy. One day, he thought, he must write about the crossover between the two without slipping into cheesy metaphors of people 'renting' and 'vacating' their physical bodies, and without describing apartments as temporary coffins awaiting the arrival of the real, smaller coffin to be displayed in the center of the living room where it formed a pleasing mise-en-abyme with the larger apartment-coffin. Without removing his index finger from the Rentals page, Jack read a few obituaries at random. It didn't take him long to conclude that the genre of Obit Lit was one of the very few genres immune to experimentation and innovation. Obituary writers would occasionally vary the short text (sometimes in the form of a poem) that was supposed to condense, while disavowing, the incommunicable grief of those left behind into a pretty, idealized image, but the overall tone remained consistent, the vocabulary limited, and the structure unchanging, indicating the failure to which any attempt to make death the subject of the literary imagination was doomed from the start. Despite the obit's claim to art it is never going to be a piece of literature, Jack thought. It will always remain closer to journalistic reportage, whose function is to report on an event that has indisputably—irreversibly—taken place.

He read that Mildred Thompson had passed away quietly in her sleep at the age of 92. He read that after a prolonged battle with cancer Solomon Dahari, age 68, had passed on in the hospital, surrounded by his loving family. Mandy Jenkins had been snatched from her loving husband all too early, just a month after their wedding, but he knew she was in a better place now, a statement that made one wonder whether Mandy's loving husband felt relieved that someone else had finally offered Mandy what he feared he would have never been able to offer her himself. Phil Atkinson, 4 years old, had died in the arms of his loving mother Laura. Jack pored over the photograph of the 4 year old Phil trying to stuff a big piece of cake into his mouth. There was no mention of the cause of death. Perhaps he had choked on the cake while his mother was far away, upstairs in the bathroom, doing laundry perhaps. Now every time she was invited to another child's birthday party, or to an office celebration, she would listen, horrified, to the sounds of pleasure and approval coming out of the mouths of other people, children and adults alike, as they voraciously consumed the very thing that had killed her son. She would politely decline the piece someone would inevitably offer her, they would insist, she would decline again, less politely, they would hand her a plate anyway, reassuring her that she can eat as little as she wants, just have a taste, it's raspberry chocolate mousse cake, she would finally push them away, the raspberry chocolate mousse landing smack on her blouse, sending her into a hysterical fit as she desperately tried to clean it off, running into the bathroom, obsessively splashing water over the stain, finally taking it off, throwing it in the toilet, flushing, unsuccessfully, standing over the toilet, waiting, looking at the water in the toilet rise up to the brim and overflow the toilet bowl, running down its sides and over her feet, her stained blouse floating, triumphant, on the surface of the water. Some time later she would emerge from the bathroom, in her bra, wet hair stuck to her scalp, her face devoid of any expression. The others, having spent the last several minutes in her absence updating each other on her personal tragedy, would stop whispering and turn around to look at her with uniform pity. No one would know what to expect from her at that moment. Some would replay the famous scene from Carrie in their mind.

Jack tried to imagine Phil's mouth, lips pursed, inside the little coffin. Of course there was no mouth there anymore. He then thought of an old man he had met years ago during a trip to Venice. He had taken the boat to one of the nearby islands, Torcello, where all the houses were painted in bright colors, like a Disney movie set. The man, whose name Jack suddenly remembered even though he had not thought of him for years—Eugenio—had invited him into his house, offered him coffee with grappa, and showed him old photographs of his family, all of whom had passed away a long time ago. Eugenio had pointed at the fading photograph of his sister and had proceeded to tell Jack, in Italian (a language Jack did not speak) the story of her unhappy marriage and her last years when she took care of Eugenio despite her own heartbreak. This was about 9 years ago. At the time Eugenio must have been around 90, which would make him close to 100 now, in the unlikelihood that he was still alive. He had been in surprisingly good health at the time but had confessed to Jack that every day it was becoming harder and harder to sit in the living room and drink his grappa surrounded by the silent portraits of the people who had once loved him. He rarely went out, except to buy cigarettes—yes, he still smoked, even at his age—and spent the greater part of his days inside the house, having one-sided conversations with his dead relatives. It had come to the point where he spent more time with the dead than with the living—they had nothing more to offer him, he told Jack. He confided in Jack that he longed to move permanently to the world of the dead in which he had already been living for a long time anyway. Eugenio had then casually asked Jack whether he could spare some sleeping pills or any other drugs he happened to have on him. However, the only drugs Jack had on him were regular, over-the-counter painkillers. No, that wouldn't do, Eugenio had sighed like a doctor who has just exhausted all possible options to save his patient, except of course Eugenio was trying to save himself by putting an end to his own life. Jack had hugged the old man and gotten back on the tourist boat that would take him to the next island. He had felt the cool breeze on his face and smiled at the impossibly blue water, never looking back.

Soon Eugenio's imploring face had lost its specific outlines, his exaggerated gestures had become frozen into a single ambivalent gesture, the smell of espresso and the taste of grappa had been washed over by the expensive red wine Jack had ordered at a restaurant on the next island. Eventually, Eugenio's house and everything in it, from the portraits on the wall to the pile of old shoes behind the door, had shrunk into a miniature doll-house that could fit more easily amongst Jack's numerous other memories from that trip. For the next nine years Eugenio's candy-blue house, along with Eugenio in it—a miniature, realistic looking doll of an old man with white hair—had remained tightly pressed in between the leaves of other memory-images, never claiming Jack's attention. Eugenio, however, had had to live out those years, month after month, week after week, day after day, counting the hours, the minutes, the seconds that still separated him from what he believed was going to be the crowning achievement of his life—his death. The thought of Eugenio drinking coffee with grappa for nine years, alone or standing outside his blue house smoking, staring at the other candy-colored houses across from him, suddenly filled Jack with such unbearable sadness that he wanted right then and there to get on the first plane to Venice, jump on the small tourist boat, swim if he had to, to the island of Torcello, to see if Eugenio was still alive and, if he was, to give him all the sleeping pills he had on him that day nine years ago, which he had then refused to give him out of some stupid sense of ethical obligation that prevented him from assisting others in ending their lives. Perhaps, he thought, filled with hope, Eugenio had died a long time ago, perhaps even the same year. Who knows, he might have died the very same day, after Jack's boat had left the island. Perhaps the very night when Jack lay in his hotel bed in Venice, Eugenio's dead body under his dead parents' portraits, was already stiff. What a relief it would be to know that the nine years of living while he should have been dead had never happened.

Jack shook his head, lifted his left hand and brought it down with force on the table, although what he really wanted to do was slap himself in the face. He didn't want to admit to himself that he felt in some way responsible for Eugenio's unnecessarily protracted suffering. But wasn't it presumptuous of Jack to assume that the old man did not want to live nine more years? Wasn't it sheer arrogance to wish for something on Eugenio's behalf, as if he, Jack, knew better than Eugenio himself what the man feared or hoped for? Who was to say that Eugenio might not have actually liked living alone with his memories, that he might not have felt abandoned and useless but, on the contrary, safe, content, surrounded by the people he loved and postponing the pleasure of eventually joining them when his own time came? Jack had simply imagined how *he* would feel if he were Eugenio, developing a whole scenario based on that hypothetical premise and tossing aside the real Eugenio, who was after all of no interest to Jack except as a curious souvenir from a picturesque Italian island as seen on page 56 of *The Lonely Planet Guide to Italy*.

But the worse part of it was that he had not done this to Eugenio alone. Jack recalled an obese Italian woman of undefined age—obesity made people ageless—lying prostrated in front of his hotel in Florence. She never moved a centimeter so he assumed she was handicapped, as testified by the crutches lying on the ground next to her, although the dress she wore (the same dress she wore every day) was so long and voluminous that the lower part of her body and her legs remained obscured. He had no idea if she slept there as well—all he knew was that every morning when he left the hotel she was there and every evening when he returned after dinner she was there. Unlike Eugenio, whose general features Jack could reconstruct if he made an effort, the Florence woman was faceless from the very beginning and remained faceless to this day, perhaps because she wore a colorful kerchief on her head, which distracted one from the particularities of her dirty face underneath, and because her flesh, sprawling generously on the pavement, produced only a vague perception of something big, round and supplicatory obstructing one's exit from the hotel onto the street. Usually she lied face down, her arms holding a small plastic cup stretched out in front of her. The cup was empty but the ground in front of her was littered with change: people threw coins at her but rarely scored inside the cup. Because of the position of her body, face down, she never looked passers by in the eye and never said a word to them, unlike most beggars who were in the habit of listing all the reasons for their current misfortunate state as well as all additional misfortunes they would have to suffer if the kind people passing by didn't have a heart and spare some change.

The woman kept silent. Her only supplicatory gesture was to slightly raise the plastic cup in the air when she heard someone's steps approaching and bring it back down when they were gone. Most people gave her money, no doubt grateful that they didn't have to look her in the eye. But regardless of the average tourist's generosity—for it was only tourists who gave her money, the locals simply crossed over to the other side of the street—the amount of money she was making per day according to Jack's calculations was negligible and, in his opinion, could not justify demeaning herself in that way just to be able to buy some bread, hoping that tomorrow will be a good day and she will make enough money to buy another loaf of bread, and so on ad infinitum. He was sorry for the Florence woman, sorry on her behalf, just as he had been sorry for Eugenio on his behalf, as though these two were not only incapable of taking care of themselves but were also incapable of experiencing the feelings proper to their situation, as if they could not really see their situation for what it truly was without the help of someone capable of more nuanced feelings, someone with a better *sentimental education*, in short someone like Jack.

Even as he felt sorry for the woman on her behalf Jack was also angry, and although he would did not like to admit it to himself, a little bit envious. He envied the woman's resignation to her misery, her inert persistence to exist even if it was only for a loaf of bread and a few rotten apples, her mind-blowing inability—or was it a natural talent?—to feel down and out about her no-exit situation while others, those far more privileged than her, had to resort to yoga and self-help audio books to learn to wield the Power of Now. This woman was already living in the Now, driven only by the desire to continue to be, unburdened by regrets and expectations. Did she really deserve to be pitied? Then again, when she lied on the ground, plastic cup in hand, did she congratulate herself for 'being in the Now'? Every time he entered or exited the hotel Jack thought about these things, growing increasingly preoccupied with the woman's misfortune, so much so that he never dropped a single coin in her cup. He found himself making short, pointless trips just so he could enter and exit the hotel as many times as possible, observe the woman, and develop further his philosophical analysis of her condition. She never disappointed him: she was always there, completely still, in exactly the same position he had last left her, a safe anchor in the kitschy sea of souvenirs and grandiose domes presided over by the Basilica bells' sublime toll and the church organ's tragic dirge.

The morning when he checked out of the hotel and walked outside...she was not there. He panicked. His first thought was to run back inside and inform the hotel reception that 'the Florence woman', as he had christened her, was missing. He then realized the absurdity of reporting a homeless beggar missing. He circled a few times around the building, checking other hotel entrances for the familiar colorful pile of flesh and fabric but came back empty-handed. Once his initial panic subsided he was able to ask himself some logical questions, such as whether the Florence woman might not have simply moved to another, more lucrative location. Perhaps she was not handicapped at all, perhaps her crutches had been just for show, perhaps the talent for 'living in the Now' that Jack had endowed her with was a strategy to swindle unsuspecting tourists. The worst part of it was that if this really were the case all his philosophical reflections would be invalidated. After an hour-long useless search he was forced to give up and take a cab to the train station. As his train was pulling out of the station he glimpsed a colorfully dressed figure lying on the ground by the newspaper kiosk but just then the train made a sudden left turn and the woman disappeared from view. Was she still there now, nine years later, prostrated in front of his hotel?

He ordered another coffee and turned on his laptop. First he searched the photo gallery on the website of his Florence hotel. Nothing there: most of the pictures were of the hotel's interior and those of the exterior were extreme long shots. What he needed were tourists' amateur photos of the hotel. After checking out several sites he landed on the photo-stream of a Japanese tourist—it included over 200 pictures from Florence only. It was fairly easy to identify the ones from the street where the hotel was located as it was one of the main streets in Florence. They were all dated July 2014. He scrolled down and… There she was! The same dress, the same head kerchief, the same spot in front of the hotel entrance. Jack could not believe his luck. The Japanese tourist must have stood above the woman, pointing the camera down at her head. There was something different about that head now. Although he never saw the face, he remembered a full head of dark brown hair: now the woman's head was crisscrossed by streaks of silver. Since her face was invisible it was impossible to determine the woman's age: there was no stable reference point from which to measure how much she had aged. She could have been very young nine years ago, around twenty, which would make her silvery hair now a sign of premature aging. Or she could have been middle-aged nine years ago, in which case her greying hair would have been a normal sign of aging. But she could have also been very old nine years ago, but looking younger than her age, which would make her current silvery streaks a sign that time had caught up with her and she had begun to age at a pace typical of those her age. In any case, one thing was clear: the Florence woman had spent the last nine years prostrated on the same small stretch of pavement, frozen in an eternal, abstract Now.

"Coffee?"

Jack closed a few of the multiple tabs on his computer screen. The constant proliferation of commercials opening and playing automatically continued to infuriate him.

"Coffee?"

He looked up from the screen. The voice had not come from a pop-up commercial. A real waitress stood in front of him, coffee pot in hand.

"That's some depressing reading material," she commented, nodding at the Obit section. She bit her lower lip. "Oh, I am sorry. I didn't mean to pry."

He reassured her that she wasn't bothering him: he was simply checking the Obit section for any mechanical errors; it was part of his job. The waitress, who introduced herself as Jennie, sat down across from him, eager to discuss the nuts and bolts of his 'exotic' profession. He would have never imagined that obit writing would bring in the girls. He told her it was just a job like any other, nothing glamorous about it. She was not convinced and pointed out, apologizing for saying something so obvious, that he wrote about "death." She put her cigarette in her mouth for a second so she could sign the quotation marks around "death" with her hands.

"Death is the one word that is meaningless without quotation marks," she said. She was determined to impress him—that much was beyond argument.

"Actually, it's reality," he corrected her. "Reality is the one word that is meaningless without quotation marks." He paused. "At least according to Nabokov."

She blushed.

"But you are onto something with that misquote," he reassured her. "After all, the whole point of obituaries is precisely to put death between quotation marks and to keep it there."

He could see from the confusion on her face that her metaphor-recognition skills were stretched to the max. She must have been aware of that because she changed the topic.

"What was the most difficult obit you have ever had to write?"

"Do you mean difficult because it was about someone I knew or difficult from a writer's point of view"?

He wondered what the home library of a waitress in a small city like Abberc. looks like. He would guess it contained mostly popular novels and fashion magazines, with a token copy of *Ana Karenina* and *The*

Catcher in the Rye thrown in for good measure. The idea of spending some time in such an apartment and reading books he would have never read otherwise, making himself a cup of hot chocolate and lounging on the comfy sofa with a floral design, flipping through the latest issue of *Elle*, was as seductive as the idea of sitting in a leather armchair, in an academic's home, surrounded by tastefully selected beautiful works of art, and flipping through the brittle pages of an old library copy of the *Third Critique of Judgment*. Jack thought how reassuring it must be to live in someone else's apartment, "reassuring" because he would feel that life had already begun there, that the place had already been 'warmed up' with the habits and memories of its previous owner—his habitual movements through the apartment, the automated actions he had performed every day, every week, for years, rituals that the owner had come to resent and feel constricted by, and from which he probably wanted to escape. A coffee pot stained after years of use, a few hairs on the bathroom floor, a forgotten piece of cheese in the back of the fridge—to Jack these little time capsules, these leftovers from someone else's life, a life that felt more real to Jack than did his own life, seemed priceless. He wondered if he was only capable of living his life by borrowing other people's lives, like a prisoner condemned to death lives the rest of his days 'on borrowed time'. He loved the feeling of waking up in someone else's bed, smelling the laundry detergent with which the covers had been washed in preparation for his arrival—the smell of laundry detergent, regardless of the brand, always made him feel instantly at home, as if all his childhood memories had been soaked in detergent—reaching out to silence the alarm, his outstretched arm repeating the same movement the apartment owner's arm must have executed thousands of times, walking barefoot to the kitchen, making coffee in the Other's used coffee pot, watering, with a sleepy hand, the Other's plants, looking out the Other's window over the rooftops of the Other's city, inspecting the dark shadows under his eyes in the Other's mirror, sitting in the Other's chair and turning on the Other's reading lamp, sipping the Other's aromatic coffee from the Other's coffee cup marked, on the inside, by several rings of coffee stains, marking the passage of time like tree ring dating.

Jennie was saying something. He had to stare at her moving lips for a while to unmute her. He did not recall how their obit conversation had ended and he had missed the beginning of her monologue but he was able to pick up the lost thread easily. She was talking about an inspiring interview she had watched on the morning edition of her favorite talk show 'For Women, By Women, About Women.' It was an interview with a celebrity, the most successful female talk show host on TV. The Morning Edition Talk Show Host (METSH) was interviewing the Most Successful Talk Show Host (MSTSH) about her relationship to 'the spiritual.' MSTSH, wearing a dress from Armani's 2014 Spring collection (Jennie took pride in being able to identify correctly the provenance of any sample of haute couture) and having undergone about six tanning sessions to achieve the desired shade of bronze, had opened her heart and soul to METSH and shared with her some intimate thoughts about the nature of 'the spiritual' and her personal relationship with it, something the paparazzi would never be able to capture in one of their numerous photographs of her, something that only she could condescend to reveal. METSH had thanked MSTSH for being willing to share with the TV audience something so personal and had mentioned, purely as an aside, that she, too, was a very spiritual person. MSTSH had smiled magnanimously at METSH, granting the latter the right to have her own, understandably minor relationship with the spiritual (after all, she was just a METSH, not a MSTSH). MSTSH had then proceeded to expand on the necessity of 'freeing yourself from the worldly'—where 'the worldly' was understood to be the opposite of 'the spiritual'—and finding 'the inner you.' When she said 'the inner you' Jennie placed her hand over her heart and half-closed her eyes as if she was having a spiritual orgasm. MSTSH had gone on to describe her journey from the worldly to the spiritual. Although she had always enjoyed dressing up and going to charity events, cocktail parties and fashion shows after a while she had begun to feel that 'something was missing.' Feeling suffocated by the glitz and champagne, and longing to get away from it all, she had left the capital and travelled to one of the depopulated villages up in the mountains two hours south of the city (here METSH pulled out a map and showed the TV audience the exact location of the village where MSTSH's amazing spiritual transformation had taken place in case any of the TV viewers wanted to have their own, needless to say lesser version of it). It was there, standing by the chicken coop, her Prada shoes sinking in cow shit, her nostrils twitching approvingly at the smell of the adjacent pigsty, her un-coiffured hair flapping in the wind while its split ends slapped her in the face, that she had found humility and felt with absolute clarity that she was capable of renouncing the world. At that point METSH had interjected that MSTSH had not really renounced the world—after all, here she was in the TV studio, all made up and, by the way, wearing a gorgeous dress—to which MSTSH had smiled and explained that renouncing the world was something one did mentally: there was no need to parade one's spiritual transformation by making it actual; indeed, that would be vulgar. Jennie looked slightly embarrassed when she said that and Jack wondered whether it was because Jennie had tried to have a spiritual journey of her own by actually leaving town and retreating to some sleepy village only to discover that her journey, in MSTSH's expert opinion, was vulgar and inauthentic.

Jack said goodbye to Jennie. He could tell she was waiting for him to ask for her number but as much as he sympathized with her selfdoubts and her inefficient search for the spiritual he could not stomach another one of her monologues. He told her he would come back to see her sometime. She smiled, relieved that he had not found her annoying or boring, and he walked away feeling guilty that he had. As he walked down the street the street lights came on, one by one, illuminating his non-spiritual journey in search for a new rental apartment. He had nowhere to sleep that night but strangely enough that fact did not trouble him as much as it should have. He stopped in front of a small cinema plastered with old posters of obscure art-house films. The only person in the cinema was the hip-looking college girl behind the ticket window busy underlining with an orange marker passages in a Business Management textbook. In Jack's long literary career there had been several cutaways to other potential careers, including one in the film industry. Every time he saw a critically appraised film he considered mediocre he would rush home and scribble down ideas for what he believed would be a much better film that he would write and direct, eventually shocking the whole film establishment with his unsuspected, raw talent.

One of the drawers in his desk was filled with wrinkled sheets of paper containing the seeds of promising, intellectually rich yet unpretentious instant cult films. At one point he had had an idea for a film based on the true story of a criminal arrested for murder and given a life sentence. In prison he joins an amateur theatre group. What starts out as a hobby turns out to be the criminal's true calling. Soon enough his performances attract the admiration of his fellow inmates, the guards, the prison administration and finally the Director of the prison, himself a failed artist. At the request of the prison administration the criminal is appointed as principal instructor of a new course, Acting for the Camera. In his spare time he offers private, one-on-one acting lessons to inmates, guards, prison administrators and, on some occasions, members of their families. His theatrical fame spreads, eventually reaching Hollywood. A recently anointed film director hears about the Actor, as the criminal has come to be known by that time, and realizes this is his unique chance to *épater la bourgeoisie*. The aspiring film director requests an appointment with the Actor, in his prison cell, which has meanwhile been transformed into a changing room. He is placed on the waiting list. Theatre and film directors compete for the Actor's attention, pitching to him projects, each one of which is "an intimate character study" demanding superb acting skills like those of His Truly. The general admiration for the Actor notwithstanding, film and theatre professionals are not allowed to hold auditions outside prison, which necessitates the constant transportation of cameras and crews in and out of the Actor's cell.

Eventually the prison administration decides that in the interest of efficiency and security it would be worth their while to set up a recording studio in the Actor's prison cell and move his bed to another cell. Gradually the studio fills up with camera equipment, an editing suite, audition tapes, and a variety of genre-specific costumes. The walls are decorated with movie posters of classic movies all primed for a remake starring the Actor. Acting schools in New York and L.A. send their most promising graduates to do an intensive internship with the Actor, whose acting style is now the subject of a new study by theatre and film scholars, who see it as the long-awaited rejection of the New Sincerity of Mumblecore. Not only do audiences agree with this assessment but—here is the kicker, the plot point that would make Hollywood pay attention—they begin to lobby for the Actor's release from prison so he can pursue freely his artistic vocation. Moral dilemma anyone? Should artistic excellence trump criminal guilt? Should the Actor get away with murder simply because he is a great actor? Hollywood likes moral dilemmas, which was fortunate for Jack since moral dilemmas happened to be his specialty, perhaps because dilemmas, as opposed to *problems*, appealed to his general ambivalence concerning all matters, from art through morality to what brand of coffee to buy at the supermarket.

Jack had another idea for a film about a hard-core atheist—'the Atheist'—down on his luck in the current economic climate. The Atheist is forced to accept the only job offer he is fortunate enough to receive after months of looking for employment—supervisor at a children's Christian camp. Failing to overcome his resentment toward all things Christian he begins brainwashing the minds of his young Christian mentees with subversive readings of their favorite Biblical passages, emphasizing the bloodshed and the violence therewith and illustrating it with spontaneous dramatic reenactments during the mandatory late night Bible Readings Around the Fire. When the parental body and the camp's administrative body are informed by an anonymous, well-meaning Christian of the Atheist's diabolical agenda to sow the seeds of skepticism in the innocent lambs' pure hearts, the Atheist is fired. Moral dilemma: should the Atheist resist the temptation to impose his own system of disbelief on those over whom he holds institutional power, or should he take advantage of the authority he's been given to enlighten the minds of the youngest members of society and support them through the nasty withdrawal symptoms that must surely accompany their rejection of the opium of the masses?

A fat drop of water slid down Jack's left cheek and settled between his lips. He sneaked into the nearest building, a post office, just before it started pouring. The guard warned him they were closing in five minutes. Jack raised his collar and was just about to go back outside when he saw a hiring notice stuck to the front window—the Post Office was hiring an entry-level clerk for the Undeliverable Mail Office. No previous postal experience was required. He copied down the information.

8.

THREE DAYS LATER HE RECEIVED a phone call from Human Resources inviting him for an interview. Interviews were conducted by the Post Office Manager himself, an overweight man in a wrinkled suit with sagging eyes and drooping cheeks that produced one of the most miserable expressions Jack had ever seen. The Manager put the folder with Jack's application materials on the desk in front of him and crossed his hands on top of it as if he had already made up his mind about Jack. He began with the usual questions. Why did Jack choose to apply for this job? Why did he believe it would be a great fit for him? What skills would he bring to the job? What did he expect in return? The Manager introduced every question with a heavy sigh as if to underscore the great displeasure he felt in having to pretend to be interested in Jack's rationale for applying for the job. The job required a lot of patience, he warned Jack. Jack assured him he was a very patient man. It also required a fair amount of heavy lifting and dragging (of bags and boxes of undelivered mail). Jack assured him he was in excellent shape. The manager didn't look convinced. He heaved another sigh and leaned forward as if to suggest he had hoped to avoid telling Jack what he was about to say but it had proven impossible. The working hours were long and tedious, he told Jack. The Undeliverable Mail Office was in the basement. There was only one window, a tiny one in the bathroom. Former employees had found the lack of sunlight and fresh air taxing. The man previously holding the job Jack was applying for had suffered a nervous breakdown brought about, according to the doctors, by an unfortunate incongruity between the man's predisposition to neurasthenia and the Undeliverable Mail Office's (UMO) ten-

dency to unlock deep psychological traumas in the employees working
there. When Jack interjected that he had assumed neurasthenia to be a
nineteenth century invention the Manager assured him that he would
be surprised how many supposedly imaginary diseases, especially psychological ones, had crossed over from the realm of the imaginary
into that of the real in the post-existentialist, post-psychoanalytical
era. Jack dared not ask the Manager to explain his terminology—he
simply made a mental note that the Manager fancied himself a con-
noisseur of human psychology. The Manager asked again whether
Jack was psychologically fit for the kind of isolation associated with
the job: if he were offered the job he would have to spend long hours
in the basement where UMO was located, up on his feet, in more
or less total isolation from his colleagues in the other departments
housed on the floors above him. Jack confessed this was the ideal job
for him: all he wanted was some peace and quiet and it sounded like
this job would provide him with just that. The manager sighed again,
this time in solidarity with Jack's sentiment, and slid a sheet of paper
across the table, asking Jack to sign at the bottom after confirming
that the salary specified in the contract conformed to his expectations.

The Manager then gave Jack a tour of the facilities, starting at the
top floor of the Post Office's building and working their way down to
the UMO in the basement. To Jack's surprise while all other offices
were easily accessible to get into UMO one had to go through two security doors. The first one opened with a special magnetic card and the
second one with a small key the Manager removed from his keychain
and handed to Jack with a gloomy expression on his face. Jack pushed
the door open, expecting to find a small room with a low ceiling, walls
dripping with water because of poor isolation, and dozens of old dirty
cotton bags filled with undelivered mail rotting on the floor. Instead, he
was standing in the middle of a spacious, sterile room with very high
ceilings, white walls and fluorescent lighting. In one corner stood a big

metal container filled with letters of all sizes, shapes and colors. On the wall next to the container hung a small metal crate. The Manager took it down and instructed Jack to observe carefully. He then proceeded to use the crate as a ladle, scooping up envelopes from the container and carrying them over to the table in the middle of the room.

The Manager emptied out the crate on top of the table and began sorting out the envelopes. He made four piles: the first pile for letters with an incorrect address, the second one for letters with an incomplete address, the third one for letters with no return address, and the last one for letters with correct receiver and sender addresses. Jack asked what was wrong with the letters in the last pile. The Manager looked surprised. There was nothing 'wrong' with the letters in the fourth pile of course. They did reach their destination as planned but there was no one waiting for them there, because the addressee was dead. In some cases they had been dead for a long time, while in others they had died recently—months, weeks or even days before the letter arrived. It was then up to the Post Office, in this case Jack, to inform the sender of the change in the addressee's status (from living to dead) by returning the sender's letter back to them and attaching a form—# 2139—in which the Post Office expressed its sincere condolences for the loss of X (name of receiver). A copy of that form—in fact, a copy of *all* correspondence—had to be filed with the Manager as evidence that the sender had been notified of the situation because, unfortunately, all too often it happened that the sender kept sending letters to the same address in utter disregard for the official notification, the aforementioned # 2139, they had received that the addressee had passed away or in utter ignorance of that turn of events. And this, the Manager pointed to another pile, is what the fifth pile was for: repeat letters or, as they were officially known, 'post-2139 letters' (letters the sender sends after they have received the # 2139 notification of the addressee's death). The Manager did not hide the fact that in about 40% of post-2139 cases the fault did not lie entirely with the sender but, rather, with the UMO clerk, who had send the #2139 notification to the wrong address—the notification would then be returned to its sender, in this case the UMO clerk (from now on Jack). In those cases, the UMO clerk would have to write a new letter—there was a special form for that, the #9321 form— to the sender and attach his first letter—the #2139 form—to it, explaining the situation and apologizing on behalf of the Post Office.

At this point Jack interrupted the Manager. Shouldn't there be a sixth pile, Jack asked, a pile for #2139 letters that had been returned to the Post Office not because the UMO clerk had sent them to the wrong address but because the addressee—in this case the sender of the original letter to the dead addressee—had also died in the narrow window of time between sending their letter to the (unbeknownst to them) dead addressee and receiving the #2139 notification from the Post Office? The Manager seemed pleased, to the best of his ability to experience such feelings, that Jack has asked this question, because, you see, he had intentionally not mentioned this case to see whether Jack would think of that possibility himself. The fact that he had suggested that he had indeed grasped the rationale for UMO's existence and its complex rules. Yes, there was a sixth pile. It was usually the smallest one as it was rare for a sender not to be aware of the addressee's death and then to die himself (herself) just before he/she would be informed of it. It was an interesting case that raised all sorts of questions about the nature, or even the possibility, of communication in the first place. After all, what, if anything, could be said to have been communicated between A (sender) and B (receiver) if 1) B was inactive (dead) and thus incapable of receiving any form of communication and 2) A was equally inactive (dead) and thus incapable of receiving the communication that B was incapable of being communicated to? The Post Office kept up the semblance of communication taking place by sending back and forth the actual letter and then a series of notifications of the failure of the original letter to reach its destination. The actual sender and addressee were secondary, if not irrelevant, to the flow of communication the Post Office was able to sustain through its various forms and declarations that kept circulating in this phantom land circumscribed by two deaths in the absence of any actual (living) agent to interrupt or put an end to this self-perpetuating illusion.

In one well-known case the situation had escalated to the absurd as the Post Office continued to send back and forth notifications, notifications about those notifications, and reminders about those notifications about notifications, five years after the deaths of the respective sender and addressee. It took a change in city planning, which led to the demolition of the building in which the sender had lived before his death, to stop the postal flow: in short, the sender's mailbox had to be literally destroyed, blown to smithereens, for him to be finally declared incommunicado. At least that's what they had thought at the time because, as it turned out, this was by no means the end of the story. Two years later a new condominium was erected in the place of the demolished building and the quasi-communication that everyone had assumed had exhausted itself started flowing again. The #9321 form, which had been bouncing back and forth for two years, unable to land in a real mailbox as a result of the sender's building's demolition, was finally delivered to the new mailbox of the new occupant of the now deceased sender's apartment. The new occupant, being alive, was more than capable of redirecting the communication flow and this is exactly what he did: he took it upon himself to respond to the notifications he was receiving, redirecting the #2139s and #9321s he was getting back to the Post Office and, in addition, writing letters of complaint to the Manager of the Post Office and to the Ministry of Communication itself. However, since the sender's address had come back 'online' again, after two years of being offline, except that the number of the mailbox had changed from 7 to 6, all correspondence addressed to the new occupant shifted from the category 'return to sender because of death' to 'return to sender because of incorrect address', causing further confusion at UMO. It was for these reasons, the Manager concluded, that the UMO clerk's position was so important: he had to be always on the alert for such shifting and sliding between categories (and piles) of mail to prevent any serious mail meltdown.

The Manager checked his watch. He had spent too much time expounding on the sixth pile method, he informed Jack, and had very little time left to go over Record-Keeping, Fact Cross-Checking, and Artifacts Handling (the handling of artifacts collected from undeliverable mail). Each of these three departments had its own terminology but in the interest of time the Manager suggested that Jack familiarize himself with it by consulting the UMO General Semiotics Manual downloadable from the UMO website. The Manager turned on the computer and showed Jack the website. He pressed one of the keys, bringing up an overcrowded Excel spreadsheet filled with numbers, names, addresses, and abbreviations. Over the next two hours the Manager attempted to explain the UMO's sophisticated record-keeping system, breaking down every single cliché Jack had associated with the UMO as a department whose very existence depended on miscommunication, misinformation and misunderstanding. For every incorrect address, misspelled name or dead addressee the UMO's superb record-keeping system produced a stream of data that was verified five times and then cross-checked with data from other departments in order to trace the error in communication back to its original source. In those cases that had given the office its other name—Dead Letter Office—that is, in cases when a letter could not be delivered to its addressee on account of the addressee's death, UMO collaborated with the Office of Crime Investigation in order to confirm the veracity of the addressee's changed existential status, because, believe it or not, there had been a few cases where the addressee had manufactured their own

'death' with the sole purpose of avoiding communication with a particular sender. Whenever there was reason to suspect foul game—that
is, fake death—Jack had to contact the Office of Criminal Investigation
and speak to Inspector Goodfellow. In those cases where the mail was
undeliverable because of an error in the addressee's or sender's address
Jack had to contact the Address and Registration Department and request #609, an address-tracking form, which he had to fill out and send
back to them so they could trace down any alternative spellings of the
name over the last ten years.

The Manager checked his watch again. They were running out of
time so Jack would have to familiarize himself with the rest of his duties
by reading the UMO manual. There was one other thing the Manager
wanted to mention, however. It was not in the UMO manual because
the Post Office had not yet passed a law dealing specifically with such
admittedly rare cases—those cases were better left to Jack's discretion.
The fact of the matter was that sometimes, once or twice a year, the
sender of an undeliverable piece of mail would prove unwilling, or unable, to accept the news of the addressee's death and attempt to get the
UMO clerk—from now on, Jack—involved in their personal drama,
writing personal letters to the clerk, in which they would share their
personal epistolary drama with the clerk and expect the latter to com-
miserate. Although the Manager did not want to make a gender-biased
generalization the majority of these types of senders, who crossed the
line and derailed the professional relationship between Post Office customer and Post Office employee into a personal one, were women. Jack
was well advised to be on the alert for such romance-deprived customers, whose handwriting often gave them away. Jack was to consult section IV, sub-section 'a', in the UMO Manual, which offered recommendations on various strategies of dealing with them that had worked in
the past. He was also welcome to suggest new strategies, drawing on
his own experience. The bottom line was that Jack was to follow the es-

tablished protocol under all circumstances and consult with the Manager whenever he was unsure about the proper course of action. He was to report at work the following morning at 9am. Dress code was casual though the Manager recommended that Jack wear the lab coat hanging in the closet to avoid getting ink stains on his clothes, which often happened after handling envelopes on which the address had been inscribed in ink. Lunch break was from 12 to 12:45 and although Jack was free to take his lunch anywhere the Manager suggested that it was most convenient to take it in the UMO office so as not to lose his concentration. Given the uncontrollable amount of human error with which the UMO clerk was confronted all day long, the only way to stay in control of the situation was to overcompensate for the randomness of communication and keep the margin of error to the minimum by eliminating any and all potential sources of distraction. For that reason, as well, phone calls to and from the UMO office during working hours were strictly prohibited.

With the prospect of a paycheck waiting for him in two weeks' time Jack felt confident enough to afford a hotel for a few nights while he was trying to secure more permanent accommodation. The hotel he finally chose was at the end of an arcade flanked with antique stores, second-hand bookshops and smoky cafes suffused with old world charm, decorated with smoky mirrors and populated by old men in old-fashioned berets that seemed to have been born with a glass of whiskey in hand. After checking in Jack came back down to the arcade, where an old philately store had caught his attention. He scooped a dozen of random postcards and held them like a hand of cards: greetings from the Alps from Sara to her dear cousin H., a get well soon card from Colin to his aunt in Manchester, where she was recovering from some unnamed women's illness, congratulations on your wedding from Philip to his dear niece Elizabeth, a love note from one H. to his beloved J., whom he had had the misfortune of seeing only briefly at K's soiree but whose smooth, pale skin and intensive dark eyes had clearly left a strong impression on H., condolences on your loss from C. to H., et cetera. Sometimes the choice of postcard was obvious given the nature of the missive; other times the message, written in tiny letters, in cursive, on the back of the postcard did not correspond to the image on the front. For instance, the love note from H. to his beloved was written on the back of a postcard that pictured the magnificent gates at the entrance to the World Expo, an image about which there was nothing intrinsically romantic. On the other hand, Sara's simple greeting from the Alps to her cousin H. was written on the back of a mildly erotic postcard featuring a young woman bending over a man to show him a passage in a book, her décolleté revealing a pair of breasts that would eventually shrivel, sag further and further down, and rot away under the ground along with the hand that had lovingly drawn the 'a' and 's' in "Alps." Morbid reflections on the transitory nature of existence are *de rigueur* when contemplating an object from the past bearing the traces of a particular human existence and, really, is there anything more melancholic than an intimate message sent between two people long ago dead? But it was not the lovers' mortality that fascinated Jack as he flipped the postcards to inspect both the front and the back. No, what he couldn't wrap his head around was the indestructibility of the feeling expressed in a few clichéd words scribbled down in a hurry, the letters now faded from the sun and immediately recognizable as belonging to another era by virtue of their overly refined calligraphy.

He pored over H.'s love note to J., inspecting the flourishes at the end of the 'e', 'a' and 'o'. There was nothing special about the flourishes per se: the period's saccharine language was frequently accompanied by an equally flowery calligraphy. Jack put down H's postcard and picked up C.'s greeting to her cousin H. The vowels were embellished with the same flourishes. He checked the address: H's love note was sent from 78 rue Jean-Pierre Timbaud and was addressed to J. at 102 rue Saint Maur, Paris. C's postcard to her cousin H. only specified the destination: 78 rue Jean-Pierre Timbaud. Was this a coincidence, or was H., C's cousin, the object of something more than her affection? Chances were he could find all sorts of connections, familial or romantic, between many of these senders and addressees spanning different times and spaces, simply because at that time the number of professional photo studios was still fairly small and the odds of strangers having their photographs taken at the same studio were rather high. It was not that unlikely that H. and J. knew one another and were, perhaps, involved in a lurid love triangle of unrequited love, C. pining after H., who was himself madly in love with J., who of course didn't care for him. One could draw a diagram of all these broken hearts, tracing their intimate relationships, their common histories and their clandestine rendezvous across Paris, eventually reconstituting the city itself from the ephemeral geography of the heart. One could write a Madame Bovaresque novel about that time in history, drawing only on the passionate correspondence between these people long reduced to a few trivial words on the back of a wrinkled postcard.

Jack parted at random the thickly stacked row of photographs in front of him and reinserted the virtual lives and loves of H., C., and J. back into the collective memory of the world. All other shops in the arcade were already closed except for a tiny antique shop crammed with the usual bric-a-brac that would be impossible to *détourner*, because it consisted of things that had long ago lost their use, remaining suspended in the liminal space outside Chronological time and Euclidian space, a space that elevated every object into a work of art and, at the same time, reduced every work of art to an artifact from a particular historical era. The store was still open not because the owner was still hoping to lure in unsuspecting tourists exploring the arcades upon the recommendation of their off-the-beaten track guidebook, but only because he had fallen asleep in the back of the store, indistinguishable from the other dead things around him. Jack wondered if the man had an apartment of his own or he lived in a small room behind the heavy curtain: he seemed to have been born already old and half-blind, having spent the better part of his life digging through other people's forgotten memories. The random objects displayed in the store, allegedly up for sale, had become over the years the owner's home, furniture that he pretended to want to get rid of but that he secretly hoped to keep for himself. This explained the exorbitant prices he had assigned, somewhat indiscriminately, to the objects for sale—if he even bothered to write them down, since more often than not antiques were displayed without a price tag—as well as the casual indifference he exhibited whenever customers tried to bargain with him. At first he would indulge them and bargain with them for a while, but eventually he would inform them abruptly that he had already promised the item in question to another customer.

Every object in the store led a double existence: first, as a cult object and, second, as part of the owner's personal home décor. During the store's regular working hours objects existed as artifacts dating from a particular time period, exemplifying this or that style, but at the end of the work day all objects would regain their usefulness: the 19th century wooden desk became the owner's kitchen table, the Bauhaus chairs were used for sitting and reading, and the rugged landscapes on the wall expressed the owner's longing for his early childhood in the Highlands. The most trivial actions of the store owner—this Postmodern Emperor of Stuff—were propped by the most random selection imaginable of architectural and artistic styles: he drank his coffee sitting in an ultra-modern Bauhaus chair, took a nap on a gorgeous 17th century sofa and read the newspaper under a fin de siècle lamp. Sometimes, when he was feeling slightly more generous, the store owner would select a few objects that were not dear to him, place them in a box and put the box outside the store, pricing every object in the box at one or two euros, a token price signifying his indifference to the object in question. Jack rummaged through the box: empty perfume bottles, a broken candlestick, an ink pen, a few old photographs and a cook book with faded pictures of unidentifiable gourmet foods.

The owner came out of the store and removed the price tag from the box.

"Free," he told Jack.

It would be an offence to the man's antiquarian sensibility to pass over such a rare offer: a free, useless object. In the world of antiques the uselessness of an object determined its price: the more useless an object, the higher the price. By that logic the most useless objects—like the ones in the box—were also the most expensive ones. Jack could not say 'no' to the incredibly good deal the storeowner had proposed to him so he picked up one of the empty perfume bottles and a small letter knife, which he dropped in his pocket. The storeowner nodded as if to congratulate Jack on his excellent choice.

Later that night, lying under the bed covers in his hotel room, Jack examined the perfume bottle sitting on top of the side table. The moon hit the side of the empty bottle creating the illusion that it was half-full. Jack raised himself in bed with both arms and brought his face closer to the bottle's opening. A faint, overly sweet scent tickled his nose. He thought that for a long time he had been going to bed late.

The following morning he woke up with a sneeze. The air smelled sweet, as if someone had smashed several bottles of perfume on the floor. He opened the side table drawer and rolled the empty perfume bottle into it. He arrived at the Post Office a little before 9am and headed down the stairs to the basement where he would spend the next eight hours. The lab coat smelled like detergent. Good. It would neutralize the saccharine perfume smell still clinging to him. He pushed the container with yesterday's mail close to the table in the middle of the room, poured out some of its contents and picked up an envelope at random. For the first few hours everything went smoothly. With a few minor exceptions most of the letters were undeliverable because the addressee had moved away without leaving a forwarding address. The office was quiet and cool, the only sound coming from the ceiling fan. Jack had never suspected that cataloguing could have such a soothing effect. He raised his right hand, in which he held an official Post Office stamp with the date, and brought it down on the envelope: 'Return to sender'. After a few hours of doing this his movements became sufficiently automated and he didn't have to think about what he was doing—communicating the failure of communication.

Some time in the afternoon the Manager stopped by to check up on Jack. He was generally satisfied with the work Jack had done, with the exception of a few cases where Jack had taken some interpretive liberties in deciding whether a particular letter was undeliverable because the addressee could not be identified or whether it was undeliverable because the sender could not be identified. The Manager pointed out that these were two totally separate cases and that he was surprised Jack was confused about the difference between them. Jack pretended to be confused about the difference between the two, rather than struck by the absurdity of the distinction between the two, and reassured the Manager that he would read up on it in the relevant section of the Manual. Before leaving the Manager pulled out an envelope from his pocket and threw it on the table.

"I almost forgot. I received this letter yesterday. It's addressed to UMO."

Jack checked the return address.

" 'The Flying Dutchman.' What's that?"

"An art gallery, down by the river. Go and check it out when you get off work tonight, will you?"

At half past six Jack stood in front of a small storefront-turned-gallery on Southport street # 231. He pushed the glass door open. A college kid—he could not have been older than 21—looked up from the book he was reading. He was a 'true hipster', that is someone for whom 'hipsterism' was no longer just a matter of style consisting of a few recognizable elements, such as a moustache, a checkered shirt and dark blue jeans. This kid was a hipster, in the same way a wooden chair is made out of wood.

"Can I help you?" the true hipster asked, looking up from either *Portnoy's Complaint* or *Infinite Jest*.

The walls were covered with envelopes of different sizes, colors and shapes, hung from the ceiling by invisible strings. They all bore the familiar "Return to sender" red stamp.

"The title of the exhibition is *Return to Sender*," the kid explained.

"I work at the Undeliverable Mail Office," Jack grinned in response. "I suppose this makes me the ideal audience for this."

"You must have received my invitation then," the hipster said. "I am Benjamin by the way." He waved his hand without getting up.

"We did not receive an invitation. But we did receive this letter from your gallery." Jack pulled out the envelope and showed it to the true hipster.

"This is an invitation to the show," the hipster explained. "I thought it would be nice to use one of the works in the show as an invitation, in line with the 'Return to Sender' theme."

"Did you read the letter?" Jack asked.

"I've read them all. To be honest, I am not sure which one I sent to you. I picked it at random."

"You should probably know that it's a murder confession addressed to the police."

"Ah, yes, I remember that one. I hope you didn't take it seriously," the hipster giggled apologetically.

"What do you mean?"

"I mean it's a fictional confession to a murder that never took place.

A work of art, like all the others," the hipster pointed to the envelopes suspended from the ceiling. "You can read more about the concept of the show in the artist's statement. It's in the catalogue on the little side table by the entrance."

"Who is the artist?"

"William Brown, but he goes by his initials: W.B."

"'The W.B'?"

"You've heard of him?"

Who hadn't heard of him? Over the last year William Brown, or W.B., the recently anointed darling of the art world, had had major shows in London, Paris, Berlin, Rio de Janeiro and New York. The most renowned art critics had published glowing reviews of his work in the top art journals. A retrospective was planned for the following year even though some claimed he was too young to have one. No one knew exactly how old he was because no one had ever laid eyes on W.B., which further compounded the sense of mystery surrounding him. His works had been acquired by MOMA and the TATE museum. He had given one single TV interview, with his back to the camera. Women who had seen the interview had commented on his broad shoulders and his attractively tussled hair; they were convinced he was handsome, single, prone to bouts of nostalgia and melancholy, most likely raised by his mother, with whom he enjoyed a special connection, a delicate soul in a muscular body with an intense stare and long lean legs. Jack was amazed at the amount of detail about W.B.'s personality and physique people were able to deduce from a few elliptical statements W.B. made in his only interview, and from the way he sat, with his back to the camera, in an uncomfortable interview chair.

"I suppose you didn't meet the man himself?" Jacked asked.

"He had his assistant deliver the work." The hipster looked up at the envelopes hanging from the ceiling. "It's heartbreaking, isn't it?"

"Heartbreaking?"

"You haven't read the artist's statement yet, have you? It's his most personal work to date. Please have a look yourself." He pointed to the artist's catalog on the side table. Jack opened the Comments book lying open next to the catalog. The last entry read: "Heartbreaking! Another superb demonstration of the idea that tragedy is at the origin of all great art!" Jack flipped through the rest of the comments. The general sentiment was the same: W.B. had mastered the art "of channeling suffering into art," he had told "in simple, almost childish terms a moving love story," with which "everyone who had ever loved and lost would identify!" The love story in question was summarized, in the artist's statement, in 500 words + endnotes. It was the story of his brief but fateful encounter with a woman the night before he departed on a yearlong trip around the world. He was smitten with her and she seemed to share his feelings. He sent her postcards from the various places he visited, expressing, on the back of the postcards, his deepening feelings for her. She didn't respond to his letters but that didn't discourage him. He continued to write to her, hoping she would eventually write back. A few months later he started receiving his own letters, stamped "return to sender." Finally, he received a letter from the Undeliverable Mail Office. That letter was displayed on the wall near the gallery entrance. It read as follows:

> Dear W.B., I am writing to you in my capacity of Chief Clerk in the Undeliverable Mail Office, London Postal Services. In case you are not familiar with our office, we are in charge of all mail sent to a London address that has, for one reason or another, failed to be delivered to its proper addressee. The possible reasons for this failure are too many to enumerate. Here we are concerned with only one of them—unfortunately, the most unpleasant one. I am very sorry to inform you that the addressee of your letters, Olivia Lacker, 12 Saint George st., passed away several weeks prior to your first letter to her. You may find some consolation in the knowledge that her

failure to respond to your letters was not the result of indifference or cruelty
on her part; put differently, death is something she could not have helped.
We were able to retrieve your address from the city's public records,
to which we have unlimited access. As unpleasant as it is for us to
have to relay to you this news—I am referring to the untimely death
of your addressee—we believe it is our duty to do so. Please let us
know whether you would like us to return to you the remainder of your
undeliverable mail or you'd prefer to give us permission to destroy it.

Respectfully,
UM Office, Chief Clerk

Jack thought of W.B. tossing and turning in a hotel bed somewhere in Japan, picturing the tiny beauty mark on Olivia's chin, her short bangs, her slightly protruding collarbone, and of Olivia lying two feet under, mute, having long lost her status of an addressee, unless one wanted to expand the notion of an 'addressee' to include a bunch of chemical elements held together by a name on the tombstone (to be distinguished by the concoction of chemical elements held together by the name on the adjacent tombstone) just on the outskirts of a city park known for its biodiversity. For months W.B. had remembered and imagined caressing and smelling a piece of flesh that used to designate a face he had come to know as 'Olivia's face', unaware that this same piece of flesh had followed its own course of life, independent of W.B.'s memories of it. It was almost unthinkable that this rotting piece of flesh could lead several simultaneous parallel lives: as an idea or a memory in someone else's mind, as an addressee of a letter, as a name written out on a small piece of paper stuck to a mailbox, as a bag of bones across which scurried ants and worms, as a series of letters engraved on a block of stone that looked incomprehensible from the point of view of, say, a Vietnamese man, as a name listed in alphabetical order in the city's birth and death registry, as a name to be quoted one day during a conference presentation on the subject of declining birth rates in first world countries by a scholar of population growth and decline, who would, years later, join the subject of his conference paper, having become himself just another number in the death registry.

Jack tried to conjure up the face of the woman W.B. must have seen, in his mind's eye, as he composed his letters to her, but all he saw were a pair of empty eye sockets that seemed to bore two holes in the glossy postcard paper. He checked the date on the last postcard from Japan: almost four months after Olivia's death. And yet she was not dead, at least not fully dead. Her existence was sustained and artificially prolonged not by a few plastic tubes plugged into a complicated machine in a hospital room somewhere but by a few short lines written with her in mind. Her ontological status i.e., her addressee status, did not depend on her but was determined by W.B.: for as long as he considered her a legitimate addressee, for as long as he wrote to her, she was not free to die. It had taken a letter by the Chief Clerk at the UM Office to finally 'unplug' her.

After declining the hipster's invitation to write something in the Audience Comment Book Jack went back to the office where he spent the rest of the workday cataloguing dead addressees and the occasional dead sender. He was slow at first but gradually he got the hang of it and was able to do five dead addressees in less than an hour, a personal record. He was grateful the clerk before him had developed an algorithm, accompanied by a helpful diagram, of the sequence of steps one had to go through from the first step—confirming the correct spelling of the addressee's name on the envelope—to the last step—matching the spelling with the spelling of the same name on the death certificate of the dead addressee and on the dead addressee's tombstone, if a picture of the latter happened to be available. The algorithm functioned like this:

1) Confirm that the name and address on the letter are those of a

real person (occasionally senders liked to play pranks by using a real address but addressing the letter to a literary or film character e.g. Care of: Mildred Pierce, 20 Vanauley street, suite 413, London 4G8).

2) Google map the address to verify that it exists (compare several maps to make sure the sender did not create an imaginary address by superimposing several different maps and photo-shopping in or out some parts of them).

3) Check the Post Office records to see if mail had been delivered unproblematically to that address in the last year.

4) Check the addressee's average response times to successfully delivered mail in the last year. Response times varied among Post Office customers but also within the post office history of a single customer: sometimes an addressee would respond to a disproportionately huge amount of mail very quickly but take their sweet time responding to a single letter they had received in three months. This was a crucial step, because the relative response time was used not only as a measure of the addressee's attention to mail, and by extension to life, but also as a measure of their being alive: average response times were essential in establishing the likelihood of the addressee's being alive or not—a disproportionately long response time was often reason enough to suspect that the addressee was no longer living.

5) Verify the addressee's name and identity (the two were not synonymous) and, where possible, their occupation, family status and family history. Is there anyone who can confirm that the addressee is alive and well and, vice versa, is there anyone who can confirm that the addressee is dead or hospitalized?

6) If there is reason to believe, based on the evidence collected in steps one through five, that the addressee is alive and well, that their average response times to DM (Delivered Mail) is within SMD (Standard Measure of Deviation), that their attention to mail, and to life, has not been disproportionately diminished or damaged beyond re-

pair, that their existence can be confirmed by external witnesses and reviewers, that they satisfy all requirements to define themselves as potential addressees, go directly to their place of residence (which has already been confirmed in one of the preceding steps) to verify that a real, physical mailbox with their name on it does exist, that it has not been vandalized, that the lock on it is fully functional and reliable (to rule out potential TDM i.e. Theft of Delivered Mail), and that it is located at the appropriate height (there had been cases where all other conditions had been met, from the existence of the addressee to the existence of the address and of the mailbox, but there was an insurmountable incongruity between the addressee's height and the height at which their mailbox had been mounted, making it inaccessible to anyone shorter than 1.65cm);

7) Conduct one-on-one interviews with the addressee's neighbors to confirm or deny any suspicions that might have arisen in step 4. The problem here is that longer response times are often correlated with poor addressee-to-neighbor level, quality and frequency of communication, that is, an addressee's failure to respond in a timely manner to their mail, which might be the result of their inability to do so (on account of being dead) cannot be verified by talking to their neighbors. The neighbors need to be able to recall the last time they saw the addressee: if they see the addressee frequently and all of a sudden they don't see the addressee any more it is easy to surmise that some unexpected, unfortunate event (death) has befallen the addressee, making him/her visually scarce. Getting a warrant to search the addressee's apartment, after their mailbox has been found fully operative and the neighbors have confirmed, through cross-interrogation, the addressee's existence, is easy; getting a search warrant in the absence of conclusive evidence from the addressee's neighbors that the addressee really does reside at this address is difficult if not impossible. For an addressee to be no longer capable of being the addressee of DM it is

necessary to establish that there was a point when they were capable of being one—in short, and this is not at all obvious, for an addressee to be suspected of being dead it is necessary to establish first that they have been, at some point in the past, alive.

8) If all else fails, if the addressee's neighbors are of no use in establishing the addressee's existential status, if it's impossible to get an official warrant to search the addressee's apartment, there is no other option but to break into the apartment to establish, first-hand, the reason why mail has failed to be delivered successfully to the addressee.

The above algorithm took care of the majority of UM cases, except one: the most psychologically complex case of the so-called 'indifferent addressee' also known as 'the unresponsive addressee' and, in some accounts, as 'the spiteful addressee.' This was the type of live addressee with a fully functional mailbox, residing at the correct address, who simply refuses to check their mailbox, either out of indifference or out of sheer spite (hence the two sub-categories, depending on the motive for not checking their mailbox). Alas, confirming the existence and address of an indifferent addressee was utterly useless. There was really nothing the Post Office could do to prevent the mail sent to such an addressee's mailbox from being returned to the Post Office. They could keep resending the mail, in the hope that the addressee would eventually break down and check their mailbox, even if it was just to take out the mail and destroy it. Unfortunately, the unresponsive addressee never opened her mailbox. She would let the mailbox overflow with mail, thereby forcing a postal employee to collect the mail lying on the floor, under the mailbox, and to take it back to the UM office. The Post Office was truly helpless in the face of the unresponsive addressee: they could not sue the addressee (ignoring one's mail was not /yet/ considered a crime), they could not declare the addressee unfit to be an addressee (a spiteful disinterest in one's mail, and in life, was not considered evidence of an underlying mental disorder), and they could certainly not try to 'talk the addressee into being so kind as to check their mail regularly' (this would be a violation of the addressee's rights, as described in the Charter on Addressees' Rights: being spitefully indifferent is a basic human right that even an otherwise powerful institution like the Post Office could not challenge).

The algorithm described above concerned only one part of the equation, the addressee. Things got even more complicated when one took into account the sender. Jack's predecessor had begun working on a second, parallel algorithm to establish a sender's existential status—in response to a case where a piece of UM had bounced back to the sender only to bounce again, this time from the sender, who had in the meantime become the addressee of UM—but had been unable to finish it on account of his nervous breakdown. Thus, because he had to work with an unfinished and, frankly, untested sender algorithm Jack spent twice the amount of time on cases of 'sender UM' than he did on 'addressee UM' cases. And even with the double amount of time he spent on UM sender cases he still spent less time than he was spending on writing back to senders, whose own status had not changed after their mail had proven undeliverable. Now, the Manager had explained to Jack that once a piece of mail proved undeliverable on account of the addressee's death, it simply bounced back to the sender, with a 'return to sender' note on it, and that was the end of it. It was not the Post Office's prerogative to explain to the sender why their mail had not been delivered successfully: the only thing that could be reasonably expected from the Post Office, and from the UM office, was a notification that the mail was 'undeliverable'.

The Manager had underscored several times that under no circumstances was Jack to get personally embroiled in the addressee-sender relationship. It was not his place to send personal notes or offer condolences to a sender should their addressee die and thus fail to acknowledge receipt of the sender's mail. Jack followed the established protocol dutifully: establish the addressee's death, cross out their name on the envelope, stamp the envelope 'return to sender', write 'no person of this name resides here' across the back and throw it in the respective pile.

One day, about two weeks after his visit to the Flying Dutchman art gallery, he came upon four identical looking envelopes: off-white, square, with the names of both addressee and sender written in pencil, in the same handwriting. Each envelope contained a single postcard: one from Barcelona, one from Mexico City, one from Sydney, and one from Istanbul. The first postcard featured the most beautiful square in Barcelona (according to the caption) surrounded by palm trees, filled with children playing soccer and old people looking at them with a benign expression on their faces. He flipped the postcard. The following message was written on the back in neat, round letters, betraying a hand that had not yet suffered keyboard atrophy: "Dear Olivia, I arrived in Barcelona last night. I should have taken those bed bugs reports more seriously but I was so adamant about 'roughing it' that I refused to admit to myself how much depends on a clean mattress and a hair-free shower. I shall think of your hot breath, tucked behind your freshly flossed teeth, as I lay my head down among those little beasts tonight. Yours, W.B."

W.B? The W.B.? Jack picked up the second postcard. It featured a close up of a small teacup, the kind in which traditional Turkish coffee is served, against the magnificent background of the Bosphorus, its lights sparkling cinematically in the distance while a single old barge moved phlegmatically through the vast blue expanse of the Aegean. On the back the following message was written in the same hand: "Dear Olivia, I have not yet received a letter from you. You will respond, won't you? This morning I was having tea on a terrace overlooking the sea. Suddenly I smelled you. I felt the presence of a woman. She walked very close to me, her knee brushing against mine. I opened my eyes, certain that I would see your face looking down at me. It was another woman, a stranger. I felt ashamed, as though I had betrayed you by confusing you with another. Forgive me. Yours, W.B."

The third postcard was the familiar bird's eye view of the Sydney opera. W.B. was beseeching Olivia to write to him, describing the moments of despair and self-doubt her continuing silence had plunged him into. The fourth postcard from Mexico City was a long shot of a beautiful church in front of which several old women were selling trinkets or begging. On the back W.B. had written that he had left his hotel room only for half an hour, to buy this postcard. The rest of the time he had remained in bed, feverishly thinking about Olivia, composing in his mind the message she was now reading, revising it over and over again, never quite content with the words, which could not properly express the emotional and intellectual numbness to which her unresponsiveness had condemned him.

All four letters were sent from hotels in four different parts of the world, which explained why they were not sent back to W.B. after their failure to be delivered. The Post Office offered the 'return to sender' service only to customers with permanent addresses in England. Jack entered Olivia's full name in Google. It took a few clicks to confirm that Olivia Lacker, residing at 12 Saint George st., twenty-nine years old, had moved to a new address. She was far from dead: she had simply moved in with her husband soon after her 'fateful encounter' with W.B. Perhaps the two really met, perhaps W.B. even fell in love with her for real, and who knows, perhaps they even had an affair, but one thing was certain: Olivia was not dead. Had W.B. manufactured Olivia's 'untimely death' to fit the concept of *amour fou* around which his art show 'Return to Sender' was structured? Was the infamous W.B., after all, a fake?

Jack closed his eyes and tried to picture the envelopes he had seen in the Flying Dutchman art gallery. He had assumed that the Return to Sender stamp on the envelopes hanging from the ceiling was fake but now he recalled that there was a slight discoloration on the right side of the first 'R' in 'Return', just like the discoloration on the real stamp he had been using at work. W.B. could not have procured these envelopes from any other place but the UM office itself. The only people who had access to the UM office were Jack, the Manager, and the janitor, a half-witted man who seemed as interested in the job of sorting out other people's letters as Jack was in reading psychoanalytic analyses of literature. Jack remembered the Manager mentioning that Jack's predecessor had left the job a few weeks before Jack was hired after suffering a 'nervous breakdown'. Could it be that W.B. was none other than Jack's predecessor?

Jack spent several days researching everything he could find about W.B. on the Internet. According to the artist's bio circulated by art journals and periodicals W.B. had gone to a prestigious if little known art school somewhere in the rural United States. Oddly enough, there seemed to be hardly any continuity between the early stages of his career in the US and his later, more established career in London and on the continent. There were numerous unaccountable delays between the media coverage of his work and his appearance on the art scene. It was almost as if his artistic career was unfolding in reverse. Instead of starting small, as a little known young artist who gradually makes a name for himself and earns the attention of the big shots, W.B.'s first works seemed to be preceded by a great deal of publicity: numerous reviews had been written about his work, multiple invitations and commissions with a thematic focus had been extended to him, and all this before his work had even been exhibited! According to Jack's calculations there had been a three-month delay between him reading a review of W.B.'s work for the first time and actually seeing the work, or rather a reproduction of it in an art journal, for the first time. The reproduction in the journal had very poor resolution but the lengthy description of the work seemed, at the time, to make up for the difficulty in actually seeing the work. In fact, come to think of it, every image Jack had ever seen of a W.B. photograph or installation had been of a similarly poor quality. W.B.'s work was so rich and thought-provoking that it gave rise to the best art criticism in decades, if by 'best' one meant the type of criticism that could stand on its own, in the *absence* of the artwork. Anyway, the artwork was just a crutch.

And what if the crutch did not exist? What if the work, even its author W.B., did not exist? What if the artist known as 'W.B.' was just an invention, a figment of a postal employee's sick imagination? What if after years of maintaining the semblance of communication through directing and redirecting the only material evidence of it—thin white envelopes—it had occurred to Jack's predecessor, the former Chief Clerk of the UM Office, that it is possible to sustain the illusion of something real long after the real has disappeared or died, like a star that has long gone cold but that still shines bright in the night sky? What if one evening, as he was locking the door to the UM office, having sorted out the dead addressees and the dead senders in their respective piles, Jack's postal predecessor had decided that he, too, could exist like that, like a dead star, a fake light that has lost its source, an undelivered letter suspended forever in the postal circuit, never to arrive at its destination, an artwork that exists only as long as art critics write about it? What if 'W.B.' was just a name endlessly circulated by art journals and gallery catalogs, a name concealing a hole in the artistic firmament, a fraud created impulsively in a moment of postal boredom?

Jack recalled the various personas he himself used to invent back in his book reviewing days. Does the creation of an artist result in a fraud or can it be considered itself a work of art? You start by building a website where you post numerous reviews of the artist's work, interviews with the artist, recordings of artist talks he was invited to give, interviews with curators, mentors, friends, family members. Once you have weaved a delicate, complex web of professional and personal relationships that are psychologically believable (it wouldn't hurt to involve a professional psychologist at this stage in the invention of the artist, someone who understands the narcissism and ego-mania shared by all artists) you begin to expand the artist's existence beyond the virtual realm: you solicit reviews of actual exhibitions, you circulate the artist's name in the academic community. The citation machine works by inertia: after a name is dropped in it, it is automatically reproduced in another text, then in another one and so on, until the name of the artist becomes a shorthand for a particular quality of an already existing—real—work of art or, if things go well, a shorthand for an entire style without the need to actually produce evidence of that for which the artist's name has become a shorthand. Before the artist's name has crystalized into something real, material, signified with a noun, it dissolves into an adjective—its particular nature is assumed without ever having to be demonstrated or explained.

In short, the invention of the artist follows the logic of touristic discourse. A given place begins to exist as a tourist attraction through the staggered, well-planned proliferation of tourist brochures about it. A travel destination depends on the existence of a travel guide, which provides directions to the place (e.g. is it better/faster/cheaper to reach it by bus, taxi, train or plane?). The comfort and quality of the trip to the place determines the existence of the place: the place is thus a matter of the leather seats in the train compartment, the number of stops on the way to the place, the quality of the restaurant service, and the cleanliness of the on-board bathroom.

The beauty of it all is that at no point in this process of inventing the artist does one have to give any veridical evidence of the artist's work: all one has to provide is the discourse around it. To counter in advance any petty demands to 'prove' the artist's existence all one has to do is have the guts to take the stereotype of the exceptional, almost

pathological privacy of the artist to the next level, where the pathological shyness and asocial, private nature of the artist extends to the
artist's works as well: the artist is so very private that he cannot bear to
reveal or share with the public his own work, forcing the public to be
satisfied with believing in it, that is, believing in its existence (a much
stronger form of belief than the simple belief in the artistic qualities
of the work or in the artist's ability/talent to continue to produce it).
Withholding the artist's work from the public, offering them only the
artist's claim that the work exists—though he can't show it to them—is
the ultimate proof that the invention of the artist has been successfully
completed. If one manages to execute this properly one can even afford
to be less original in composing the artist's backstory. Any old stereotype will do, though the most popular one remains the rags to riches
story: the raw talent, the years of starving, the accidental discovery
of the artist and so on. If the artist becomes famous too easily or too
soon you can always pull him out of circulation, wait a bit and then
send him back into circulation, as it were, in reverse: a successful artist
masquerades as a raw, undiscovered talent until he is discovered again,
and the whole thing repeats itself. The artist's inventor can repeat this
algorithm for inventing an artist an infinite number of times, correcting any glitches with each subsequent repetition and improving the
coherence and believability of the story.

There was one way Jack could test the validity of his inventing-the-
artist theory. He took out a blank sheet of paper and wrote the following:

> Dear W.B., You must be wondering why I have not responded to any of your
> letters. I have not forgotten our time together and I will always remember
> it fondly but there is someone else in my life now and I don't want to
> jeopardize this new relationship by living in the past. I hope you understand.
>
> Yours, Olivia

Jack reread and tweaked the letter several times until he was fully was satisfied with its vagueness and mediocrity. The strength of clichés was never more obvious to him, especially in matters of the heart: what better way to turn off a lover than to clothe yourself in clichés, destroying their romantic image of you? He sealed the letter and copied W.B.'s address from the online address registry, wondering what the Manager would say if he got wind of all this. Writing personalized responses to customers was, of course, a direct violation of Post Office regulations regardless of whether the postal employee did that out of good intentions, for example to inform the UM's sender of the reasons for the delivery failure. You may feel as sympathetic as you like, the Manager had warned Jack, but do not, under any circumstances, get involved! Every customer is a lawsuit waiting to happen. Jack mailed three copies of the letter accompanied by a copy of the *Return to Sender* catalog he had picked up at the gallery: one to W.B., one to the Flying Dutchman art gallery, and one to the Chief Editor of *Contemporary Art*, the journal that claimed to have 'discovered' W.B.

Over the next few days all major newspapers, periodicals and journals that featured an Art Column ran a short article by Lionel Trilling, an art critic who had written extensively on W.B.'s work. Trilling wrote that *Return to Sender*, the latest show by acclaimed 'enfant terrible' W.B., had recently come under anonymous attack for faking the real life story on which it claimed to be based. The critic went on to say that 'the W.B. affair', as it came to be known, had stirred up the old philosophical debate about the relationship between life and art, truth and fiction. Could an artwork be held accountable for 'faking it' given that 'faking it' was inherent in the very definition of art? Did the knowledge that the story on which *Return to Sender* was based was fake affect negatively our aesthetic appreciation of the work? Did it matter that the dead addressee at the center of W.B.'s work was actually alive?

A few days after the publication of Trilling's piece in the journal

Contemporary Art Jack stopped by the Flying Dutchman gallery. Benjamin the hipster briefed Jack on all the latest developments related to the affair. Apparently W.B. had contacted the gallery and asked them to issue a statement that all accusations against him, including the claim that he had 'faked' Olivia's death, were without substance. The statement was supposed to end with a reminder that, in the words of none other than Lionel Trilling himself, W.B.'s art was "concerned with destabilizing the artificial border separating art from life" and that, therefore, anyone who claimed W.B's work was 'fake' was launching nothing less than "a personal attack on W.B.'s artistic vision."

Several weeks passed by. Although the brief storm Jack's anonymous attack had caused in art circles died down attendance at the Flying Dutchman gallery was declining: people felt cheated out of a good tragic story after reading Olivia's (i.e., Jack's) response to W.B.'s desperate love letters (Jack's letter had been reproduced in all major publications and a copy of it was hung on the gallery wall, right next to W.B.'s artist statement). Just when it seemed that the W.B. affair was over, plunging Jack into another long spell of postal ennui, things took a turn for the better, or at least for the interesting.

On November 17 the Sunday paper ran an obituary of a young woman who had been found stabbed to death in her apartment. There was nothing unusual about that except that the woman's name was Olivia Lacker, residing at 33 Isabella street, previously of #12 Saint George st.

A few days later, Jack was sorting out, as usual, the double-death pile—dead addressee and dead sender—when he came upon a dusty, bulging envelope addressed as follows: "To Whom It May Concern, mailbox #?, 619 Paladin street." Jack sneezed and reached into his pocket for a paper tissue and cried out in pain. He took out his hand: his middle finger was covered in blood. He slowly put his hand back in his pocket and took out a small letter knife. He looked at it incomprehensibly but after a few moments he remembered that several weeks earlier he had gotten it for free (along with an empty perfume bottle) at the antique store next to his hotel. He wiped his blood off the knife's edge and cut open the envelope from the side. A small object rolled out of the envelope into his hand: it was a letter knife, the same as the one he had just used to open the letter, only this one was covered in what looked like old blood stains. Jack unfolded the handwritten letter:

Dear Sir, I am writing to confess to the murder of Olivia Lacker. I am not a psychopath. I fully understand the gravity of my act. I feel morally responsible for taking another human life and I am nothing if not willing to accept my sentence. But I have a dilemma. Although I have no doubt that I deserve to hang I am also intellectually certain that I have succeeded at what many others have failed miserably: executing the perfect crime. While my heart and reason tell me I must rot in jail for the heinous crime I have committed, from a logical point of view I cannot be convicted of a crime unless I am apprehended. Given that I have committed the perfect crime the chances of me being apprehended are zero. I thus find myself in an impossible and, believe me, painful situation: I am overcome with feelings of guilt and self-hatred but, at the same time, I am unable to come forward and turn myself in because my intellect does not allow it. I am in perennial check, unable to checkmate myself, if you will excuse the clumsy chess metaphor. Whenever I recall the face of the woman I murdered I feel morally and emotionally anguished and I long for my deserved punishment. Yet as soon as I feel that I want to die something inside me shifts and my guilt transforms into pride. I waver between self-hatred and self-admiration, unable to give myself up completely to either.

I cannot make a choice between the two. Only you can make that choice for me. If you succeed in arresting me I shall finally be free of this torture. I will embrace my punishment as fully deserved, by which I mean both morally and logically deserved. Otherwise I shall remain forever torn between suffering morally yet being intellectually satisfied with myself, and suffering intellectually—in the event my perfect crime is proven imperfect— while being morally relieved.

Please find enclosed the murder weapon, a letter knife. My life is in your hands. I await your answer.

John Doe

John Doe a.k.a W.B., Jack thought. Apparently the only way for W.B. to reclaim his artistic credibility was to give his audience what they wanted. They had felt cheated out of a desperate lover writing to his beloved without knowing she had died. Well, they finally got what they wanted—even if the beloved's death came with a considerable delay. She was dead now, sacrificed in the name of an artwork demanding the death of the addressee.

Jack turned over the letter. There was a drawing on the back: a letter knife, seen from the front, the back, and the side. He examined the text under the drawing through a magnifying glass: "A copy of the murder weapon: an ordinary letter knife available at any philately shop in town. Price: 3 pounds. The one enclosed herewith is not the actual murder weapon but a faithful replica. The bloodstains are fake. They were added to give the reproduction a more authentic appearance. The original can be easily identified by a slight discoloration on the inside of the handle and a small inscription on the edge: G.H. (the initials of the company that manufactured this limited edition of letter knives just before going bankrupt)."

Jack picked up the magnifying glass with one hand and the letter knife—the one he had used to open the letter—with his other. He saw the initials right away: they were etched into the metal edge exactly as described in the letter: "G.H."

It was lunchtime. He took off his lab coat, placed the two letter knives in two separate plastic bags, switched off the lights and locked the door twice.

Whenever he wandered about aimlessly, with only a vague idea of where he was going, he inevitably ended up at his destination without looking for it, but if he ever tried to find a place he had previously stumbled upon by accident he almost never could find it again. Places seemed accessible only when he was *not* looking for them. Having gotten lost twice he was about to give up when he suddenly found himself standing in front of the same antique store where he had gotten the perfume bottle and the letter knife. In the broad daylight every object in the store had reverted back to its artifactual status rather than being part of the storeowner's private home décor. The box of 'free items' in which Jack had found the letter knife was where he had last seen it: on the table in front of the store, next to the folders with old postcards and faded family photographs, only now the objects in the box were priced at two pounds.

Jack cleared his throat. The storeowner, hidden behind two matching 19th century dressers, looked up from a book he was reading. Jack apologized for interrupting the man's reading and explained that he was curious about an object, a letter knife to be precise, that he had acquired for free from this store several weeks ago. Did the storeowner happen to know the name of the manufacturer and the year of manufacture? The man listened to Jack patiently and then corrected him: none of the items in this store were 'free'. All items in the box were at a reduced price, two pounds, but they were definitely not free. Was Jack insinuating that there was nothing of value in the store? Did he perhaps think two pounds was too much for a 19th century letter knife? The man kept rephrasing his rhetorical questions as if he was afraid his sarcasm would be lost on Jack. Jack assured the man that he had never presumed to underestimate the difficulty of making one's living out of other people's past but that, nevertheless, he was not mistaken about the letter knife, which he had indeed gotten for free. They went on like that for a little while longer until finally Jack 'remembered' that he had indeed paid two pounds and the man, softened by Jack's voluntary surrender, admitted to having no recollection whatsoever of the circumstances under which he had acquired the letter knife in question: he kept a record of all larger items but the provenance of the smaller ones, particularly something as trivial as a letter knife, was anyone's guess.

Exhausted by the preceding useless intercourse, and surprised by the unexpected 19th century flavor of his own internal monologue, Jack asked one last question: did the man recall whether he had acquired the items in the 'free box' separately, at different times and from different places, or were they all in the box when he got it? The man could not remember. Jack gave him twenty pounds and left the store carrying the box under his arm. Twenty meters further down the road he threw the box in the river. To think he could reconstruct a murder from a few random objects that may or may not have belonged to the same man was ludicrous. He watched the box fall into a little vortex of river junk and walked away, feeling the sharp edge of the only piece of evidence of a murder lying in his pocket. He wondered about his own interest in this case. Was it moral? Intellectual? Was he really interested in solving a crime for the sake of bringing the perpetrator to justice? Was he tempted by the intellectual challenge the murderer had extended personally to him? Or was he simply suffering from a case of postal ennui himself?

The most shocking thing about the murder weapon was not so much its utterly banal nature—an everyday object a copy of which sat on everyone's desk—but the fact that it could be deployed and redeployed for the same purpose over and over again. It had killed one person already and it could—would—kill again. The letter knife was immortal, waiting to insert itself between the next duo of humans, making one of them into a perpetrator and the other one into a victim. There was nothing to stop Jack from occupying either one of these vacant positions. Put differently, the fact that nothing was stopping Jack from killing or being killed simply meant that he would either kill or be killed. After it was all over, after Jack had killed or been killed, the knife would end up in another shopping arcade, in another box of 'free items', to be picked up by another insomniac flâneur.

Back at the UM office everything was exactly as he had left it yet he had the impression that the room was smaller, the piles of paperwork messier, the handwriting on the envelopes sloppier, and the errors in the UM catalog sillier. He realized that the UM office had lost its metaphorical dimension—it was no longer a space raising philosophical questions about the possibility of communication, or provoking reflections about the conventions and aesthetic qualities of a new sub-genre of epistolary literature. The UM office was now just a room filled with useless paper destined to be recycled. The absence of an addressee or of a sender that had earlier seemed to spawn endlessly fascinating philosophical paradoxes was now an annoying detail Jack had been hired to keep a record of for reasons that were becoming more and more unclear to him. Strictly speaking, he reasoned, none of these letters had a missing addressee, even those whose addressee could be conclusively proven dead. On the contrary, they all had the same addressee: Jack. They had failed to reach the person whose name was scribbled on the front of the envelope but they had all reached Jack: after all, they would never be considered 'undeliverable' without his acknowledgement of their receipt. One could go even further—and Jack did—and posit that a piece of UM became truly 'undeliverable' only if Jack did not respond to it.

The notion of 'undeliverable mail' put into question the assumption that the sender and addressee in a communication flow pre-exist that flow rather than being constituted by it. Incommunicability, or the undeliverability of mail, rendered the ontological status of both sides of the communication flow equally indeterminate. If Jack's ability to be the addressee of undeliverable mail depended on his ability to be absent i.e., dead, his ability to be the addressee of a murderer's confession implied his identification as the murderer's next victim.

Jack took out a sheet of paper and wrote the following response to John Doe a.k.a W.B:

> *Dear Sir, I am sorry for my belated response. First of all, I would like to draw your attention to the fact that you failed to provide a return address. I urge you to correct this egregious omission on your part; otherwise I am afraid you won't be able to benefit from my assistance, which, I assure you, I am eager to provide.*
>
> *Now, to the matter at hand. I would like to thank you for extending us the courtesy of turning yourself in, thereby saving a lot of police resources, which have now been re-directed for deployment in other urgent police operations. What I am about to say next won't be to your liking I am afraid. As much as I praise your unabashed willingness to co-operate with us by confessing to the murder you have committed I am less satisfied with your equivocation—under the pretext that you are 'morally confused'—when it comes to actually allowing us to put you behind bars. I sympathize with the moral turmoil and existential angst you are going through. I am even mildly amused by your intellectual arrogance—I refer, of course, to the quasi-intellectual challenge you pose to us, mocking—prematurely I should add—our ability to identify your whereabouts. However, at the end of the day—and at the end of your cliché-ridden letter—I find your 'theory' of a clash between your moral sense and your intellectual wit facile, unconvincing, and, frankly, disappointing. It's one of the oldest, most predictable ways of setting up a dilemma. Yes, I am a man of literature. I am familiar with genre conventions, character types and plot twists, and I am suspicious of anyone claiming to have committed the perfect crime but then offering the most clichéd, from a literary point of view, account of it. I don't trust such a man, or should I say such a poseur, because I know that the author of the perfect*

crime must be, by definition, a superb storyteller. A mediocre storyteller—one who falls back on the modernist trope of an unresolvable conflict between reason and sentiment, between the superego and the id—cannot be the criminal mastermind he claims to be. I realize this might sound a bit harsh but I am afraid any confrontation with mediocrity makes me lose all inhibitions and drives me to call a (clichéd) spade a (clichéd) spade.

Rest assured, Sir, that you shall be apprehended within a fortnight.

Regards,

Chief Inspector Jack Sturrett

9.

THE METHOD HAD TO FIT the crime, about which two things could be said: first, the motive for Olivia's murder was to make real the fictional metaphor around which W.B.'s art show was structured; second, it was possible that Olivia's murder, like the fictional metaphor it was supposed to make real, had not actually taken place, that the murder was just another cleverly executed ruse, another piece of fiction. What W.B. didn't know—couldn't have known—was that Jack was, in fact, quite experienced with 'fictional murders', having reflected on the subject at length in a work of fiction he had authored himself back in the days when he was moonlighting as a screenwriter.

Jack realized his response to W.B.'s murder confession had inconspicuously moved their exchange out of the realm of the fictional and into the realm of the real, up to now his least favorite one. If there was one thing he and W.B. shared it was an interest in taking metaphors and fictions literally. For Jack's part it was a way of injecting some seriousness in what he perceived as the increasing 'levitation' of life and art, the tendency to take everything ironically. The W.B. affair had raised the question of responding to an artwork as though it were a message addressed to *you* and demanding a response. One did not normally read a novel and then write a letter to one of the novel's characters to ask them about their beliefs and opinions. One did not normally assume that a letter hanging on the wall in an art gallery demands a response. But perhaps one ought to, Jack thought.

His thoughts were interrupted by the turn of the key in the door. The Manager opened the door and stood at the entrance without closing it. He walked around the table, very slowly, inspecting the piles of unsorted mail.

"You don't seem to have made a lot of progress," he pointed at the piles of UM.

"I am confident I will catch up…" Jack mumbled.

"Are you sure you are confident?"

Jack was about to say something but the Manager raised his hand slightly as though he had estimated the minimum height at which he could lift it and still enjoy the full dramatic effect he intended it to have.

"I think we can both agree that the work you have been doing here is sub-par. I have to say I am not surprised. You predecessor had similar difficulties, which were only compounded by his seemingly uncontrollable tendency to open certain letters and tamper with their contents. You will receive your severance package by the end of this month. As of tomorrow you are no longer an employee of this office."

The only thing that concerned Jack at the moment was not the fact that he would have to look for another job but that once he left the UM office he would no longer be able to receive any future undeliverable correspondence from W.B.—and he had every reason to believe that there *would* be further correspondence. W.B's letters would continue to be forwarded to the UM office but someone else, Jack's successor, would receive them and file them in the proper file for they would have absolutely no significance for him.

Once the Manager had left Jack stuffed W.B.'s letter in his pocket and collected his belongings. He walked in the direction of his hotel thinking about, what else, murder. It was as if murder was the only thing to put things in motion, to put him, Jack, in motion, as if the only way he could ask 'who' 'what' 'where' 'when' and 'why', and actually take an interest in the answer, was if the object of these questions was dead. 'Where' someone or something was, mattered only if he/she or it *was no longer there* (because he/she/it was dead); 'why' someone did something mattered only if his reasons could be criminalized as 'motives'; 'who' someone was mattered only to the extent that he/she was endowed with criminal agency. The meaning of life seemed to depend on its criminalization, on the criminalization of *agents*, *reasons* and *actions*, on their transformation into criminal masterminds performing criminal acts with criminal motives. Action that did not result in complete obliteration was not active enough; a mind that did not conceive of the obliteration of another mind was not living up to its full potential; reasons that were not meticulously planned and rehearsed and that did not go back to some unresolved psychological trauma were not real reasons, that is, motives.

Back at the hotel the concierge gave him the key to his room and informed him that he had no new mail. In the elevator he wondered about the usefulness of being informed about the lack of something (e.g. mail). When he got out of the elevator he tripped over several long cables zigzagging across the hallway. He followed them to their source, a room two doors down from his own. Inside the room three cameras were pointed mercilessly at the bed, on the edge of which sat an aging woman in a resplendent white dress. A man dressed as badly as the average assistant director came up to the door and told Jack that they were shooting a film and that they would appreciate it if he could refrain from walking up and down the hallway.

Jack locked himself in his room and lied down on the bed without taking off his shoes. He held W.B.'s letter above his head. Paladin street. He closed his eyes and said the words out loud: "Paladin street." There was a familiar ring to it. "Paladin street. Paladin. Paladino. Paladino street! Next stop Paladino street!"

The name of the street was misspelled. It was 'Paladino', not 'Paladin', street, one of the stops on the very first route of the tourist double decker Jack had explored when he first arrived in town. He could picture clearly the name of the street on a plaque hung over a small bakery, in a sleepy neighborhood on the opposite side of the river. W.B.'s letter had failed to be delivered simply because of one missing letter.

Of course, there was also no mailbox number and no name but these problems suddenly didn't seem insurmountable. He got off the bed but sat down again—he was supposed to stay in his room while the film shoot was going on. He wondered what he would look like with a wig and his thoughts drifted away to memories of school plays, costumes too big or too small for him, and the unbearable heat under the stage lights.

Later that evening, after the film crew had wrapped up the shoot, Jack headed towards Paladino street. The idea how to continue receiving W.B.'s letters occurred to him as he stood in the middle of an art gallery on Paladino street. The art exhibit was called "Conceptual Art," a term that had worn off over the last several decades but had been given new life—or so the curator of the exhibit claimed—in this 'bold, original take on the concept of a concept', or what the curator referred to as 'post-post-conceptual art.' Every work in the exhibit conveyed, literally, the concept that had inspired it, without however giving it material expression. In the curator's words, every work celebrated the 'autonomy of the concept' by freeing it from a physical form that would only drag it down into the trivial realm of the real. The concept behind the exhibit was to take the idea of 'conceptual art' literally and exhibit 'concepts' as artworks.

But how does one exhibit an abstraction, a mental image? What would the catalog for such an exhibition look like? How does one determine the price of a concept? Jack imagined an artist negotiating the price of a post-conceptual painting exploring the concept of 'death'. "This one would run you a couple of thousand pounds," the artist would say. The client and the artist would argue back and forth for a while until the artist would offer the client a deal: he would paint the moment right before death, which 'is a little less expensive.' And how would one even title such works? One couldn't call a painting like that simply 'Death'. Perhaps all one could do is add the prefix 'post' in the title, indicating that the 'post-conceptual' move takes place only within the mind of the gallery viewer, rather than across the canvass itself, since it is in the very 'nature' of the concept—if one could use such an inappropriate word to describe something immaterial and abstract—to be purely mental.

Before entering the gallery Jack quickly carried out two (abbreviated) phenomenological reductions of the artworks he imagined he would see inside, and then, just to be on the safe side, an extra reduction of the mental act of phenomenological reduction itself. These preliminary steps left him mentally exhausted but rather pleased with himself: by the time he made his way to the center of the gallery space he was convinced that he had already seen, in his mind's eye, the exhibit and that he would only have to glance around to confirm that his notion of post-post-conceptual art was correct.

He was wrong. After excising any material trace he could think of from the image of the artworks he had constructed in his mind, the only thing left, the only thing he expected to see on the walls, were the captions of the artworks without the artworks themselves. But the curator had done him one better. As he looked around the gallery Jack failed to find anything—anything at all—for his eyes to latch on. Nothing obstructed his view or, rather, *there was no view*: his look was dissociated from any possible object. Even the whiteness of the walls was not something he could be said to be looking at. There were no prepositions to properly describe the relationship between his look and whatever else existed 'outside' it precisely because there was no 'outside'. There were no little pieces of paper with the captions of individual works to orient his look. There was nothing to indicate where one work ended and another one began—no caption, no frame, no slight variations in the gallery lighting to indicate the borders separating artworks and the distance between him and them. The only limits or frames—if one could call them that—were those barely sensed jumps in the continually unfolding spool of his self-awareness. He understood that the only works of art in the gallery were the concepts—some highly developed, others barely formed—within his own mind as he strolled through the white cube. The exhibit did nothing less than dramatize the movements of his own mind.

On the way out he noticed the Comments Book whose unabashed materiality seemed so aggressively literal in the rarified post-post-conceptual air around it. He did not write comment on the exhibit but wrote down his name: Charles Worthington.

Charles Worthington lived at 619 Paladino st., mailbox #12, the address from which W.B.'s undeliverable mail had been bouncing back to the UM office. 'Charles Worthington' was Jack's ingenious solution to the problem he was faced with after being fired from the UM office: how to continue his correspondence with W.B., a disgruntled postal employee turned con artist turned murderer, in order to prove the latter's involvement in, and perhaps responsibility for, Olivia's death. Very little was known of Charles. Jack preferred to keep it that way. As usual, he would 'fill him out' gradually.

Jack arrived at 619 Paladino street a bit before dusk. All he could see were the outlines of a small house overgrown with grass and hidden from view by an oak tree whose branches fell protectively over the roof and extended all the way over the fence and kept slapping Jack in the face as he tried to climb up the fence and look inside the little garden in which a few poppies drooped lower and lower to the ground. After several unsuccessful attempts to jump the fence he found a hole in it through which he managed to squeeze in.

The door was not locked. Inside the state of the house was ambiguous: it could have been abandoned a long time ago or just a few days ago. It was neither dirty, nor clean, neither well furnished nor barely furnished, smelling neither of musk nor of fresh air. It was in a sort of in-between state, as if the owner had left in a hurry expecting to return.

It took Jack half an hour to find the mailbox: it was overgrown with grass and hidden from the street by the bottom half of a tree trunk cut down for no apparent reason other than perhaps to hide the mailbox from the street. The mailbox was empty. No wonder W.B.'s letters could not be delivered: the street name was misspelled and the mailbox hidden. These two obstacles were easily removable, however: the address could be corrected, the mailbox made visible to the mailman. Once this had been accomplished—the house cleaned up a bit, the grass mowed, the metal fence fixed—its sole inhabitant, Charles Worthington, could be allowed to make an appearance and, most importantly, receive mail.

10.

THE FOLLOWING MORNING, having affixed a plaque with his name and address to the mailbox, Charles Worthington sat out on the porch drinking coffee.

Over the next few weeks Charles explored his neighborhood, chatting with random people in grocery stores, drugstores and bars, building up a sense of neighborly familiarity and resisting his neighbors' skepticism vis-à-vis his claim that he had been living in that neighborhood 'for a very long time.' One of Jack's winning strategies, which he had perfected over long hours of insomnia, was to construct a shared past and inconspicuously insinuate himself in it. He would start from some blanket, noncommittal statements that did not require any proof because they were merely rhetorical, statements about 'how things' used to be (always better than they were now), 'how the neighborhood had changed' (always for the worse), 'how difficult it had become to trust anyone, even your neighbors' (he would heartily agree) and 'how city planners should think more seriously about public space' (this he would agree with but with some qualifications, just for the sake of argument, because argument, he reasoned, builds stronger, lasting relationships by leaving traces of resentment in the other party thereby perpetuating their memory of him and of the things they shared with him, namely disagreement). Gradually, he would intersperse those general statements—the building blocks of the fake past he shared with his neighbors—with more concrete ones, such as those about "Stuart's horrible hedge job," "the unfortunate side effects of home schooling in the case of the Smith twins," and "the unexplainable phasing out of blueberry muffins—everyone's favorite—at the local bakery." Once he had laid down the base for a fake common past—trivial statements about time (statements about social degeneration and disintegration) and shared timely concerns about trivial things—Jack would focus on one-on-one 'interviews' with individual members of the community, in the course of which he would make numerous mental notes about very specific incidents in each member's life, incidents that Jack could casually bring up later on in a totally different context and in an off-hand manner as a quick reference or an inside joke they were all in on and that therefore did not need to be expounded upon. He would take a firm stand on all of these incidents and purposefully contradict himself, saying one thing to one neighbor and the opposite to another, then pulling back and letting them gossip about him. Becoming the object of gossip was his ultimate goal, a sign that he had succeeded in making others talk about him spontaneously, the way they talked about blueberry muffins or the Smith twins, just another detail of their daily lives. The moment he no longer had to put any effort into making others address him or talk about him was the moment he knew Jack Sturrett had successfully become Charles Worthington.

To assuage the doubts and fears of the most skeptical members of the community, who insisted that they had never seen Charles around, Jack created a simple, believable back-story for Charles based on the bits and pieces he collected from conversations with his neighbors. They told him the house's previous tenant had been a civil servant (they thought he used to work at the Post Office but they were not absolutely sure), the misanthropic type that barely leaves the house. On the basis of a few scant details Jack invented himself as the civil servant's brother. He told them he was not particularly close to his brother, who, in true misanthropic fashion, had managed to alienate himself from the rest of the family. The reason the neighbors hadn't seen his brother, Jack explained, was that his brother had spent the last year in a home for patients suffering from mild psychotic symptoms, taking out his bitterness and resentment on nurses, who were unfortunately obliged to take it. Charles was taking care of the house in his brother's absence but he hadn't really spent much time in it: his job involved a lot of travelling, which is why he hadn't had the pleasure of socializing with his neighbors as much as he would have liked to, a grave omission he was hoping to correct in the near future. His neighbors found the story believable—after all, they had all, at some point in their lives, had to deal with an unwieldy, carbuncular family member. As time went by Charles and his neighbors bonded over their shared sense of victimization at the hands of a misanthropic family member they could all collectively hate.

Gradually Charles developed a certain image of himself, one that left a distinctly positive impression on the other members of the community, who came to see him as a reliable man of high principles, sound morals and strong beliefs and opinions about 'things that mattered' such as the insufficient height of the Timbledons' hedge, the potholes in Mr. Keaton's driveway, the unseasonably warm temperatures, the difficulty of finding an eligible partner in life despite the new dating options made possible by social media, the preposterously expensive necklace Mrs. Landon in #45 wore sometimes etc. On several occasions Jack overheard some of his neighbors talking about a man they described as 'serious, predictable, slightly boring but reliable, a real homebody, and a neat dresser'. It took him a while to realize they were referring to Charles. Jack was pleased with the pace at which Charles was developing a belief system of internally coherent opinions about the world—in one word, a 'personality'.

If Jack's wardrobe consisted of a few pairs of identical jeans, four shirts and one sweater with a ripped shoulder, which he had patched over with a piece of leather, Charles was quite the dandy. He didn't dress extravagantly, however. Two simple rules governed his style: conformity and inconspicuousness. From his very first day at 619 Paladino st. Charles wore a wig with a receding hairline, with a few silver streaks here and there, to conceal Jack's thick dark hair. He considered buying several wigs, each representing a different stage in his hairline recession—one for the weeks following a (virtual) haircut, another one for the middle period, and a third one for the days preceding a much needed haircut—but then decided against it. The wig with as little hair as possible was the easiest one to maintain: people did not generally pay attention to balding men i.e., they did not expect their hair to grow dramatically.

Jack bought a very nice pair of moustaches that faded ever so slightly when exposed to the sun over an extended period of time, just as a real moustache would. On the nights he spent at the hotel—which was four times a week, four nights that Charles was 'away on business', as he told his neighbors—he would pace around the hotel room, trying out different gaits for Charles. He finally settled on one, simple and straightforward, like Charles himself: with every step the feet are raised just above the ground, not too high but not too low either, to avoid tripping, then the right arm goes up in the air in a measured, steady movement, not too excited but not too apathetic either, the left arm follows, copying the movement of the right hand, the torso, slightly inclined forward, moves forward, keeping up with the movement of the arms, the head remains steady throughout, chin up, Adam's apple tucked in, ears tucked in as well (Jack found the sight of a man walking with his ears flapping in the wind undignified), stomach tucked in, nostrils free of any flare, mouth slightly open to allow ventilation (Jack found the sight of slightly parted lips equally ridiculous but unfortunately he had not yet found an alternative way of ventilation). The wig had to be secured at all times as individual hairs tended to slip out in the course of executing all these movements.

One evening, while taking a break from practicing Charles' gait in his hotel room, Jack turned on the TV to watch *Accounting*, part of a documentary series, *Work*, exploring the history of some of the most common professions in the world (at the end of this week's episode he watched the trailer for the following week's episode about gas station attendants). Silent, black and white images of accountants bent over their desks in cramped fin de siècle offices flickered across the screen. Jack was fascinated by the small round glasses the now dead accountants wore out of necessity—bad lighting conditions, long working hours—rather than as a fashion statement. He combed the antique stores in Abberc. until he found a pair that looked more or less like the ones he had seen sliding down the noses of the now dead accountants.

Jack quite enjoyed the (fake) sense of maturity and reliability Charles projected with his overall demeanor and appearance, the sense of someone one might call 'a pillar of society.' It pleased him to think that whereas the average person's doppelgänger represented the freedom to indulge in all kinds of socially prohibited activities and to satisfy 'perverse' desires, his self-invented doppelgänger was anything but a libertine. While for anyone else the function of the doppelgänger was to liberate their primary personality, let it engage in actions otherwise found reprehensible, vulgar, absurd, ridiculous, nauseating or, in some cases, punishable by law, Jack now felt truly free only when he could relax into conformity and mediocrity, a state in which no scruples prevented him from peppering his dull conversations with random quotes by famous people. In the middle of a conversation about the relative usefulness of two brands of lawn-mowers, one British, the other Dutch, Charles would always find a way to lighten up the otherwise dreary exchange by smuggling in an entirely irrelevant quote from Voltaire—for example, "False wit is a fatiguing search after cunning traits, an affectation of saying in enigmas what others have already said naturally, to hang together ideas which are incompatible, to divide that which ought to be united, of seizing false relations"—which was so obviously *not a propos* the subject matter of the conversation that Charles's interlocutor would be embarrassed to bring it up for fear of not seeing some hidden level of appositeness that had escaped his unliterary mind. Although many of his neighbors considered Jack's proclivity to illustrate his own discourse with quotations from academic and literary sources (which, they assumed incorrectly, he had read) a personal idiosyncrasy as well as a sign of intelligence, he himself had always believed the constant referencing of other people's opinions to support one's own unfocused thoughts to be a despicable form of ventriloquism indicative of a feeble mind. This is exactly why he allowed, even encouraged, Charles to practice it—Charles was, at his core, a conformist, a man who tends to the hedge around his house, making sure its height and color match those of his neighbors'.

Time went by, presumably. Jack kept busy at the house, cleaning, reading, and watching Charles's neighbors. He checked the mailbox every day but did not find anything other than junk mail. It was kind of extraordinary that junk mail was always deliverable even if it was incorrectly addressed. People often wonder how long after someone's death their fingernails continue to grow but no one ever wonders how long after an addressee's death she continues to receive junk mail, or why, despite the person's inability to continue to be the addressee of their junk mail the latter is never forwarded to the UM office. Most often junk mail continues to be delivered to the dead addressee's mailbox until a new tenant moves in and makes the mistake of opening the mailbox. Once the mailbox has been opened the mail inside—real and/ or junk—is considered delivered.

The heated debates around the difficulty of determining the exact moment when a piece of mail is to be deemed 'delivered' are equaled only by pro- and anti-abortion debates. In both cases timing is everything. Once the mailbox has been opened, the junk mail inside cannot be aborted, that is returned to sender or forwarded to the UM office. If one wants to stop receiving junk mail the best course of action is not to open the mailbox for a very long time (the time varies), letting the junk mail accumulate and rot inside until it's not possible to open the mailbox any more, in which case the postal employee is forced to remove the contents of the mailbox himself so that he can put in—yes, you guessed it—more junk mail. By opening the mailbox the next tenant declares his willingness to continue to receive the previous tenant's mail. In short, from the point of view of junk mail, all addressees are mutually exchangeable. And why not, Jack thought. All people—all potential addressees—read junk mail in exactly the same way: they do not project any of their subjectivity onto it, they do not interpret it, there are no conventions or stylistic features in junk mail that individual addressees could respond to in radically different, subjective ways. Junk mail is *not* a literary genre. It does not demand interpretive skills. Or does it?

Jack interrupted his reflection on the semiotics of junk mail to examine the piece of junk mail Charles had just pulled out of the mailbox. It was an invitation to two new shows opening at The Flying Dutchman. The title of the first show was printed in small font under a reproduction of a black and while photograph of a man lying in the grass, in the middle of a small clearing in the forest: *Criminals on Vacation.* Underneath was some information about the second show, *Other Lives,* illustrated with a photograph of a young woman sitting at a large kitchen table in the middle of a dining room, surrounded by several groups of men and women. If one looked closely one could see several 'copies' of her popping up in the middle of each one of these groups. According to the explanation underneath the photograph this second exhibition explored the parallel hypothetical lives of the artist, 'the paths not taken.'

An unfamiliar woman sat at Benjamin's desk at the Flying Dutchman. Jack was relieved he didn't have to make small talk with the hipster, whose level of self-possession and poise had infuriated him from

the very beginning. He circled around the gallery, looking at the photographs without reading the captions and short explanations printed
on small pieces of paper and glued to the wall. All photographs were
black and white, dated between 1920s and 1950s, and all featured a
single individual or a group of people against some kind of natural
background. The ambiguous composition of the group photographs
made it difficult to tell who the focus of interest was supposed to be.
Even if one of the people in the group stood apart from the rest it was
not immediately clear that he (or she) was what the viewer was supposed to focus on. There was nothing memorable about the people
or their surroundings: one would find photographs like these in any
family album. They were not a record of some important event, a mile-
stone in personal or family history but simply random photographs
taken on the fly, without much concern for composition. The men and
women in the photographs were engaged in various leisure activities—
picnicking, fishing, singing, playing tennis, cooking outside or sleeping in the grass.

In one photograph a charming young man, naked from the waist
up, his body bronze from the sun, had jumped up in the air to catch a
tennis ball. He was smiling, a disarming boyish smile. The other people
in the picture, a group of young men and women, were laughing and
pointing at him. The caption read: "Samuel T. Clemson, age 19, vacationing in Switzerland with his sister, August 1922. Convicted of a first-
degree murder for stabbing to death Dorothy Keller, age 57. Executed
on December 13, 1922." Jack examined the young man's face again, the
high cheekbones, the little blonde hairs sticking out of his chin like the
first fuzz on a young goose, the sensuous lips, the Adam's apple sunken
to the bottom of his throat, the bright eyes. Samuel's hands were reaching up to grab the tennis ball. His whole body was moving toward it
with a single-mindedness that was surprisingly lacking from the young
man's face, which was relaxed rather than focused. His eyes were half-

closed. Jack thought that most people, when they are happy, close their eyes completely, or at least half way, as if sight is an obstacle to the full enjoyment of a moment of pure pleasure like this one. Samuel was enjoying the summer breeze, the sun, the fresh mountain air, the three young girls giggling at his efforts, his own young body sprung in the air, light, taut, beautiful, immortal.

Until December 13, that is. Jack moved closer to the photograph. He searched the young murderer's eyes, looking for a glimpse of a malicious streak, a calculating mind. Did he already know Dorothy Keller when he jumped up in the air to catch the tennis ball? Did he already know, at this moment, mid-air, that he would murder her? Had he already planned the whole thing? Perhaps he had the idea right then, in that moment? Perhaps he had been wondering about it for a long time, trying to figure out what to do with her, short of murdering her, for days, weeks, or even years, and in that very moment he decided, with absolute certainty, that there was no way around it, that he had to kill her. Or perhaps he had already made the decision but had been struggling to come up with the best strategy, going through various options, discarding them one by one, worried that he is spending too much time on details, that he is overthinking it. Then, suddenly, in the moment he reached out for the tennis ball he pictured clearly how he would do it. Then again, perhaps he had already done it. Jack squeezed his eyes and looked even closer at Samuel's eyes. He was so close to the photograph now that Samuel's eyes disintegrated into dozens of miniscule black dots. Was there a glimmer of regret, sadness, self-hatred, boredom, or had he already forgotten about his deed?

Another photograph was a long shot of a secluded, rocky beach overgrown with moss, enormous trees swaying in the wind. A woman in her late thirties or early forties stood at one end of the beach, arms wide open, her wet, transparent blouse flapping in the wind, her hair loosened up, falling over her bare shoulders. Three figures—a man and two little boys—ran toward the woman's open arms from the opposite end of the beach and of the photograph. The boys were flailing their arms around, the man was laughing too, but it was the woman's face that captured Jack's attention. She was ecstatic. The caption read: "Geraldine Carther, 39, vacationing in an unknown resort on the Mediterranean. July 9, 1948. Convicted of three first-degree murders: her husband, Jonathan Carther, 43, and her two sons, Edward and Donald Carther, 9 and 10. Murder weapon: poison. Executed on January 5, 1949, after two botched attempts." It was not clear whether the 'two botched attempts' referred to the three murders or to her execution.

The gallery sitter asked Jack not to get so close to the photographs. He stepped away from the wall. Samuel, the murderous tennis player, remained suspended in mid-air—eyes half-closed, lips partly open, unaware of his impending execution.

11.

ONE MORNING JACK LOOKED OUT the kitchen window and saw the mailman. Jack opened the front door and walked casually to the mailbox. The mailman searched his mailbag and finally produced a postcard without an envelope. He was about to slip it in the mailbox when he noticed Jack.

"Here you go," he said, glancing at the postcard before handing it over to Jack. "Everyone's on vacation except us. Not fair, is it?"

Jack pretended to smile. The mailman walked away, offended by Jack's under-appreciation of the literalness of postal humor. The postcard, which turned out to be a hyper-real color photograph, featured a gorgeous view of what looked like the Mediterranean sea. It was taken from a spacious terracotta terrace. A man, half-dressed, sat in the shade of a palm tree sipping a cocktail, his face hidden under a wide-brimmed summer hat. Jack turned over the postcard and immediately recognized the handwriting: "John Doe vacationing in a Mediterranean resort. Guilty of a first degree murder, not convicted yet, anxiously awaiting to be apprehended, hoping not to be disappointed."

A sudden gust of wind rushed through the window. Jack looked down: he was slicing an orange. Outside a few kids from the neighborhood were playing pick-up soccer. The mailman was nowhere to be seen. Jack looked around. John Doe's postcard was propped up against a pile of mini DV tapes on one of the bookshelves. He had no recollection either of putting it there or of coming back into the house after the short exchange with the mailman. He picked up one of the tapes: it was labeled "March 24." When did he bring the old rushes of his London life to Charles's house? He put the tape inside the mini DV tape player—which he was equally surprised to find on the kitchen table—and fell back on the couch.

When he woke up the sun was setting. The tape had come to an end. The only sound in the house was that of auto-rewinding. Without getting up he dragged his laptop on top of his belly, pulled himself up a little and began typing:

> *Re-watching the tapes from six months ago. I would not have remembered them if it were not for the difficulties I've been having, the last several days—or is it weeks? It started with little things: forgetting that I had already done something and trying to do it again, forgetting that I hadn't done something that I should have done, forgetting to check the mailbox or checking it several times over an hour. One day I left the house to go back to my hotel room, and it was only when I went down to the hotel bar later that evening that I realized I had forgotten to change back into my clothes. When I told the bartender to put the drinks on my tab he looked at me strangely and said I had not started a tab yet. Thought he was joking. Said to him, "Jack Sturrett, room 16." He stared at me like I was talking gibberish. At that moment I caught a glance of Charles's reflection in the mirror behind him. Apologized and went back straight into my room to take off the wig and moustache. When I returned to the bar later the bartender poured me a drink and told me 'confidentially' that a man had been looking for me and had tried to pass himself off as me. I acted shocked, then indignant, finally made a joke out of it: who in their right mind would want to be me?! Several days later I was taking a break from mowing the lawn, smoking in the front yard of Charles's house, when Mrs. Hulley walked past. When she saw me she looked around, as if expecting to see someone else, saw no one, left. A few minutes later she returned with several*

concerned neighbors. They wanted to know where Charles was. I asked them if they were joking. They weren't, they told me. I laughed awkwardly and scratched my head. My hair was thick and wavy. Stunned, I turned around and looked for my reflection in the window: I had forgotten to change into Charles's clothes and put on the wig! I told Charles's neighbors he had hired me to mow the lawn and if any of them needed their lawns mowed I would be happy to do it and would even give them a discount.

This was cutting it close. I cannot slip like this anymore. Don't trust myself. Went to see a doctor about it. A psychiatrist. He tried to reassure me. Said it's normal not to be able to recollect every second of every action. Said most of our movements are automated – the fact that I have no memory of every individual second of every automated movement doesn't mean I am unaware of it. Said the normal way to recollect something is to recollect it in its entirety. The opposite of that—breaking down the event into individual sections and each section into moments or seconds would be sheer madness. I was not convinced. Told him if I add up all the seconds of all automated movements of which I remain unconscious my daily amount of temps perdu would probably be over an hour or something crazy like that. He advised me not to apply Proustian logic to everyday life. It makes for a beautiful metaphor but causes psychological disturbance, he said. I disagreed.

I resolved to monitor myself more closely.

I began taping myself put on and take off my disguise and keeping track of any unwanted fluctuations in the amount of time Jack takes to become Charles and Charles takes to become Jack. If I noticed that one was slacking off and taking longer to become the other I took the necessary measures to balance things out. This self-monitoring eventually paid off. The tape records showed clearly that Charles spent considerably less time becoming

Jack than the other way around. Granted, the transformation Jack-Charles involved a more complicated procedure than the transformation Charles-Jack—I had to put on the wig, the moustache and the slight stomach pouch I had ordered online from a movie make-up company. Still, the difference in the amount of time devoted to each transformation—one hour versus twelve minutes, respectively—was too big to ignore. The more I watched the taped make-up sessions the more convinced I became that Charles simply didn't care about the authenticity or veracity of his performance. Sometimes he was so careless that he remembered to remove only half of Charles's make-up—he would remove the moustache but keep the wig, or vice versa—and he would walk back into the hotel looking ludicrous, his face a composite of two faces: Charles's nose, Jack's mouth, Charles's eyebrows, Jack's thick hair, Charles's glasses etc. His face would resemble an abstract work of art challenging basic rules of composition and aesthetic unity, making absolutely no sense. However, as little as he resembled himself Jack would always manage to sneak back into the hotel thanks to the hotel's transient nature: hundreds of people walked in and out any given day and no one really made a concerted effort to check their internal consistency. However, after the lawn-mowing incident I was constantly on the alert, making sure Charles looked like himself at all times lest he attracted the attention, and suspicion, of some of his more incredulous neighbors, who seemed to notice the tiniest incongruity in his appearance from day to day.

After a period of adjustment I believed I had finally found the right balance between becoming Charles and becoming Jack, though I was still concerned about the possible side effects of this constant identity-switching. I continued to monitor myself and tape my two parallel lives as Jack, a hotel guest, currently unemployed and keeping mostly to himself, and Charles, a well-adjusted middle-class bachelor with sound views on culture, climate and social mores. The more I examined my self-records the more difficult it was to shake off the impression that Jack had gotten the worse part of the deal. I could see the changing in and out of Charles was beginning to take its toll on him: for instance, he began keeping a diary in which he wrote extensively about his (paranoid?) doubts that he might be suffering from depersonalization or some form of dissociative disorder.

Gradually things got worse. I noticed that Jack, paranoid that he might be schizophrenic, began spying on himself, trying to account for every moment his primary self could not recall. Eventually he resolved that the best way to prevent any potential personality split or multiplication of personalities was to invent his own double himself, prophylactically so to speak. He reasoned that if double and multiple personality are the result of the failure of the primary personality to satisfy conflicting desires and needs and negotiate between multiple incongruous different self-images, then the only way to prevent the disintegration of personality he felt was looming over him was to consciously create a separate personality corresponding to the desires and needs not met by the primary self, in short to double himself before his unconscious did it for him (or rather to him).

According to the entries in his diary that I had a chance to read, when he was occupied with something else, he did manage to create his prophylactic double; unfortunately, that did not assuage his doubts and suspicions. As he explained in his diary, he was now afraid that the double he had created himself would also be afraid of a possible doubling or multiplication of personality. The problem was that Jack had created his double to be as psychologically believable as possible: he had not merely duplicated his physical appearance but his whole psychological make up, including his own skepticism about the internal coherence of his identity. Thus, his double suffered from the same fears, doubts and suspicions of unaccountable time—temps perdu—that Jack suffered from. Jack realized that creating new doubles was not a viable solution to the problem since the more doubles he created in an attempt to account for lost time, the more the amount of lost time increased as it was now spread among multiple versions of himself and difficult to synchronize, let alone monitor.

On Thursday afternoon Jack left Charles's house, in full Charles get-up, and got on the bus. He got off the bus at the usual stop but instead of going back to the hotel he decided to go for a walk. He was running out of make-up supplies, and Charles's wig needed to be replaced. The Don't Be Yourself: It's Boring! Makeup store had opened recently downtown, right next to the Post Office. Jack stopped in front of the Post Office to check his reflection in the mirror. His hat was askew and he tried to readjust it. The trick, he knew, was to push it slightly to the right to compensate for the slight asymmetry of his skull. He pushed it once but in his reflection in the Post Office glass door the hat slid in the same direction instead of in the opposite direction as it should have (given that things were supposed to be reversed in the mirror). He took off the hat and smoothed down the few remaining hairs crisscrossing the surface of his balding head, or rather the wig imitating a balding head. He put on his hat again and pushed it once again to the right. Once again the hat in the mirror slid in the wrong direction. Frustrated, he took down his hat, squeezed it under his arm and was about to walk away when the revolving glass door of the Post Office opened. A man came out of the building, turned right and walked down the stairs without noticing Jack. It was Charles. No, it could not have been

Charles because Charles was right here, standing in front of the glass door, trying to remain calm. But if it was not Charles, it had to be someone who looked like him, someone wearing the same wig, the same hat slightly pushed to the right, exactly as Charles's reflection in the mirror, which Jack now realized had been the man whom he had seen exiting the building. Jack readjusted Charles's hat as best as he could and followed the Charles look-alike, who had already made it to the bottom of the stairs.

They passed through a lively shopping arcade but Jack didn't hear anything. It seemed to him that he had gone deaf or that someone was holding a big seashell close to his ear—the only sound that reached him was the thundering, dull sound of waves crushing against the shore. The inside of his ear was wet and he felt something trickle down his neck. Was he bleeding? He touched his neck: sweat. His neck was sweating. Charles's neck. Charles's neck, he heard a voice say. Keep calm, he ordered himself. You are Charles. You pretend to be him. You are dressed like him. It's that simple. That man who looks like Charles is a mirage. The real Charles, the pretend-Charles, is standing here right now. There is no other Charles. He was just tired, that's all. Exhausted. He raised his hand and spread out his fingers. One, two, three, four, five, six days. He had remained Charles for too long without a break, touching up his makeup every day. He had never done that before. He should go back to the hotel and change, right now, instead of chasing imaginary doubles.

To reestablish the balance between Jack and Charles, Jack spent four days in the hotel, sleeping, reading, and dining alone in the hotel restaurant. On the fifth day he put on Charles's clothes, wig and moustache and took the bus to Paladino street. Everything looked exactly as he had left it five days ago. Of course, he thought. Did he expect the house would vanish? He put the key in the lock.

"Good morning."

Jack pulled the key out of the lock and turned around. He was standing in front of the house on Paladino street. He looked down. There was a suitcase in his right hand. Mrs. Hulley was leaning over the fence, trying to peep inside the hallway behind him.

"Are you going on a trip?"

He said he was actually coming back from a five-day business trip. Mrs. Hulley puckered his lips up.

"It was a simple question. I wasn't trying to pry into your personal life."

"I never implied anything of the sort," he said.

Well, if that was the case, she said, she wanted to know why he felt the need to lie to her that he was coming back from a five-day business trip when he had talked to her just the day before. Jack smiled, pretending to remember—yes, of course, they had talked about…His voice trailed off. Somewhat softened by his apologetic voice she told him she was concerned about him. She had always found him a bit odd but the other day, when she witnessed how surprised he was to see his own name on the mailbox, she sensed for the first time that this was not just an eccentricity but something "worth looking into." And when, in response to his question who had been collecting his mail she had told him that of course he himself had been collecting his mail, he had fainted—then she knew something was wrong.

Jack managed to get rid of her somehow—but not before multiple apologies and attestations to her genial personality without which this neighborhood would not be the same—and locked himself in the house. He rolled down the blinds, removed his makeup, removed his wristwatch and looked at it. Whatever happens now Jack must not lose track of time. He must account for every second.

He sat at the kitchen table and turned on his laptop:

Just learned I came by yesterday. Don't recall anything. Seems he has finally won. He was here yesterday, without me. No one asked about me. Feel pleased he was believable but resentful that he didn't give credit where credit was due. This sort of thing does not happen every day. Must write about it. The style should be experimental so as to reflect the extraordinary subject matter. Or maybe the other way around: the style should be plain, even boring. Short declarative sentences and very few adjectives and adverbs – this would contrast nicely with the unprecedented nature of the story. 'Unprecedented'. Adjective. Strike that. Why are adjectives and adverbs considered signs of 'style' while no one gives a damn about nouns?

The pendulum of the big antique clock in the corner swayed gracefully from left to right, right to left. How did a voice in Jack's head materialize as a man wearing a nice jacket, a wig and a fake moustache? How did a wig, a fake moustache, a pair of pants and a nice jacket become a real voice in Jack's head? Rewind. He had found the antique clock already in the house when he moved in. He moved in after he was fired from the UM office. He was fired from the UM office for failing to process UM in a timely manner. He had failed to process UM in a timely manner because he had gotten side tracked by W.B.'s mail. He had chosen the house on Paladino street in order to be able to continue receiving W.B.'s mail. Good, that's good! Must keep track of everything that happened up to this moment.

Naturally there would be some slippages here and there. The gallery catalogue from the *Criminals on Vacation* exhibit for example. He did not recall taking it home from the gallery yet there it was on the kitchen table in front of him. Jack took off Charles's glasses and stared at Samuel T. Clemson's photograph, which now appeared unfocused, a murky composition of lines and shadows. He put on Charles's glasses again and the photograph came into focus. What is the 'punctum' in a photograph of a murderer? How is the experience of punctum different from the experience of shock or surprise? Is it true that the essence of photography can be interrogated and arrived at only in relation to love and death? Do all photographs—even those that do not anticipate or presuppose a murder—have a punctum? Can one get at the punctum by blowing up the photograph? Is it something invisible, concealed or, on the contrary, something obvious, on display, easily ignored and, because of that, most likely to prick you? Is Sontag right that the passivity of the photograph constitutes its aggression, that taking a picture of something does not ascribe or reveal its historical or moral value but merely affirms its quiddity?

Jack closed the *Criminals on Vacation* catalogue. He knew he was merely biding his time, waiting for Charles to make an appearance. Perhaps he had already done so. Perhaps it was Charles who was having these thoughts.

Why would anyone consider the doubling of personality a form of mental pathology? As soon as we acknowledge the extraordinary sense of relief and calm it brings with it—not having to take a stand, to commit, always wavering—it becomes clear that it's actually a privilege to be split in that manner. Life is hard enough as it is: it certainly gets easier when one takes turns living it. So what if one is not always on the same page? The less one knows about the other one the better. It's not recommended to get too chummy with him. Keep your distance. Distance makes the heart grow fonder. It's the best method for reintegrating a split personality.

That, along with a cleansing of personality to be prescribed on a case-to-case basis. Results may vary depending on the strength of the primary personality. Now, personality *cleansing* should not be confused with the *distilling* of personality, which is a more invasive procedure. For a distillation of personality to be carried out successfully the presence of at least two personalities is required, one of which will be distilled into the other. The choice of the personality to be distilled is a difficult one and will often demand a serious tête-à-tête between the two parties involved as they evaluate the pros and cons of distilling either one of them. If one of the personalities, usually the weaker one, agrees to sacrifice herself in the name of the greater good the distillation process can begin right away and the prognosis is usually very good. However, in most cases the two parties fail to reach an agreement, at which point a third party has to be brought in as an arbitrator. The third party could be external to the personality—in the interest of objectivity—but it's also true that an outside party would lack the intimate inside knowledge of the situation that a party from within the personality would be privy to. Ultimately, it is recommended that the person undergoing the distillation develop a third personality—a token one, there is no need to flesh it out completely—that possesses characteristics of *both* personalities and is thus better positioned to evaluate what is in the person's best interest.

One disadvantage of the third personality strategy used in personality distillation is that because of its *internal* whereabouts it is liable to become contaminated by the other two personalities and, in the worst-case scenario, it might lose its privileged arbiter status, turning itself into a possible target for distillation. In those rare cases the prognosis becomes exponentially worse as a fourth, fifth, sixth, or seventh personality needs to be developed from scratch to serve as a potential arbiter in the distillation process. Unfortunately, more often than not these extra personalities are created in such a slapdash fashion that none of them are equipped to carry out the distillation procedure with the sort of determination and quasi-scientific rigor required in psyche treatments. Sometimes one of the newborn, least developed personalities is so prematurely conceived and born, lacking in experience but cunning, bratty and malicious, a real upstart, that it distills older, more fully developed personalities into itself—a process known as reverse distillation—producing a most unpleasant psychic odor in the process. As a general rule a cleansing of personality is always the method of choice, although in some cases personality cleansing is recommended as a preliminary step to the distillation of personality, precisely because it is less invasive and almost free of undesirable side effects.

What is cleansing and how does it differ from a distillation of personality? Some amateurs maintain that there is no significant distinction between the two, pointing to the semantic proximity in their official names. To 'cleanse' and to 'distill' both mean, they argue, to produce something purer than what you started out with. What they fail to acknowledge, however, is that 'distillation' results in the extermination of larger psychic units—entire alternate personalities to be precise, as in the case of three personalities being distilled into one—whereas 'cleansing' takes place within a single personality (and within each individual alternate personality in cases of multiple personality). Cleansing is usually done for prophylactic reasons e.g., to prevent the sedimentation of one's cognitive apparatus; ideally, it should be done every three months, along with one's haircut or pedicure appointment. Unlike distillation, which requires a fairly elaborate set of instruments and is best done at a designated distillation facility, cleansing can be done at home or even in the street i.e., there is an element of improvisation in cleansing that one doesn't get with distillation.

There is another, more radical method of personality cleansing, which Jack decided to try out right now. He closed all the windows, pulled down the blinds and the curtains, switched off all lights, cleared some room in the corner and sat down, eyes closed, hands on knees, feet tucked under. The first thing to say about this radical form of cleansing is that it is not just another form of meditation. In meditation the purpose is to slow down one's thoughts and examine each one of them

carefully before discarding them one by one. Meditation demands focus, patience and perseverance, three qualities Jack lacked. The form
of cleansing better suited to people of his temperament—restless, anxious, neurotic—works precisely by exaggerating these qualities. The
goal is not to slow down one's mental processes but, on the contrary, to
accelerate them—to think more, think chaotically, think faster, without however allowing oneself to slip into meta- or self-observational
mode. This type of radical cleansing involves over-saturating oneself
with impressions, perceptions, and memories, leaving no gaps, no
breathers in between.

Cleansing in the sense of 'emptying one's mind' is the vulgar, ple-
beian version of the radical cleansing described above. Emptying one's
mind is not that difficult. Most people on the subway have mastered
the perpetual blank state, one wash away from the last centrifugal toss
and turn, just before they empty the entire contents of their mind, all
tangled up, and hang it out to dry. But very few of them are capable of
the more radical form of cleansing-as-self-saturation: they lack either
the requisite cerebral thickness or the agility and speed of neural connections necessary to fire up the cerebral flow and keep it going for a
long time.

12.

THE WINDOW WAS OPEN and the shutter was banging against the wall. Dusk had fallen. Ennui had befallen Jack. It was a free-floating, unmotivated ennui—the worst kind. He had learned to recognize its onset and departure, learned also to go through its successive stages faster but with the same amount of indifference. In the time it took him to open the window and secure the shutter he was able to leapfrog through all stages of ennui—from dissatisfaction and disappointment with the world to a total disinterest in his own dissatisfaction and disappointment with the world.

Two figures stood on the other side of the street, with their backs to Jack. He recognized Mrs. Hulley. The face of the man she was talking to was obscured by the shadow but the rest of his body was visible. He wore grey corduroy jeans, a Scandinavian sweater and a brownish jacket. There was something familiar about him. When he turned around and walked away it was clear why he looked familiar. It was Charles.

It could not be Charles, of course. He resembled Charles. Charles was here, emerging slowly but surely from a shallow but long stream of consciousness, like some pre-historical amoeba testing out the atmosphere with its primitive senses to see if life would suck just a little bit but not completely, because the amoeba was exhausted from searching for minimal to average living conditions. Consciousness streams that one would consider livable—without hoping for any special perks—were not, contrary to popular onion, readily available. Indeed, they were hard to find these days and, predictably, their market value had risen. The average stream of consciousness used to be guaranteed a duration of at least 75 years, with periods of high and low tide, which expanded or narrowed down the stream's average width. The contemporary average consciousness stream was a sorry sight by comparison: it remained dry for the better part of its duration, usually because of poor mental irrigation, and when it was finally irrigated it would flood the surrounding rational fields, submerging them for years under a foul, mushy layer of undisciplined observations, inherited beliefs, and lukewarm metaphors.

The amoeba crawled out on the shore just when Mrs. Hulley walked past Jack's house.

"Goodbye," Jack said, his head still wrapped up in the gooey placenta of his consciousness stream.

"You mean 'Good evening,'" Mrs. Hulley corrected him.

"It was very nice talking to you, Mrs. Hulley."

She responded maliciously that the only conversation the two of them had ever had was the one about rental prices when he first moved in, months ago.

"You have a strange sense of humor, Mrs. Hulley," Jack laughed awkwardly. He did not recognize his own voice. She told him that she was not known for having a sense of humor and repeated that she had not seen him for at least a week. True, she had just talked to a fellow who looked very much like Charles and the first time she saw him (the fellow had been coming around quite often lately) she actually did mistake him for Charles—the resemblance was uncanny—but of course now she knew the fellow was not Charles. No, no, Jack interrupted her. She had not made a mistake: that other fellow was him. He hoped Mrs. Hulley would appreciate how difficult it was for Charles to share with her something very personal and confidential. He made a dramatic pause and then told her he suffered from a dissociative disorder, which he had kept a secret until now on account of the stigma still attached to disorders of that kind. Mrs. Hulley listened to his 'confession' with great interest. Then she declared authoritatively that although she was not a psychologist in her opinion he did indeed seem to suffer from some kind of personality disorder but not from the one he thought. Dissociative disorder was one thing, she said with conviction; claiming that one's alternate personality—the fellow she had just talked to—was a real person of flesh and blood, or that a real person—that fellow again—was merely a mental projection, was a far more troubling matter.

After Mrs. Hulley had expressed her opinion on Jack's mental state he went back into Charles's house and sat in front of his laptop. He pressed 'return' and didn't lift his finger from the button until he had scrolled down several blank pages—he didn't want his continued self-monitoring to be skewed by previous records.

Following the brief encounter with Mrs. Hulley several possibilities presented themselves. Will jot them down here in clear, declarative sentences and in the third person. Amazed at the clarity and rigor that speaking and writing in the third person always brings with it. One seems to write with greater conviction and fewer self-doubts. The third person is particularly adept at identifying the first person's incommensurable attitudes, self-contradictory statements and beliefs and thus acts as a natural corrective of the first person's inherently skeptical attitude. The first person is often blindsided by his own privileged view and is therefore rather untrustworthy.

Daily observations, by the third person, suggest that the first person likes to lounge about until noon, rolling around in bed, staring at the ceiling, absent-mindedly considering a new paint job, listening to the water dripping from the shower, and in general not doing much. The first person likes crisp bacon, black coffee, squeaky wood floors, musky eau de cologne, old stamps, random lists, bare feet, and a lot of attention. The first person tends to be secretive and is often not privy even to his own secrets. The first person often feels lonely and alienated and depends exclusively on the third person to save it from the doldrums.

Naturally the two have very different ways of going about things, a result of their different attunement to the world; what is less well known, and not sufficiently discussed, is their very different way of sitting at the table. The first person has a distinct preference for lifting his feet up on the table and supporting his head with one arm, which is carefully folded under the chin. By contrast, the third person generally crosses his legs under the table and props his head with both hands, looking down at the unpredictable patterns of lines in the wooden surface of the table. Sometimes the two debate which way of sitting at the table is more advantageous, although they are both aware of the irrelevance of such arguments given their very different sets of priorities. During these debates the first person often gets all fired up and has a tendency to blurt out things without thinking them over first, especially when it has had one too many whiskey shots. In times like these, when having a normal conversation with the first person becomes nearly impossible, the third person calls up the second person and the two of them keep each other company as they wait for the first person to sober up. Then the first person's predisposition toward paranoia is exacerbated—it seems to him that the third person and the second person are conspiring against him. In particular, the first person suspects the third person is constantly observing him, keeping a record of his potential slippages and failures to respond to judgment calls.

But the first person has resolved to put an end to this silly contest of one-upmanship. The third person's failure to appreciate the first person's ability to emancipate himself from his inherent narcissism, to expand beyond his blindsided self-

centeredness, works in the first person's favor. The first person is perfectly capable of playing the role of another and of being aware of himself as playing a role. Unfortunately the first person finds it challenging to write about himself without the third person's constant interference. Even now, the third person is adamant about being the ultimate authority on Jack's precarious position in the wake of his encounter with Mrs. Hulley. The third person insists on reconstructing Jack's narrative trajectory without any input from the first, let alone the second person. There he goes:

> Jack is fired from the UM office. He devises a plan that will allow him to continue reading W.B.'s letters: Jack (hereafter Jack 1) invents Jack 2, who moves into the address where W.B. has been sending his letters. Jack 2 wears an elaborate disguise to distinguish himself from Jack 1. For a while the plan seems to work. Jack 2 moves into the building—under the name of 'Charles'—and insinuates himself in the community, gaining his neighbors' trust and gradually transforming himself into a respectable addressee. He is now in a position to receive W.B.'s letters i.e., to intercept them before they bounce back to the UM Office. In this way Jack 2's presence at Paladino street shifts the status of W.B.'s letters from 'undeliverable' to 'delivered'. The UM office no longer receives any letters from W.B., which means the Office no longer returns W.B.'s letters to him, stamped 'Return to Sender'. Now that W.B. is no longer receiving his own letters back he must deduce that his letters are actually being delivered, ipso facto, that there is an addressee to receive them, though it might not be—in fact, cannot be—the addressee W.B. intended.

At first one might think there are multiple possibilities to account for this state of affairs: e.g. the addressee might have returned to the vacant address and resumed receiving W.B.'s letters, or the addressee to whom W.B. was addressing his letters is not the same as the addressee who eventually returned to the address. However, the fact that W.B. kept on sending his letters to the same address even after having his letters returned to him numerous times suggests that having his letters delivered was not W.B.'s priority and perhaps not his intention at all! What kind of person continues sending letters after they have been returned to him multiple times? Is W.B. in denial of the addressee's fate (death)? Or does W.B. intentionally write letters to an addressee he very well knows cannot receive them?

Perhaps the question is not how much W.B. knows about the addressee—whether he knows the addressee exists or not—but whether W.B. himself is aware that he is sending the letters. Perhaps W.B. has a double, W.B. 2, similar to Jack's Jack 2 a.k.a. Charles, with the difference that Jack is aware of Jack 2's existence because he invented him, whereas W.B. might not be aware of W.B. 2's existence because W.B. 2, in contrast to Jack 2, is a real alter. But if W.B. 2 is real he must be living in the house on Paladino street and is thus able to receive the letters sent by W.B. But wouldn't that mean that W.B. 2 knowingly forwards the letters to the UM office?

What is at issue here is the distribution of knowledge, a rather messy and questionable one. Let's go through all possible options, but first a word about methodology. Glossing over Peirce, in the chapter from

The Limits of Interpretation devoted to Borges and entitled "Abduction in Uqbar" Umberto Eco distinguishes between three ways of reasoning: deductive, inductive, and abductive. In deduction, one posits a general rule and then demonstrates how the case he is trying to solve is an instance of that rule. In induction, one begins with a representative sample of cases and on that basis draws a conclusion about what the rule governing them ought to be. In abduction, one reasons by analogy: one begins by assuming a completely different rule from the one he would normally assume if he were following the deductive approach, then one tests the hypothesis that the case he is trying to solve is actually an instance of that rule and, finally, if the hypothesis is confirmed, one accepts the rule. The method of reasoning employed here is, obviously, of the abductive kind.

W.B. knows he is writing a letter. He believes he is writing to X, a real person with a real address, when in fact X is the name of W.B.'s alternate personality, W.B. 2, of whom W.B. is not aware of course. W.B. 2 receives the letter—since his real name is X—but because in cases of double or multiple personality disorder the second personality is aware of the primary self, W.B. 2 is aware of who wrote the letter, namely W.B. 1. Initially, W.B. 2 simply forwards W.B. 1's letters to the UM office, just to fuck with W.B. 1's brain, to amuse himself by confusing W.B. 1 and forcing him to wonder why his letters are not being delivered. But when W.B. 1 continues to write and send those letters, despite the fact that they are all being returned to him, W.B. 2 begins to wonder whether W.B. 1 is really unaware of W.B. 2's existence. W.B. 2 grows paranoid. Perhaps, he reasons, W.B. 1 actually knows that W.B. 2 exists. Perhaps the primary self is as knowledgeable about the alternate self as the latter is about the former.

Ok, let's assume that W.B. 1 is aware of W.B. 2's existence. One possibility then is that W.B.1 intentionally sends the letters to his own double, possibly as a way of reintegrating W.B.'s personality: after all, if the primary self is communicating with the alternate self that implies that they are both aware of each other, because in order for any form of communication to take place, including the epistolary kind, one party in the exchange must be capable of acting as a sender and the other party must be capable of acting as an addressee. But if W.B.1 is intentionally writing to W.B. 2, the reintegration of W.B.'s personality is no longer a goal: it must have been already achieved before W.B. 1 wrote the first letter to W.B. 2, which is predicated on their mutual acknowledgement as parties in an exchange.

Let's try to imagine what form this kind of communication might take in concrete detail. W.B.1 and W.B. 2 are the same person i.e. they occupy the same physical body. When W.B.1 is writing a letter to W.B. 2 he is sitting at a desk in his home, wherever that is—this is still unknown—and when the letter is delivered, it is delivered in a red mailbox outside the house on Paladino street where W.B. 2 lives. But of course W.B.1 and W.B. 2 occupy the same body. So a few days after W.B.1 slips the letter in the red mailbox in front of his apartment building—wherever that is—he gets on the bus and travels to Paladino street, walks over to the red mailbox in front of the house and opens it. The letter is inside. W.B. 2 picks up the letter he has written to himself and walks back into his house. At that moment W.B. 2 is at an advantage because he knows that the letter is from W.B. 1, i.e. from himself, whereas W.B. 1 knows that he has sent the letter to someone real but doesn't know that this someone is himself. To recapitulate, W.B. 1 doesn't know that he is writing to himself, whereas W.B. 2 does know that he is receiving a letter written by himself.

There is another possibility, however. Perhaps W.B.1 and W.B. 2 do not live in separate places i.e. W.B. 2 does not reside in the house on Paladino street. So when W.B. 1 is sitting at his desk, in his apartment—wherever that might be—he is already writing as W.B. 2 i.e., W.B. 2 has already supplanted W.B. 1. But then the question arises: whom is W.B. 2 writing to? Is he writing to another person altogether (a person other than W.B.) or to W.B. 3 (another 'part' of W.B. who lives in the house on Paladino street)? This latter option leads to infinite regress, because there is no reason to assume that the person writing the letter is W.B. 2 (who has taken over W.B. 1): it is equally possible that W.B. 3 is writing the letter, having already taken over W.B. 2 and W.B. 1, and it is equally possible that the person writing the letter is W.B. 4, having successfully supplanted W.B. 1, W.B. 2, and W.B. 3.

Perhaps Mrs. Hulley's hypothesis is closer to the truth after all: the addressee of W.B. 1's letters, she argued, the one residing in the house on Paladino street, is not a single man but in fact two men, both of whom keep denying the other's existence, although for different reasons. Jack 1 invents a double, Jack 2, and inscribes Jack 2 as the addressee of W.B. 1's letters by moving in under the name 'Charles' (a.k.a. Jack 2) in the house on Paladino street. Jack 2 looks physically different from Jack 1 thanks to a carefully designed disguise. Now, if we go back to the above mentioned hypotheses on W.B. 1 and W.B. 2 and choose the version in which W.B. 2 is living in the house on Paladino street, where he receives the letters W.B.1 writes to him(self), and if we take into consideration Jack 2's confusion at being taken, by his neighbors on Paladino street, for someone else, we would have to conclude that there must be a very strong physical resemblance between Jack 2, the invented, disguised version of Jack 1, and W.B. 2, who is *not* wearing a disguise: he appears, on the surface, indistinguishable from W.B. 1.

On one hand, this hypothesis has the advantage of revealing something that Jack 1 has been struggling to discover for a long time, namely what W.B. looks like: W.B. looks like Jack's invented double. On the other hand, however, the psychological confusion this discovery causes cannot be underestimated. Remember that Jack pretends that he has an alternate self, Jack 2, whereas W.B. is not pretending: he is really split between W.B. 1 and W.B. 2. What happens when, first, W.B. 2 (the alter who checks the mailbox on Paladino street and perhaps lives there as well) sees Jack 2 and, second, when Jack 2 sees W.B. 2? When W.B. 2 seeks Jack 2, who, remember, is an exact copy of him, W.B. 2 thinks he is seeing himself i.e. his primary self W.B. 1. If W.B. was not aware that he suffers from a double personality disorder this must be the moment when he learns—or he thinks he learns—that he has a double (W.B. 1). We know, of course, that he is mistaken: W.B. sees a real person, Jack 2, not his own (imaginary) double. In short, W.B. 2 takes Jack 2, a real person, for an extension of his (W.B.'s) own personality, for his own imaginary double. On the other hand, when Jack 2 sees W.B. 2 he thinks that what he thought was just a game of pretense— disguising himself as another person, Jack 2—has turned real. In short, Jack 2 convinces himself that W.B. 2 is his own imaginary double turned real. In both cases, Jack and W.B. deny each other's reality, believing the other to be nothing more than a mental projection of their own personality, their own imaginary double.

The third person remembered, without the first person's help, the day he passed by the Post Office headquarters and stopped in front of the entrance to readjust his hat. He looked at his reflection in the glass or, rather, he looked at what he thought was his reflection until he realized the reflection was reversed and it could move on its own, independently of the third person. It was not the third person's own reflection but a real man, one who looked exactly like the third person. The third person then realized that this is what must have happened: W.B. 2, who was forwarding W.B. 1's letters to the UM office, with or without W.B. 1's instructions, or perhaps against them, must have gone to the Post Office to inquire why his letters (to himself) had been successfully delivered instead of forwarded to the UM office. The post office officials must have thought his inquiry odd and must have asked him why he was complaining that he was actually receiving his mail. They must have asked him why he didn't send his letters directly to the UM office if that was his desired addressee. It must have been in the course of that conversation with a disgruntled postal employee that W.B. learned that someone had moved into the house on Paladino street.

The above are all the possible ways—with the exception of others—in which Jack's current ontological status can be interpreted, according to the third person. Given these insurmountable facts, what is the most convincing diagnosis of Jack's mental condition and is there anything particularly original about it?

The third person believes there is. In most cases of psychopathology the patient has trouble distinguishing the real from the unreal and mistakes his mental projections for real people. Treatment usually involves helping the patient realize that his world is populated by phantoms created by his own sick mind, which gives the illusion of material existence to imaginary things. But where is the harm in suspecting real things of being mental projections? If anything, the third person thinks, it seems like a sign of circumspection.

Jack put the laptop to sleep and lied down on the bed without undressing. He wondered why people keep diaries. The diary is a literary form fundamentally different from any other genre of literature as it is written with the intention—the prohibition—not to be read. There is a difference, however, between writing something and then deciding not to share it with anyone, and writing something with the specific intention of not showing it to anyone. The moment of negation does not follow the act of writing but is constitutive of it: the diary's author writes with the intention of not being read. At first glance the diary resembles a letter returned to its sender after failing to reach its addressee. However, the letter is returned to the sender as a result of a failure (postal or human, as in the case of the dead addressee discussed above in great detail) whereas the diary does not 'fail' to be read, because 'not being read' is part of the intentional structure of the act of diary writing. The success of the diary depends on its 'failure' to be read. One keeps the diary a secret from others so as to share this secret with oneself, or rather with one's future self.

The diary is the most narcissistic literary form: it's a genre in which narcissism is not only allowed but fully legitimated. There are established genre conventions to which a diary must implicitly conform if it is to be granted the status of a diary. A list of the pieces of furniture in one's house, as personal as those objects are, or a sample grocery list does not constitute a diary. These are not 'proper' expressions of narcissism. The diary works with a narrower definition of the self: only the most private, the most salacious and usually forbidden thoughts and feelings are recorded therein. To the extent that the diary's author takes pleasure in baring his soul on the page, doing a soft porn striptease in front of an audience that includes only himself, it might be more accurate to categorize the diary as a subgenre of either pornographic or erotic literature. It is a kind of psychological exhibitionism, a piece of masochistic memoir embellished with self-lacerations, painful regrets and wishful thinking.

The diary serves many different functions but preeminent among them is that of retrospectively positing a self where there was none. When a man opens the first page of a notebook and writes down "Diary" he experiences the shock of self-inflation. Every thought or feeling he happens to have acquires a super-significance it never had before simply by virtue of the fact that now it's going to be entered secretly into a flimsy notebook. The man passionately fills the pages of the notebook with every thought that crosses his mind, intoxicated by the sheer abundance of words, verbs and adjectives he manages to come up with, an excess of language he mistakes for a sign of inner life. After several weeks of studiously doing an inventory of every thought, feel-

ing, image and observation that crosses his mind he is shocked to realize the meaninglessness, randomness and banality of these long grocery lists, which never come together to form a coherent inner world.
Frustrated, the man tears apart the diary and falls into depression.

And then something unexpected happens. The man's awareness of
his failure as an 'author' sparks up something suspiciously close to a...
'self'. The sense of failure, the disappointment and disgust he feels with
himself, he is surprised to discover, become the foundation of a real
sense of self. The sense that one has failed to be oneself, the skepticism
that one's 'self' even exists—these are the painful but necessary pre-
conditions for the emergence of a proper 'self'. Boredom too, though it
is unclear whether boredom is a precondition for the emergence of a
'self' or a side effect of already having one.

There is a cure for boredom—distraction—but there is no cure for
ennui. The vain attempt to overcome boredom by means of distraction
produces ennui. And yet ennui does not plunge one into depression.
On the contrary—the man falling endlessly into the bottomless abyss
of ennui is the ultimate man of leisure: he is at leisure to catalogue,
without a trace of interest or passion, every single detail of the world
around him. He simply cannot sustain for a very long time his supposed
indifference to it. The exhaustiveness of some accounts of indifference
is really quite astonishing. Take Georges Perec's *Un homme qui dort* (*A
Man Asleep*), for instance. The young man's proclaimed indifference
to the world, which he *tours* without ever *inhabiting* fully, brings the
world even closer to him, placing it under a magnifying glass: he revels
in every detail, from the six pairs of wet socks drying in his little attic
and the noise of every individual drop of water hitting the bottom of
the sink, to his invisible neighbor's cough, which might be deliberate,
mean-spirited, or unconscious. The 'man asleep' ends up producing an
involuntary inventory of the world, as though he can express his indifference only by sabotaging himself: his self-proclaimed, committed in-

difference toward the larger picture manifests in hypnotic attention to the picture's minor details. The more he tries to express his indifference to the world the more interested his account of indifference becomes and the more invested he is in it.

The *catalogue* is the quintessential expression of the 'man asleep', which is just another name for 'the tourist': the catalogue combines a lack of discrimination, which belies indifference, with a hyper-attentiveness to detail, which suggests interest. The tourist is generally regarded as not fully *present*: he comes from somewhere else, from a place that cannot be immediately verified through the senses but has to be read about and pointed to on a map, and his statements, opinions, beliefs, feelings and thoughts appear tentative and ungrounded because he is not inscribed in the invisible web of local customs. The tourist's gait is uncertain and meandering, his suitcase unzipped, his conversation dull. He is a man without a past, without a backstory.

But people don't walk around with their backstory neatly packed in a small backpack, from which they pull out whatever motive or reason they need to justify their past or map out their future. Jack, for instance, had always suffered from back problems. When he travelled he packed lightly and never took his backstory with him, unless he could simplify it, fold it, and fit it under the seat in front of him. After a few train rides the wrinkles in his backstory went so deep that moments belonging to different folds of time would become entangled, skewing the narrative trajectory. Every time he arrived in a new town he had to carefully unfold his backstory, iron down the wrinkles, and fold it again. It was easier to simply sew together a new backstory and tailor it to the place where he moved. He figured that as fictional as every new backstory was there would always be an element of his real self in it, for instance his opinion of what he considered a believable backstory in the first place.

13.

IF JACK HAD WOKEN UP and if he had thought about it as he sat, fully clothed, at the edge of the bed, in the house on Paladino street or in a hotel room, he would have eventually had to accept that this was as accurate a description of what he had just done as any. Had he walked over to the door and turned around he would have seen that he was no longer sitting on the bed. His absence from the bed would have spawned numerous interpretations, in contrast with his presence in the bed, which would have been so final, factual and undeniable that it would have been basically insurmountable. His presence would have asserted itself as a given, as all there was. His absence from the bed, however, would have be read as a consequence of him having left the room, but of course there were many varieties of 'leaving': he could have left to go to the kitchen to make himself coffee, or he could have left to go fetch the letter knife from the pocket of his jacket in order to dispose of it, or he could have left to answer the phone ringing in the other room only to learn, from a familiar voice on the other end of the line, that he had been summoned back to London to resume his job as a book reviewer, or he could have left to go out on the little balcony, water the plants, and jump to his death.

To say something of a man who is present is bound to be redundant: his presence speaks for itself. But nothing is ever self-evident when it comes to absence. Absence automatically transforms a place into a crime scene, setting in motion a reconstruction algorithm: What must have happened here? When must it have happened? How must it have ended? What must it have all meant?

If on that particular morning—Friday, 9:40am, grey skies, humidity factor above normal—Jack had gone to the kitchen and poured himself a cup of coffee nothing would have happened. He would have felt it with his whole being: he would have felt it reverberate through his entire body, then through the porcelain coffee cup and outward throughout the house on Paladino street in Abberc. He would have put on his jacket and gone out. With every step nothing would have continued to happen. He would have begun counting his steps. One. Nothing. Two. Nothing. Three. Nothing. Four.

Nothing.

Nothing would have continued to happen consistently all the way to the UM office. If he had gotten on the elevator he would have pressed the basement button. The door to the UM office would have been slightly ajar. He would have thought this to be a total breach of security. He would have recalled that the UM clerk was never to leave the UM office without locking it twice. If he had put his hand on the door handle he would have heard voices inside. If he had recognized one of them it would have been the Manager's. "The job requires a lot of patience and a fair amount of heavy lifting and dragging, mostly bags and boxes full of mail," the Manager would have said. "The working hours are long and tedious. There is only one window, a tiny one in the bathroom. If you were offered the job you would have to spend long hours in the basement, up on your feet, pretty much alone, except for an hour long lunch break." Another male voice would have reassured the Manager that he had worked an office job before and that this one didn't seem that different. The Manager would have then lowered his voice as if he was about to share a confidential piece of information. "It's my duty to let you know that one of our employees, in fact the one previously occupying the post you are applying for, found the lack of sunlight and fresh air taxing. I was forced to let him go since he was unable to perform his duties." "Now," the Manager would have spoken in his normal tone of voice again, "assuming you are happy with the salary as advertised, would you please sign here?"

APPENDIX A:
IN THE PARK (A PLAY BY JACK STURRETT)

Birds chirping, children playing in the distance.

A bench in the park.

JACK, in his 20s, dressed casually, is sitting on the bench.

SAMUEL, in his 60s, approaches the bench. Samuel wears brown pants and a checkered short-sleeved shirt.

Samuel sits next to Jack, who doesn't seem to notice him. Samuel looks quite enthused about life: he smiles, looks around, looks up at the sun, nods approvingly at the people passing by. There is something proprietary in his look, as though he owns the park.

Jack looks straight ahead. His face remains expressionless. He is not actively or arrogantly ignoring Samuel but simply not registering his presence. A few people pass by: Samuel smiles at them and even waves 'hello.'

Samuel leans back, crosses his legs and starts whistling, occasionally casting a sideway glance at Jack. Jack looks in the other direction (very naturally, not purposefully avoiding Samuel), looks down at his shoes, notices one of his shoelaces has come undone and ties it up again.

Beat.

Samuel slaps his knees and gets up. He stretches in a very demonstrative manner, hoping to get Jack's attention. Jack closes his eyes and tilts his head slightly toward the sunlight. Samuel begins to pace in front of the bench. Jack does not move. Samuel circles around the bench, looking at Jack. Suddenly he stops in front of the bench.

Beat.

Samuel coughs loudly. Jack does not react. Samuel sits down again. He watches Jack for a few seconds.

SAMUEL
Beautiful weather, isn't it?

Jack does not react.

SAMUEL
(excited)
On a day like this, you just want to…Oh, I don't know…

Samuel gestures with his hand, signifying nothing in particular. Jack does not react.

SAMUEL
Nice little park we've got here.

Samuel nods a few times as though agreeing with himself. Jack shakes his left hand, brings it up to his ear and listens to his watch.

SAMUEL
It's not going to last. On Thursday it will be in the 60s but then starting on Friday temperatures will start falling and there is a slight chance we'll see some rain.

Jack is winding his watch.

SAMUEL
A nice watch you've got there.

Jack puts his watch in his pocket.

SAMUEL

My cousin is coming to visit me on Friday. I hope Friday will
be sunny, like today. I missed the weather forecast.
Did you listen to the weather forecast?

Jack glances briefly at Samuel.

JACK

No.

Samuel is pleased that he has finally gotten Jack's attention.

SAMUEL

So you don't normally listen to the weather forecast?

Jack does not respond.

SAMUEL (cont.)

I said you don't normally listen to the weather forecast?

JACK

No.

SAMUEL

You just don't care that much about the weather.

Jack does not respond.

SAMUEL

It's all the same to you. You just can't be bothered with it.

Jack does not respond.

SAMUEL

I like the weather. I like it, and I like talking about it.

Jack does not respond.

SAMUEL

Well?

Jack begins to get up. Samuel pushes him back. Startled, Jack falls back on the bench.

SAMUEL

Well?

Jack does not respond.

SAMUEL

Come on! Make an effort!

Jack does not respond.

SAMUEL

The weather. Today. Yesterday. Tomorrow. Next week.
Next year. Pick a time. Like it. Hate it. Describe it. Comment
on it. A chance of rain. A slight chance of showers.
A 5% chance of precipitation in the morning.

Jack says nothing.

Samuel gets up and goes around the bench. Jack watches him without the slightest curiosity. Samuel takes something out of his pocket: a long piece of string. He begins tying Jack's right foot to the bench. He moves to the other side of the bench and ties Jack's left foot to the bench using the same piece of string. Jack does not protest. Samuel pulls out another piece of string from his pocket and stands behind Jack.

SAMUEL

Put your hands behind your back.

Samuel grabs Jack's hands and ties them behind Jack's back. Samuel walks around and stands in front of the bench. He is sweating heavily. He takes out a handkerchief and wipes his forehead. Jack pulls at the string but he is not really trying very hard. He looks distractedly in the distance.

SAMUEL

Now, let's start from the beginning. I am going to go back over there (he points at a path) and then I am going to walk up to the bench. Are you paying attention?

Samuel starts walking away but suddenly stops and turns around and walks back to the bench.

SAMUEL

What is your name?

Jack does not react.

SAMUEL

Listen here. I am concerned about you. I am sitting here, I am looking at you, and I just can't stop myself from getting worried about you. You can't go on like this. I can't imagine what it must be like for you, coming here, day after day, weekend after weekend, unsure of what you are looking for, afraid to hope and yet secretly hoping. Well, you don't need to hope any more.

Samuel smiles and taps Jack on the shoulder. He walks away. Jack remains alone. He is staring at something in the distance.

Beat.

He sneezes.

Beat.

Samuel reappears and walks toward the bench. As before, he looks enthused about life. He looks up at the sun, nods approvingly at the people passing by and smiles. He sits down next to Jack and smiles at him.

SAMUEL

Isn't it a lovely day?

Jack does not respond. Samuel pretends not to notice. His face still half-frozen in a grin, he takes out a pack of cigarettes and lights one. He looks around, content, and smokes in silence. He casually presses his cigarette into Jack's left hand. Jack is so startled that he does not scream. Samuel smiles generously.

SAMUEL

So what's it going to be?

Jack stares at Samuel.

Beat.

JACK
(tentatively)

A lovely day?

THE END

APPENDIX B:
MURDER, HE WROTE
(A SCREENPLAY BY JACK STURRETT)

INT. THE OFFICE OF FORD HARDER, PRIVATE EYE - NIGHT

It's raining. On the desk there is a half empty bottle of bourbon, a pile of folders, a phone, and an old Remington typewriter. DETECTIVE HARDER, suave, in his 40s, is drinking and looking absentmindedly at one of the folders lying open in front of him: there are pages filled with notes, as well as photographs of what appears to be a man's corpse.

HARDER (V.O.)
Another rainy night. I was trying to work on the Palson case, quit smoking, remember where I put Lorna's phone number, compose an acerbic mental note to Sergeant Folder at the LAPD, and think of a nice way to break things off with Greta. When I first moved into this office, seven years ago, I had already developed a rather elaborate idea of my future lifestyle: sheets of cold, incessant rain, the numbing gurgle of rainwater down old, rusty pipes, the slosh of cars outside, the occasional beam light on the wet wall of the insurance company building across the street. All that had stopped being an idea long ago. I can no longer tell the rain beating against the window from the blood throbbing in my temples.

The phone rings. Harder looks at it. It keeps ringing. Finally, someone picks it up in the next room.

SECRETARY (O.S.)
No, I'm sorry, Ms. Greta. He just left.

SECRETARY (O.S.) (cont.)
Yes, of course I'll tell him. First thing in the morning.

Harder throws the photograph on the desk, looks at the bottle of urbon, decides against it, stands up, closes the Palson folder, puts another cigarette in his mouth, looks for a box of matches. There is a knock on the door. MRS. DOYLE, the secretary, in her 50s, walks in.

MRS. DOYLE
There is a man waiting outside.

HARDER
There always is.

MRS. DOYLE
He says it's urgent.

HARDER
A sense of urgency: now there's something to be envied.

Harder sits back in his chair, without taking his hat off. A very tall man, in his 30s, wearing a bright yellow raincoat, a small suitcase in hand, walks in. He is KRATT.

HARDER (V.O.)
He wasn't a man of flesh and blood. He resembled a musical motif from one of those passionate but subdued violin concertos whose inconsolable murmur went well with the general meteorological despondency outside my window. He was a solemnly tragic adagio come out of the rain, with the same sort of perpetual melancholy that eventually settles into tired resignation.

Kratt doesn't seem to notice Mrs. Doyle and almost shuts the door in her face. Harder nods at the only other chair in the room. Kratt sits down. His raincoat and hat are soaking wet. He doesn't remove either of them. His hat hangs low over his eyes, leaving his face barely visible. Harder pours himself another glass of bourbon and points at the bottle.

                          HARDER
Bourbon?

                           KRATT
No, thank you.

                          HARDER
                    (points at Kratt's hat)
That thing's soaking wet. Want to take it off?

Kratt ignores him. There is already a small puddle under his chair.
The two men sit there for a while without saying a word. Harder is
drinking his bourbon and staring at Kratt, who continues to look down
at his feet.

                          HARDER
I like a man of few words. Leaves much to the imagination, I am told.
I'm not the imaginative kind, though.

                           KRATT
                       (defensively)
I'm Edward Kratt.

                          HARDER
I didn't think you weren't.

                           KRATT
I'm a writer. Detective novels.

                          HARDER
                 Anything I might've heard of?

                           KRATT
                         I doubt it.

There is a long pause during which Kratt continues staring at his shoes and Harder continues staring at Kratt. Harder leans back in his chair, lifts his feet up on the desk and lights a cigarette. Kratt takes an envelope out of his pocket and fiddles with it. He shifts in his chair as if he is unsure what he will do next. Finally, Kratt stands up, approaches the desk, puts the envelope down and goes back to his seat. Harder does not even glance at the envelope but waits patiently for an explanation. Kratt stands up and begins pacing.

KRATT

I've typed everything I'm going to tell you in case... in case I forget. I've been getting better the last several weeks but I wouldn't trust myself...yet. Of course you don't have the slightest idea what I'm talking about... That's understandable...I'll try to explain everything from the beginning...The beginning...The ending...It's all gone now...

Kratt stops. Suddenly he looks alarmed. His face is extremely tense. He is trying hard to remember something.

HARDER

You were going to tell me everything from the beginning.

KRATT

Yes... I'm a writer.

HARDER

Let me guess. Detective novels?

KRATT

Yes. My plots are serpentine, contorted... baroque if you wish.

Harder continues to smoke. Suddenly he appears very interested in his shoelaces.

KRATT

Life itself is baroque...

HARDER

I've said that many times.

Kratt doesn't seem to notice Harder any more. He continues pacing, talking very fast. His raincoat makes swishing sounds as he moves.

KRATT

I've written eleven novels. I remember every detective novel I've ever read. I remember everything. And I mean everything. Every cellar, every grave in every cemetery, the pseudonym of every pathetic small-time crook, every candleholder with golden incrustations on every white-clothed dinner table, every crystal chandelier hanging in every stuffy Victorian dining room, every leaf on every chestnut tree, every pearl earring hanging from every ear of every femme fatale, every diamond necklace missing from every countess' jewelry box, every rape, robbery, assault, every murder...

HARDER

You'd make a damn good cop.

KRATT

I used to work on ten different plots at the same time, all in my head. I could reproduce, on command, hundreds of plotlines, forward and backward. My mind was filled with things I didn't want to remember but that I couldn't forget. I began seeing Dr. Sloan. He had this idea...he wanted to try hypnosis...I know, it sounds ridiculous. And yet, it seemed to work...for a while.

HARDER

What was the first thing you forgot?

KRATT

I forget. In the beginning it was minor details: the color of a character's raincoat or the number of cops on a given street. I was feeling lighter every day, you know, like when you haven't eaten in a long time and you feel as if you're not walking but gliding above ground. I began a new novel right around the time I started seeing Dr. Sloan. I had the whole story in my head. It was ingenious, I mean I vaguely remember thinking that. I started writing. *Then* it happened.

HARDER

Yes, most things happen *then*.

KRATT

I wasn't careful. I erased more than I can remember. All that's left are scattered clues. I don't know how any of them fit together. So here I am.

HARDER

Mr. Kratt, I'm a detective. I follow people. I solve murders. That's what I do.

KRATT

And that's precisely what I'm asking you to do.

HARDER

You're asking me to help you remember a story you began writing.

KRATT

I'm asking you to solve a murder.

HARDER

A fictional murder.

KRATT

Every murder is fictional. Before someone commits it.

HARDER

Do you at least remember the motive for the murder?

KRATT

Nothing out of the ordinary. Obscure psychological reasons.

HARDER
Those kinds of reasons are always obscure. Who's the victim?

KRATT
I don't know.

HARDER
Forgive the petty question but who's the suspect?

KRATT
I don't know. But I'm sure it's a murder case.

Harder lights another cigarette.

KRATT
I realize the case is unusual.

HARDER
In such cases I find my usual methods most helpful. I'll need a copy of the manuscript, or at least the part you've actually written. It'll help me think. You know what else helps me think?

Kratt places a packet of 100 bills on the desk. Harder takes the money and slips it in his pocket.

HARDER
I'm already thinking.

Kratt places the small suitcase on the desk.

KRATT
I have to warn you. The setting is rather dreary. Intentionally, of course.

HARDER
(grins)
Dreary is good. Realistic.

KRATT

I thought so too.

Kratt leaves. Harder pours himself another glass of bourbon and opens the case.

CUT TO:

EXT. THE DESERT - DAY

Harder stands still looking straight ahead. He is still wearing his office clothes. It's quiet except for the WIND. There is nothing around: only little cacti and dry bushes. He looks left. Nothing. He looks right. Nothing. He begins to walk forward slowly. His movements are accompanied by the sound of RAIN and SCREECHING TIRES on wet pavement. Whenever he stops moving, we hear the desert wind; when he resumes walking, we hear the rain again. As he walks around aimlessly he overhears snippets of various conversations, some of them close by, others coming from a distance. There is no one around.

VOICES (O.S.)

"Silence. Just silence."
"Talk. And talk fast. I don't like silence."

"I just had a phone call. You were right. It was murder. Just half an hour ago, or so. In his apartment. They don't know who did it—yet."

"Bad news, handsome? You look like a washed egg."
"Get the hell out of here."

"The cards are dealt. You'll play'em. Get going."

"No car. Let's go. It's rotten here and I don't drink gin."

"What time did you leave the office?"
"About eleven o'clock."

"That wouldn't be smart. Just smart-aleck."

"You boys think I know who it was?"

"Park yourself. What's the graft?"

"Let's see your dough."

"I've got some information for him."
"About what?"

"I'm sorry—angel. I had you wrong."

"I guess he played it as clean as he could, but he couldn't help but make enemies."

"Hold it! The mitts high, sweets!"

"I could. But I don't want to get my hands dirty."

"Door was open. Expecting someone?"

"Sorry...I'm sorry."

"Call your play. I'll read you a chapter of the Bible or buy you a drink. Say which."

"There's blood on your cheek. Wipe it off."
"Go on, kid me."
"I wasn't kidding you."

"Is he dead?"
"Beginner's luck—yeah."

"That's damn cute."

A green scarf glides past him. Sheets of paper (musical scores) fly past him. The sounds of MOZART'S REQUIEM in the distance. He comes across various objects in the sand, stops to pick up every object and examines it carefully. He takes out small plastic bags from his pocket and puts each object in a separate bag. Some of the objects he keeps (sealing them in plastic bags), and others he throws away immediately, but it's not obvious why he keeps some and throws away the rest. Occasionally, right after he throws away an object, he stops, retraces his steps and looks for the object but he can never find it: he finds a different object in its place. He keeps the following objects:

An ashtray filled with cigarette butts and one lit cigarette. He puts the ashtray (without emptying it) in a plastic bag and smokes the rest of the lit cigarette as he continues walking.

A pack of cigarettes

A box of matches

Pieces form a broken vase

A cigarette lighter

A green scarf

The score for Mozart's Requiem

A single black leather glove (the right one)

Two bottles of pills

Scissors

Various tools (screwdriver etc.)

A bottle of poison

A razor

A pen

A tie (the same tie he wore in the first scene)

A black phone

A slingshot

A gun

Car keys

A woman's earring

A man's watch (broken)

He continues walking slower and slower, burdened by the increasing number of plastic bags. In the distance, the silhouette of a man appears from the right and disappears to the left. He is too far away to be identified. Harder drops all plastic bags and starts running forward, left and right, right and left, backwards, in circles, but the man is nowhere to be seen.

While Harder is running, parts of the same snippets of conversations are heard again. The sounds change order depending on the direction in which he is moving: they are reversed when he is running backwards; new sounds are added when he takes a step to the left or to the right. He begins to change directions faster and faster: the sounds are reshuffled faster and faster, gradually escalating into a cacophony of incomprehensible words. He sits down on the sand and arranges the evidence in a neat pile in front of him.

CUT TO:

INT. HARDER'S OFFICE - NIGHT

The plastic bags are on the desk. We pull back to reveal: Harder sitting at his desk, looking down at the evidence. He unzips the plastic bag containing a pack of cigarettes and a box of matches. He lights a cigarette and puts the pack and the matches back in the plastic bag.

KRATT (O.S)
You shouldn't be doing this.

HARDER
(nods at the pile of objects on the desk)
You're not exactly running out of evidence.

Harder picks up the murder weapons he has brought back from the desert: scissors, tools, razor, poison, gun, knife. He examines each carefully.

HARDER
How many murders are we talking about?

KRATT
One.

HARDER
The killer seems to have a hard time deciding on a murder weapon.

KRATT
I think I'll go with the gun.

HARDER
(approvingly)
I would too.

With the cigarette hanging casually from his lips Harder begins to unzip the plastic bags one by one, removing the objects and arranging them on the desk. He begins to examine them more carefully. He picks up the bag containing the black phone. He looks at it as if he is trying to remember something. He looks at the corner of his desk where his phone used to sit: it is not there. He takes out the phone from the bag and puts it in the place of his missing phone. He dials a number. The phone RINGS in Mrs. Doyle's office.

HARDER

Mrs. Doyle, has anyone been in my office since yesterday?
No? Thank you.

Harder puts down the receiver and picks up another plastic bag, the
one containing a pen. He takes the pen out of the bag and, with a
habitual movement, puts it in the little pocket inside his jacket. He
looks through the rest of the plastic bags, picks another one, opens it
and takes out a tie (the same one he wore in the first scene), which he
proceeds to put on. He sits back in his chair and continues smoking
calmly.

HARDER

I suppose this is what you call realism. I have to admit I
almost believed this was my phone.

KRATT

It *is* your phone.

HARDER
(sarcastic)
Of course it is. I brought it along in case I wanted to call you
long distance.

KRATT

Obviously, you were not entirely able to suspend disbelief.
You should be more careful next time.

HARDER
(points at the objects on the desk)
Do you remember any of these?

Kratt looks at the pile of objects, focusing on the ashtray.

                                                        CUT TO:

INT. DINER - MORNING

A table next to the window. A coffee cup on the table and a hand next to it. The rest of the man remains out of the frame. The hand picks up the coffee cup, the man drinks, then puts the cup down. The hand disappears from the frame, then reappears holding a cigarette. Another hand (a woman's hand) enters the frame, placing an ashtray next to the smoker's hand. The ashtray is dirty, full of cigarette butts.

                                                        CUT TO:

INT. HARDER'S OFFICE - NIGHT

Harder leans over the desk.

                            HARDER
        Well?

                            KRATT
        Someone smoking.

                            HARDER
        Did you see his face?

Kratt shakes his head. Harder points at the umbrella.

                            HARDER
        What about this?
                                                        CUT TO:

EXT. A GROVE - DAY

Here and there, propped up against a tree, lying in the grass, or hanging from a branch are posters with words or phrases written on them. Three of the posters contain the following incomplete sentences: "… pours himself another glass…" "…the splatter of raindrops on the…" "…like dead pigeons falling…"

CUT TO:

INT. HARDER'S OFFICE - NIGHT

                    HARDER
    Anything?

                    KRATT
    Sentence fragments. Someone drinking. Rain. Pigeons.

                    HARDER
    What is this? A haiku?

Kratt doesn't answer. He stands up and leaves without an explanation.
Harder pours himself another glass of bourbon.

                    HARDER
                (under his breath)
        Dead pigeons.

The sound of raindrops beating against the window grows louder.

CUT TO:

INT. DINER – MORNING

Harder sits at a table next to the window. A WAITRESS approaches
the table.

                    WAITRESS
    Good morning! Our specials today are…

                    HARDER
    Coffee. Black.

Harder looks through the window. He slips his hand in his pocket, appears surprised to find something there, takes it out: it's the plastic bag containing the pack of cigarettes and the box of matches. He looks at it for a while, then opens it and lights a cigarette. The waitress comes back with the coffee.

WAITRESS

I'll bring you an ashtray.

Harder continues smoking and sipping his coffee. The waitress comes back with the ashtray. It's dirty and full of cigarette butts.

WAITRESS

Call me when you're ready for a refill. I'm Judy.

She points to her nametag. Harder finishes his cigarette and puts the cigarette butt in the ashtray.

CUT TO:

INT. HARDER'S OFFICE – NIGHT

All clues are lying on Harder's desk. Kratt bends over the desk to examine them closely. Harder is sitting behind the desk, his feet up as usual.

KRATT

Are you sure this is the original syntax? You haven't moved things around?

HARDER

Forget about filling in the blanks for a while, alright?
There are a few more important things to discuss.

KRATT

Such as?

                            HARDER

Such as the curious fact that apart from all this junk I didn't
run into a single decent corpse. I did see a man wandering
about in what appeared to bean aimless fashion, though as
soon as he saw me he disappeared quite purposefully.

                            KRATT

Don't worry. There *will* be a body.

                            HARDER

I like to worry. It keeps me motivated. And what do you
mean "there *will* be a body"? Don't expect me to do your
dirty work. My job is to find the body. Yours is to put it there.

                            KRATT

I said the body's there. How far did you walk?

                            HARDER

Ten miles or so.

                            KRATT

You didn't go far enough.

Harder opens Kratt's manuscript to a different page.

                                                    CUT TO:

EXT. DESERT – DAY

Harder's hand picks up an object lying in the sand. It's a scarf (an
exact copy of the green scarf that we saw in the first scene in the
desert except that this one is blue).

                                                    CUT TO:

EXT. DESERT - NIGHT

Harder is sitting by a little fire, smoking and examining the blue scarf.
He turns away—it's not clear what he is doing. Several notes from a

TOY PIANO are heard. He turns around and continues smoking and looking at the fire.

CUT TO:

INT. HARDER'S OFFICE - NIGHT

The office is completely dark, except for a flashlight illuminating the desk.

KRATT

And?

HARDER

There was a scarf. Last time it was green. Now it's blue.

KRATT

I'll make a note of that.

He makes a note of it.

HARDER

Then you've got some good old specious evidence, though I must admit it adds color to the whole dreary affair.

Harder places the toy piano on the desk and plays a little tune: a very simplified version of Mozart's requiem.

KRATT

I was going to revise that part.

CUT TO:

EXT. DESERT – DAY

Harder is walking through the desert aimlessly. He comes upon a desk. DR. SLOAN sits behind the desk, diligently typing away at an old Remington. Occasionally, he stops typing and wipes the sweat off his face. There is a single sheet of paper in the typewriter and he has almost reached the bottom of the page. The page slides out and falls on the ground. Unperturbed, Sloan continues to type. A green scarf (the same one we saw in the earlier scenes in the desert) flies past him. He continues typing. Now and then he stops to check the sheet of paper that is not there. He fiddles with the typewriter and corrects several imaginary mistakes with a white-out.

Harder takes off his jacket, rolls up his shirt sleeves, pushes his hat back and rolls his cigarette from one end of his mouth to the other. He walks slowly around the desk. Sloan doesn't pay any attention to him and continues typing.

                                    HARDER
Mind if I ask you a few questions?

Sloan continues typing.

                                    HARDER
I see you're a very busy man…Still, I must, hmm, insist that you spare a few moments of your, hmm, precious time and discuss with me certain matters that might, hmm, in fact, concern you personally.

Startled, Sloan stops typing, turns around to look at something behind him. There is nothing behind him. He turns to Harder.

                                    SLOAN
I'm terribly sorry. I thought you were talking to him.

                                    HARDER
Him?

                                    SLOAN
                          (points at something behind him)
Him.

Harder looks in the direction in which Sloan is pointing. A man, dressed like a beggar, scurries behind the desk without looking at either of them, mumbling something under his breath.

                    SLOAN
What can I do for you?

                    HARDER
There has been a murder.

                    SLOAN
                   (politely)
No.

                    HARDER
                   (politely)
Yes.

Sloan continues to smile. Harder waits. Sloan goes back to typing. He stops, takes out a portable radio from the desk drawer, turns it on. Pleasant atonal music is heard. Sloan shakes his head and kicks his heels under the desk, in sync with the atonal music. Harder spits and lights up another cigarette.

                    HARDER
Harder. Private Eye. I'm looking for a suspect.

Sloan stops typing but continues kicking his heels for a while, by sheer inertia. Occasionally, he shakes his head too but it looks more like a tick.

                    SLOAN
Who?

                    HARDER
I don't know. That's why I'm looking for him.

                    SLOAN
What has he done?

HARDER

Murder, presumably.

SLOAN

And you presume it's him?

HARDER

I wouldn't be looking for him if I didn't.

Sloan waves his finger, clearly pleased with his own powers of ratiocination.

SLOAN

Aha, but you wouldn't suspect him if you weren't looking for him!

HARDER

You're quite the sophist, aren't you? So, what do you know about this bird?

Harder searches his pockets for a piece of paper to write on but finds only several boxes of matches. He opens one of them and gets his pen ready. He walks around the desk in circles.

HARDER

Keep your answers snappy: I don't have room for extensive notes. Who is he?

SLOAN

I don't know. Someone insignificant.

HARDER

That tells us something.

SLOAN

What?

HARDER

Something insignificant. Is he comfortable?

SLOAN

With himself?

HARDER

Are there others?

SLOAN

There always are. But he is not comfortable with them.

HARDER

He lives alone then?

SLOAN

Only if that tells us something.

HARDER

Unfortunately, it doesn't.

He shows Sloan the box of matches. It's filled with his notes.

HARDER (cont.)

I ran out of room.

Harder takes out a new box of matches and resumes walking in circles.

HARDER

What kind of man is he? Unpack your adjectives.

SLOAN

What you unpack always turns to be less than what you've packed, all things being unequal.

HARDER

Which they always are. Is he dangerous?

SLOAN

Is that important?

HARDER

If it's specific enough.

SLOAN

Danger is not specific.

HARDER

Are you saying he's not dangerous?

SLOAN

Not in these specific words.

HARDER

The plot rarefies.

SLOAN

It's only because the blood hasn't coagulated yet.

HARDER

So there's blood.

SLOAN

It comes with the corpse. Are you looking for one of those
as well?

HARDER

Don't get cute with me. Have you got one?

Sloan appears confused and embarrassed.

SLOAN

I forget: why are you looking for him?

HARDER

He's a suspect in a murder case.

SLOAN

That would make him suspicious, wouldn't it?

HARDER

You're quick. What's his motive?

SLOAN

To see if he could kill without one.

HARDER

What's in it for him?

SLOAN

The perfect crime.

HARDER

A worthy ideal. Arrogant yet cliché.

SLOAN

Don't underestimate the power of clichés.

HARDER

To do so would be arrogant.

SLOAN

He's smart. He knows the perfect crime can't be the result of
just another narrative twist. In other words, he's got an idea.

HARDER

Why did he put it in other words?

SLOAN

Great ideas don't exist except in other words.

Sloan clicks his tongue and starts typing again.

HARDER

What are you doing?

SLOAN

Entering my patients' data. It's important to update the files
regularly.

Harder writes something down on the box of matches.

HARDER

Any interesting cases?

No answer. Harder looks up: Sloan has suddenly vanished. The sound
of the typewriter is heard for a while, then it gradually fades away.
Harder walks to the place where the desk stood a second ago, bends
down, and buries his hand in the sand. Nothing. He stands up and is
almost swept off his feet by a young jogger fatale in sweatpants and a
T-shirt.

She looks at him annoyed but doesn't say anything. After running in
one place for a while and very obviously ignoring Harder, she sits
down on the sand and begins to stretch.

HARDER

Harder.

JOGGER FATALE

This is as hard as I like it. Why don't you try minding your
own business?

HARDER

Maybe I don't care much for trying that hard.

She stands up and starts jumping up and down, every time bringing
her knees higher and higher, almost up to her chin.

HARDER (cont.)

Sorry to interrupt your routine, but did you happen to notice
anything unusual on your way here? Say, a corpse?

JOGGER FATALE
What would he do here?

HARDER
So you know him?

JOGGER FATALE
It.

HARDER
What?

JOGGER FATALE
It. The corpse is not an animate being. You can't use a
personal pronoun when referring to him...eh...It.

HARDER
That's cute. I like a woman with a flair for semantics.

JOGGER FATALE
(sarcastic)
Will you buy me a Popsicle now?

HARDER
If you show me the body.

JOGGER FATALE
You wish.

HARDER
I didn't mean yours...though that's nice too. I meant *it*.

JOGGER FATALE
There is no body.

HARDER
You mean it's hidden away?

The Jogger stops jumping up and down and points at nothing in particular.

JOGGER FATALE
There's nobody.

Harder looks around: there is nobody and nothing in sight. He turns toward the Jogger: she has disappeared. Harder starts walking to the left. He comes across a book half-buried in the sand. He picks it up. A movie-ticket stub falls out of the book.

CUT TO:

INT. HARDER'S OFFICE - NIGHT

Harder throws a book on the desk: it's the same book he found in the desert. Close up of the book: L'ecume des jours by Boris Vian. The movie-ticket stub is already sealed in a plastic bag, lying next to the book. Harder puts his feet up on the desk and lights up a cigarette.

HARDER
I walked for four hours. In four hours—in 13 miles—not a single drop of blood. A book!

Kratt takes the book, examines it carefully, even smells it, leaves it on the desk and leans back in his chair, his eyes half-closed.

CUT TO:

INT. PUBLIC LIBRARY – DAY

Close up of a man's feet walking down a hallway. Nothing else can be seen.

CUT TO:

INT. HARDER'S OFFICE – NIGHT

KRATT

I'm not sure.

HARDER
(reads from Vian's book)
Listen to this: "Dans la vie, l'essentiel est de porter sur tout des jugements *a priori*." ' A priori.' That's a damn poetic word.

Harder smiles absentmindedly, then remembers where he is and puts the book down. Suddenly he appears very focused.

HARDER

This is what I find strange. *Everyone* I saw had *never* heard of a killer, or of a corpse for that matter. In fact, *no one* I saw had *ever* heard of a killer or a corpse.

KRATT

When you put it this way, it does sound hopeless.

HARDER

What do you want me to do?

KRATT

What you've been doing all along: continue looking for clues.

HARDER

Finding more clues will not make up for the lack of a crime, not to mention the absence of a murderer and a corpse.

KRATT

They're there. You just haven't found them yet.

HARDER

You're sure everything I need to know to solve this case is there?

KRATT
Of course it's there. Where else could it be?

HARDER
What if…

KRATT
What?

HARDER
If…

KRATT
Then…

HARDER
I'll have to think more about this.

KRATT
Keep me posted.

Kratt leaves. Mrs. Doyle comes in and leaves a stack of papers on Harder's desk. She heads for the door but stops and turns around.

MRS. DOYLE
I almost forgot.

She takes a little black box out of her pocket and leaves it on the desk.

MRS. DOYLE
Ms. Greta stopped by earlier. She left this for you.

HARDER
(picks up the box)
What is it?

MRS. DOYLE
A gift, I suppose.

Harder opens the box absentmindedly, takes out the watch, puts it on, without looking at it, opens Kratt's manuscript and starts reading.

MRS. DOYLE
It's a very nice watch.

CUT TO:

EXT. EVENING – A TERRACE OVERLOOKING THE CANYON

A man stands smoking, with his back to the camera. Harder approaches and stands a few feet away from the man, also with his back to the camera. He turns up his collar and stares at the lights in the distance. He feels his pockets and takes out the plastic bag containing a pack of cigarettes (the one he found in the desert). Without the least bit of hesitation, he opens it, takes out a cigarette, puts it in his mouth, feels his pockets again, doesn't find a lighter. He notices the man smoking a few feet away from him, approaches him and gestures that he would like a light. The man takes out a cigarette lighter. Harder nods 'thank you' and goes back to where he was standing. He continues looking at the lights in the distance and smoking.

CUT TO:

INT. PUBLIC LIBRARY – EVENING

Harder is wandering between the shelves, occasionally stopping to look at a book.

HARDER (V.O.)
It was Tuesday evening. I had had a few whiskeys at the Pink Elephant and had somehow gotten it into my head that a little library research would be the perfect finish to another unproductive day. I was also curious, despite myself, about the other eleven novels Kratt had written before his little incident.

Harder stops by a bookshelf, runs his hand over the books. As he pulls out one of Kratt's books from the shelf, he accidentally pushes another book on the shelf causing it to fall to the floor. He bends down, picks it up, dusts it off, closes it and motions to put it back on the shelf but stops. Close up of the book's cover: *L'ecume des jours*.

CUT TO:

INT. HARDER'S OFFICE - NIGHT

Harder is pacing in front of his desk, smoking. He hasn't taken off his coat and hat. Occasionally, he looks at Vian's book, still in the plastic bag, lying on the desk. Just as he heads for the door, Mrs. Doyle walks in.

MRS. DOYLE

Ms. Lorna called.

HARDER

I'm going out.

MRS. DOYLE

What should I tell her if she calls again?

HARDER

Nothing. Send her flowers. White tulips.

Harder slips the plastic bag containing Vian's book in his pocket and leaves.

CUT TO:

INT. MOVIE THEATRE – NIGHT

HARDER

One for *The Samurai*, please.

Harder feels the inside of his pocket and finds something though he doesn't take it out. His face becomes tense. He withdraws from the cashier's window.

CASHIER

I'm sorry but the 8 o'clock show is sold out.

Harder looks confused for a second. Then he smiles and appears relieved.

HARDER

Thank you. Thank you.

The cashier looks at him confused. Harder smiles again and starts walking away. He has only made a few steps when the cashier calls after him.

CASHIER

Sir. Wait. I do have one seat left. It's your lucky day.

HARDER

Are you sure?

CASHIER

I'm just trying to help you. Nobody's forcing you to see the show if you don't want to.

HARDER

I wish you were right. Unfortunately, something tells me I've already seen it.

CASHIER

Do you want the ticket or not?

CUT TO:

INT. HARDER'S OFFICE – NIGHT

Harder walks into the office. He looks agitated and tense. He goes straight to the desk, takes out all his notes, Kratt's manuscript, all plastic bags containing clues and spreads everything on his desk. He remembers something, slips his hand in his pocket and takes out the two plastic bags he has been carrying around: one containing a movie ticket stub, the other Vian's book. He puts them on top of the pile and stares at them for a long time. He rummages through the pile and finds the plastic bag containing a cigarette lighter. He holds it in his hand.

CUT TO:

EXT. A TERRACE OVERLOOKING THE CANYON – EVENING

Harder approaches the stranger smoking beside him and asks him for a light. The stranger takes out a cigarette lighter. Harder bends toward the stranger's hand and puts his own hand in front of the lighter but this time we see the two men from another angle which reveals that the lighter is the same lighter Harder brought back from the desert.

CUT TO:

INT. HARDER'S OFFICE – NIGHT

Harder is still holding the plastic bag with the cigarette lighter. Kratt walks in. Harder drops the bag on the desk.

KRATT

Anything new?

HARDER

Things.

Harder pulls out the plastic bag containing an earring.

HARDER

Does this ring a bell?

Kratt takes the earring and looks at it with great concentration.

CUT TO:

A close up of a female hand holding a phone receiver.

CUT TO:

INT. HARDER'S OFFICE – NIGHT

                        HARDER
Anything?

                        KRATT
Nothing.

                        HARDER
Nothing at all?

                        KRATT
Nothing doesn't come in parts.

The two of them stare at each other with something like resentment.

                        KRATT
It might belong to Stella.

                        HARDER
Who?

                        KRATT
The jogger.

                        HARDER
She wasn't wearing any jewelry.

They stare at each other again. Finally, Kratt stands up. Harder nods. Kratt leaves. Harder remains sitting for a while, fiddling with the earring. He puts it back in the plastic bag, stands up and walks out, passing through Mrs. Doyle's office. She is on the phone.

MRS. DOYLE
...a gift for our anniversary...No, they are small but pretty...

CUT TO:

INT. HARDER'S OFFICE – DAY

Harder walks in, passes by Mrs. Doyle's desk. She's on the phone.
She looks upset.

MRS. DOYLE
(covers the receiver with her hand)
Mr. Kratt is waiting for you.

Harder nods and walks into his office. Mrs. Doyle continues talking
on the phone.

MRS. DOYLE
I looked everywhere....I couldn't find it.

CUT TO:

INT. HARDER'S OFFICE – NIGHT

Kratt is sitting in the chair he always sits in. Harder walks in.

KRATT
Sorry I'm early.

HARDER
I'm afraid I don't have anything new to tell you. Something
essential is missing.

Kratt produces an envelope full of money and places it on the desk.

HARDER
I was thinking more along the lines of a corpse. To tell you

the truth, I find that kind of thinking very unrewarding.

Harder sighs and opens Kratt's manuscript at random.

CUT TO:

EXT. DESERT – DAY

Harder is walking very slowly and apathetically, like a man who doesn't expect to find anything. Occasionally he stops, because he thinks he's seen an object buried in the sand: however, it's only a little mound of sand. He continues wandering aimlessly.

CUT TO:

INT. HARDER'S OFFICE – NIGHT

Harder is sitting at his desk, smoking. There is absolutely nothing on the desk.

KRATT
Where are the clues?

HARDER
There aren't any. Even the irrelevant ones were gone. I suppose this is what you call writer's block.

KRATT
I don't understand. Everything you need to know to solve this case is in the story.

HARDER
Unless, of course, there's something outside it.

CUT TO:

INT. HARDER'S OFFICE – NIGHT

Harder is reading Kratt's manuscript. A few of the clues lie in front of him. Mrs. Doyle walks in, carrying a cup of coffee. She still looks upset. She leaves the cup on the desk.

MRS. DOYLE
I arranged for a dozen of white tulips.

Harder furrows his eyebrows as if he's trying to remember something.

MRS. DOYLE
For Ms. Lorna.

HARDER
Of course. Thank you, Mrs. Doyle.

Mrs. Doyle motions to leave the room.

HARDER
Is anything wrong, Mrs. Doyle?

MRS. DOYLE
It's nothing. It's just that I lost an earring Richard gave me. It kind of put me in a bad mood.

Harder nods sympathetically. Mrs. Doyle motions to leave the room. Suddenly he picks up a plastic bag from the pile of clues in front of him.

HARDER
Mrs. Doyle, is this it?

MRS. DOYLE
Where did you find it?! And why is it in a plastic bag?

Harder hands her the earring, keeping the plastic bag.

HARDER
I didn't want to lose it again before returning it to you.

He picks up his hat, grabs his coat and leaves in a hurry.

CUT TO:

EXT. PUBLIC GARAGE – NIGHT

Harder is walking through a garage, looking for his car. He passes by two men getting into their car. One of them throws the car keys to the other. Harder continues looking for his car.

CUT TO:

INT. DINER – NIGHT

Harder is sitting alone, smoking. There are several espresso cups in front of him and an ashtray full of cigarette butts. He is fiddling with the empty plastic bag (the one in which he had kept the earring). The waitress brings the check. He leaves money on the table and gets ready to leave. He looks at his watch. Close up of the watch: it has stopped. He looks at it for a long time, then gets up and quickly walks out the door.

CUT TO:

INT. HARDER'S OFFICE – NIGHT

He goes straight to the desk, rummages through the pile of plastic bags and picks out the one with the stopped watch. He looks at it, incomprehensibly. He drops it and rummages through the pile of bags until he finds the one containing the car keys. Close up of the car keys.

CUT TO:

EXT. PUBLIC GARAGE – NIGHT

A set of car keys (the same ones as the keys in the plastic bag) flies through the air, over a car, and a pair of hands catches them on the other side of the car.

CUT TO:

EXT. KRATT'S HOUSE – NIGHT

Harder walks up to Kratt's house. He rings the bell, looks around, kills his cigarette with the sole of his shoe.

> ### HARDER (V.O)
> 167 Merry Street was a dull looking California paradise. I arrived a little after seven. Kratt looked as wholesome as I suspect any man would after a good night's sleep, scrambled eggs and bacon, and several cups of coffee. He was dressed impeccably yet casually, with the sort of subdued elegance that never failed to impress me and that I didn't waste any effort emulating. His skin looked fresh as a quince, his hair soft and clean, his face surprisingly visible.

CUT TO:

INT. KRATT'S HOUSE – NIGHT

> ### KRATT
> Whiskey or scotch?

> ### HARDER
> Bourbon.

Kratt disappears in the direction of the kitchen. Harder walks around the room, looking at things. He stops in front of a small bookshelf packed with books. He runs his hand over the books on the upper shelf but doesn't take out any of them. He notices a collection of CDs and looks at the titles. Kratt reappears in the doorway. He takes out a few pills from a small bottle in his hands and swallows them.

> ### KRATT
> (points to the CDs)
> Choose something you like.

HARDER
(points to the pills)
What are these for?

KRATT
An obscure psychological problem I might not have.

HARDER
If you keep taking them, you might actually develop
some obscure psychological problem.

KRATT
If I do, then I'd have to start taking them. So you see, it's
good that I'm taking them.

HARDER
In other words, you're taking them for a problem you don't
have but that, if you had it, would be alleviated by the fact that
you have been taking them. You seem to place an alarmingly
great trust in the purely hypothetical.

KRATT
Are you suggesting I shouldn't?

HARDER
Maybe it's just me, but 'what happens' has always struck me
as more reliable than 'what might happen.'

KRATT
(sympathetic)
You must have lived an alarmingly real life.

HARDER
It seemed to agree with me. Care if I smoke?

KRATT
The ashtray is right there.

Kratt goes back to the kitchen. Harder lights up a cigarette and approaches the side table. He takes the ashtray and walks over to the couch in the middle of the room. He sits down, sets the ashtray on the table before him and continues smoking, looking absentmindedly at the ashtray, which is full of cigarette butts. He leaves his cigarette on the edge of the ashtray and continues looking at it with the utmost concentration. Kratt enters, carrying the drinks. He sets them on the table and notices Harder's tense face.

KRATT

Everything alright?

HARDER

What? ..Yes. Déjà vu.

KRATT

Happens often.

In an adjacent room the phone rings. Kratt excuses himself. We hear his muffled voice in the other room. Harder walks back to the CD collection, chooses a CD and puts it in the CD player. It's Mozart's Requiem. While the Requiem is playing, Harder continues walking around the room and looking at things. Suddenly a gust of wind sends a few sheets of paper flying across the room and landing at his feet. Harder picks them up: musical scores. He puts the sheets back on the shelf and puts a candleholder on top.

He sits in an armchair but immediately realizes that he is sitting on something. He reaches underneath and takes out a black leather glove (a left one). He looks at it, surprised. He puts his hand in his pocket and takes out a plastic bag containing a black leather glove (a right one). It's obvious that they are a pair.

Meanwhile, the music has grown louder. He reaches into his other pocket and takes out a plastic bag. Close up of the bag: it contains the score of the Requiem, smudged, covered with dust and sand. He picks up the pair of gloves again. While Harder is looking at the pair (without taking the right glove from the plastic bag), Kratt walks in.

Harder quickly hides the right glove.

HARDER

Nice glove.

KRATT

I lost the right one. Another drink?

HARDER

Naturally.

Kratt goes to the kitchen. Harder puts the right glove back in his pocket and gets up. He walks into the adjacent room. It looks like a study: a desk, lots of books everywhere, an old Remington typewriter (the same one that the psychiatrist was typing on in the desert). Harder approaches the typewriter and takes out the sheet of paper from it. The page is not finished. He looks around and notices a pile of paper at the other end of the desk. He picks up the first page but realizes it's not the first page of the manuscript so he turns the whole pile upside down and picks up the page that was lying at the bottom.

Upon reading the first several sentences, his face changes: he looks confused, incredulous. He picks up the next page, and the next one, and the next one: he glances at them rather than reading them in their entirety. Shaken, he involuntarily takes a few steps back. His body brushes against an empty vase behind him. The vase falls down, breaking into pieces. He doesn't do anything: he just stands there, looking down at the pieces. Then very slowly he takes out from his pocket a plastic bag filled with shards of glass.

Kratt appears in the doorway, carrying the drinks. Kratt looks down at the broken vase, then he notices the plastic bag in Harder's hands. Without a word Kratt turns around, goes back to the living room, and sets down the drinks on the table. Harder follows him, bringing the manuscript with him.

The two of them drink in silence. Harder puts down the manuscript and his empty glass on the table, takes something out of his pocket and throws it in the middle of the table: it's a plastic bag containing a gun.

HARDER
I thought you might need this.

Kratt puts down his empty glass as well. The two of them are looking at the gun. Kratt reaches out and very slowly picks up the bag—he looks surprised at his own action. Harder watches him, expressionless. Kratt takes out the gun and examines it as if he has never seen a gun.

Suddenly, and with an abrupt, overly anxious movement, he points the gun at Harder. Harder remains calm. Kratt continues pointing the gun: he looks focused and uncertain at the same time.

HARDER
I'm touched but don't bother hesitating for my sake. You've long missed the point where you could've turned this into a morality play. Anyway, I might think less of you if you did...

Kratt remains silent.

HARDER
Do you mind? (He lights up a cigarette)...I have to tell you, I admire a man of imagination, though of course I'm perfectly aware that in my situation, it's a bit ridiculous to flatter you.

KRATT
I didn't lie to you.

HARDER
Come on, if memory serves you well—which it certainly does, although you've been so damn modest about it— you must remember the tragic story of a literary talent losing his memory...

Harder picks up the first page of the manuscript and reads out loud.

HARDER

"It all starts on a rainy evening in October. The lights on the fifth floor of the Reynolds building are still on. The shadow of a man is moving across the room...A client arrives, unannounced. A young man. He doesn't talk much. The detective is distracted. It's late. He hasn't had enough bourbon, certainly not enough to sit there and listen to that stranger wax poetic about a book he's writing....They talk... They seem to come to an agreement...The man leaves in the rain, the same rain from which he came, of which he is made. The detective pours himself another glass of bourbon. The splatter of raindrops on the windowpane has slowed down. The raindrops sound heavier, like dead pigeons falling with an eloquent thump on the ground." 'Dead pigeons': I like that.

Harder puts down the page and pours himself another drink.

HARDER
(points at his drink)
It helps me keep up with the poetic language. Just out of curiosity: exactly how long before you came to my office did you write this?
(He points at the manuscript)

Without taking down the gun for a single moment, Kratt starts pacing on his side of the table.

KRATT

I didn't lie to you. A writer of detective novels loses his memory and tries to reconstruct the ending of his last novel. He hires a detective to investigate the crime at the center of the novel. That was my original idea.

HARDER

And voila: the perfect crime.

KRATT

You made it perfect. Do you believe in self-fulfilling prophecies, Harder? You should: your own life is a self-fulfilling prophecy. You collected the data. You analyzed it. You solved your own death in advance. There was really nothing left for you to do but die.

Kratt stops talking. He continues pointing the gun at Harder. Harder looks as calm as ever.

HARDER

Come on, you remember how to kill me, don't you? Or perhaps I should ask you this: how far ahead did you remember, Kratt?

Kratt moves the gun into his other hand.

HARDER

Do you remember this?

Kratt looks more and more tense.

KRATT
(unsure)
It's all coming back to me now.

HARDER

Perhaps. Or perhaps you're having a déjà vu.

Kratt squeezes the gun.

HARDER

Perhaps you don't really remember the ending. Perhaps you don't want to remember it. Perhaps it's not to your liking.

Harder rolls his cigarette to the other end of his mouth. He takes out a plastic bag from the little pocket on the inside of his jacket.

HARDER

When I found the gun, I also found this.

He takes out a bullet from the bag and holds it in front of Kratt's eyes. There are old red stains on the bullet and on the inside of the bag.

HARDER

I thought it was a mistake, a clue that had gotten misplaced or something, or another proof of my failure to suspend disbelief, which you were so quick to diagnose. I couldn't figure it out, see, because this puppy here (he rolls the bullet between his fingers) is a 45.

Kratt looks at the gun he is still pointing at Harder.

HARDER
(points to Kratt's gun)

This one is a 38.

A GUNSHOT. Kratt falls down.

HARDER (cont.)

You couldn't have remembered this.

The police arrive, headed by Sergeant Folder from the LAPD.

FOLDER

You'd better have a good story, Harder.

HARDER
(points at the wall)

You'll find a 33mm bullet approximately 5 inches to the left of the clock.

FOLDER
(to his subordinates)

Call the lab. Tell them to get ready for an autopsy.

Harder hands Folder the plastic bag with the bloody 45mm bullet.

HARDER

It's not necessary.

Confused, Folder takes the bag. As Folder and the rest of the police are going about their routine search of the apartment, Harder bends over Kratt's corpse.

HARDER (V.O)

"I looked at his still body. It was no different from any other corpse I'd seen. His literary flights of fancy, even his fancy flights of literariness, seemed small in comparison with this body of evidence, this incontrovertible evidence of a body lying calmly in the middle of the room on a rainy evening in October."

Harder stands up. Sergeant Folder approaches him.

Folder dangles two plastic bags under Harder's nose: one contains the 33mm bullet, the other the 45mm bullet.

FOLDER

What game are you playing this time, Harder?

HARDER

Don't underestimate yourself. I'm sure you'll figure it out.

Suddenly, Harder furrows his eyebrows and appears confused and slightly terrified: there is a little bit of sand on Folder's impeccably clean suit, right on his shoulders.

FOLDER

All the same, I'd appreciate a report of some kind. We might already have a file on this Kratt. It's important that we update the files regularly.

CUT TO:

INT. HARDER'S OFFICE – NIGHT

Harder is sitting at his desk, looking at a black-and-white photograph of Kratt's body (the same photograph he was looking at in the very first scene). Mrs. Doyle walks in. She leaves a stack of papers on the desk and picks up the empty cup of coffee and the ashtray full of cigarette butts. She drops the cup on the desk and it rolls across the desk toward Harder. The cup is full of sand, not coffee.

                          MRS. DOYLE
     Sorry. I'm so sorry. I don't know what's gotten into me
     today. I drop everything.

Harder stares at the little pile of sand on the desk while Mrs. Doyle eagerly cleans up the mess.

                                                  CUT TO:

EXT. DESERT – DAY

An extreme close up of Harder's face. Only the sounds of the desert are heard (wind, dust, crows). He looks left. Nothing. He looks right. Nothing. A green scarf flies past him. He tilts his hat over his eyes and starts walking away from the camera.

                        HARDER (V.O.)
     "I guess he played it as clean as he could,
     but he couldn't help but make enemies."

                                                  CUT TO:

CLOSE UP of the black and white photograph of Kratt's body.

                        THE END.

ABOUT THE AUTHOR

TEMENUGA TRIFONOVA is Associate Professor of Cinema and Media Studies at York University in Toronto. Her first novel, *Rewrite*, was published by NON Publishing (Vancouver) in 2014. A film adaptation of *Tourist* (2017, 100 min), which she wrote and directed herself, won "Best Feature" at Mostra del Cinema di Taranto, Italy (2018). The film has also been screened at the Philosophical Film Festival (Skopje, 2018), and the Blow-Up International Art House Film Festival (Chicago, 2017). Trifonova is the author of the scholarly monographs *Warped Minds: Cinema and Psychopathology* (2014) and *The Image in French Philosophy* (2007), and the edited volumes *Contemporary Visual Culture and the Sublime* (2017) and *European Film Theory* (2008). She has been a visiting scholar and/or artist at the American Academy in Rome, the Brown Foundation at the Dora Maar House (France), The Fondation des Treilles (France), the New York University Center for European and Mediterranean Studies, and the Pushkinskaya Art Centre in St. Petersburg. She is currently a Marie Curie Fellow at Le Studium Centre for Advanced Studies in Tours, France.

MORE BLACK SCAT BOOKS YOU'RE SURE TO ENJOY

www.ingramcontent.com/pod-product-compliance
Lightning Source LLC
Chambersburg PA
CBHW032024240626
47154CB00003B/773